TECHNICAL ADVIS
DESTRUCTIO

Ranger Vic
Ranger David
Ranger Chris

Green Beret John "Doc" Spears

Rangers lead the way!

BOOK THREE

FORGOTTEN RUIN

VIOLENCE OF ACTION

JASON ANSPACH
NICK COLE

WARGATE

An imprint of Galaxy's Edge Press
PO BOX 534
Puyallup, Washington 98371
Copyright © 2021 by Galaxy's Edge, LLC
All rights reserved.

Paperback ISBN: 978-1-949731-57-6
Hardcover ISBN: 978-1-949731-58-3

www.forgottenruin.com
www.jasonanspach.com
www.nickcolebooks.com
www.wargatebooks.com

AUTHORS' NOTE:

NICK and Jason here. We're so glad you've made it this far into the Forgotten Ruin, and there's a lot farther to go. With Book 3 we get ready to enter the main storyline of what the Rangers are doing here in the Forgotten Ruin.

But first they gotta smoke a dragon.

The first two novels were pure survival and drama. And this one has those elements. But now we're going to show you what Rangers do best: taking out a high-value target. This is the U.S. Army Rangers' primary mission, and in Afghanistan they excelled exceptionally at this type of operation. What we want to show you now is how they go about that. This book attempts to dramatically show the level of planning, rehearsal, and preparation that goes into the very narrow time window of an operation of this nature.

Six weeks of planning for something that can happen in two minutes.

So the story is told in action steps, and then the effort that went into those steps. We think you'll dig it. It's a tight story. The Rangers run their plan in real time. And we want to show what happens when all goes according to plan, and even when the unplanned enters that situation. That's what Rangers do.

In other words, this isn't a crisis the Rangers find themselves in. It's a hit on a high-value target they engineer and orchestrate. Different story, same excitement and drama.

Then...

We have a special bonus-content surprise for you after "The End" of this book. We want to give you the origin story of the Forgotten Ruin. It's arcane. It's strange. But this will begin to explain what's going on and get you ready for the rest of the series as the Rangers face their greatest enemy so far. You'll get clues along the way. If the bonus content isn't for you, you don't need it. If you just dig the action, that's fine. Some of our readers just wanted to know how the world went from the way it is now... to the Forgotten Ruin. The content you find at the end of this book is there to start you along the path, give you a greater understanding of how it all happened, and be fun in the process. Think of it as a post-apocalyptic military cyber-thriller. Just a few fragments to get you going. We'll have more for those who want it. Just let us know what you think.

And now, settle in for some Rangers Acting Hostile. RAH.

Jason Anspach
and
Nick Cole

CHAPTER ONE

THE dragon attacked Forward Operating Base Hawthorn the last night of my extra duty. The extra duty punishment I got nailed with, along with getting busted right down to private E-1, for disobeying orders when the Rangers hit the lich Toth-Azom. Now it was almost over and in just a few hours I'd be off everyone's list and free to try and claw my way back to PFC with all its rank and incredible privileges well beyond that of other lowly privates who don't have a rocker below their mosquito wings. It was late, well after oh-two-hundred, and I was at the front gate of the FOB on guard watch, standing atop the squat southwestern tower when the massive flying dinosaur hit the fortress in a sudden surprise attack.

At first, we had no idea what was happening. Later, we'd all remark that we'd noted something peculiar about the air that night. Maybe even in the days before, the air had smelled a little like chlorine gas. But no one put together that an ancient huge green dragon was about to attack our FOB just two weeks after the Rangers had put the hit on a lich and his army of the dead, leaving the smashed bones of the ruined necromancer little more than powdered chalk thanks to Sergeant Thor's fifty-caliber anti-materiel rounds moving at twenty-four hundred feet per second through the lich's dusty skull. Exploding undead mummified necromancer brains all over the worn flagstones of an old temple hill where some great long-ago battle of the Ruin had once been fought.

The green dragon's unexpected attack against the FOB looked like a massive fog bank coming rapidly onshore near some seaside port. A fast-moving ethereal greenish iridescent mist that came out of the trees beyond the kill zone atop the high crag in the late morning hours of the night. The Rangers had cleared the kill zone of old twisted olive trees that lay in front of the crumbling ruin of a fortress, but the fog that late night was like a crop duster spraying a line of chemicals right up against our front gate and then racing over the walls and swirling across the tall dark towers at the back of the old fortress we'd taken off the SEAL McCluskey.

There was no titanic roar from an elder age. No behemoth black shape blotting out the stars and moon. Just the feeling that some massive and unseen thing had suddenly displaced the volume of air directly over the fortress. And then the line of green fog washing across the walls and the kill zone in front of the fortress we had our emplaced weapons trained on.

"That's weird," muttered Tanner, who was on watch with me. Where there should have been some kind of plane, or a dragon in this case, streaking in and laying down the green mist, there was nothing to be seen as the fog started to overtake the fortress. And like I said, no titanic roar and call like some dinosaur from the ages before man.

Kennedy would later tell us the dragon had most likely cast a spell of invisibility on itself before the attack. Apparently they can do that. Dragons can use spells here in the Ruin. So—we got that going for us.

Sergeant Kang was sergeant of the guard that night. He was with me and Tanner on the southwest tower when the billowing green smoke and fog streaked over our heads and began to drift down across the outer walls, expanding over the fortress. Open space and walls and towers disappeared softly. The fog was wet and hot, and it stank like badly over-maintained pools on the hottest of bleak summer days. Immediately our eyes began to burn and sting.

"Gas! Gas! Gas!" shouted Sergeant Kang as something huge and unseen raced overhead, driving the gas-fog down, obscuring our field of fire across the kill zone. Sergeant Kang ordered us into MOPP posture, which was really just the gas masks we had to bring on guard duty. This was the only mission-oriented protective posture the Rangers had established as SOP for any kind of chemical or biological attack. Which, to be honest, they had not really anticipated, but with the Ruin being what it was, it was best to assume that some horrible thing here probably did do chemical or biological attacks. You never knew what you were gonna run into in the Ruin, so it was best to assume anything was possible.

Still, all we had was the masks. No charcoal over-suits and rubber shoes. For which everyone was thankful. Until now anyway. Our Crytek uniforms and assault gloves were supposed to cover the rest of our exposed skin. The blanketing iridescent green gas now shrouding the tower, which was all I could see, revealed exactly how much skin was exposed as necks and wrists began to sting.

Like a pro, I had my mask out of my carrier and donned fifteen seconds after Sergeant Kang's warning, remembering how I'd thought just a few hours earlier what a waste this thing was to carry around on guard because I was so

3

beat from all the extra duty I'd been doing for fourteen very hard, very long days now. I cleared my mask, checked the seals as more gas swarmed in at us, and pulled the hood to cover my neck and skin. The fog was billowing everywhere like it was a thing that could breathe in and out. A living thing. A bellows. Or a storm front.

Sergeant Kang was coughing over the comm because he couldn't don his mask and still give the alert over the net. He choked and strangled as he let the comm operator, Old Man Sims tonight, know we were under attack from gas.

Then he got his mask on.

More of the green and gray stuff billowed and swamped the parapets. Hot blasts of sudden drafts swirled the gas, and though we couldn't see it, it was clear there was something big streaking in over the fortress now, making more runs and blanketing our FOB in endless green. I had no idea what was going on for the next few seconds. But Sergeant Kang, mask on, told me and Tanner to hold the tower while he went below to get the Carl.

"Whatever it is," he barked, "it's using a close-air-support-style attack. I'll get the launchers to both towers. Watch the kill zone. We could have assaulters moving in."

Tanner and I were charged with manning one of the Mark 47 automatic grenade launchers the Forge had cranked out. There were two, one on each of the squat tower at the front gate. These were the Special Forces operations models of the fabled Mark 19. There was also a fifty team down at the actual front gate. So far that was all the heavy weapons the Forge had been able to reinforce our front door to our new home with.

My extra duty that day, after getting a final smoking, running the crag twice, again, had been weapons maintenance on the Mark 47. So I'm not saying I was pro, but I knew it, and I knew what I was doing in that moment we got ready to go live.

Tanner switched to thermal on his NVGs and scanned the trees beyond the kill zone while I took a seat behind the automatic grenade launcher. We'd already checked and cleared the feed tray both manually and visually. Linked 40mm grenades were ready and waiting to go.

I pulled back the right charging handle, then the left. Safety still on.

That was when the titanic beast finally bellowed up there in the sky and billowing fog. Letting us know it was above us and that there was nothing we could do about it, or what it was going to do next. Like some primordial apex predator from the age of dinosaurs calling out its territorial war cry, inviting all to submit to its feeding. I'm not kidding, my blood ran actually cold in that sudden instant of its cry echoing out over the walls and towers of the FOB high atop the crag. Like Godzilla, but with a snake-like hiss and rattle in the subvocal range you swore you could feel deep down in your soul.

The gas was so thick now I could barely see. And bonus round, the lenses in my mask were fogging up and I could hear myself breathing heavily because getting smashed by a sky lizard the size of three city buses has a tendency to do that to you. The fear was palpable. The blanket of poisonous dragon's breath hung everywhere and hovered over everything like a low ceiling that would never dissipate. My exposed skin was on fire and my eyes were still watering. The gas was even getting into my Oakley assault gloves and making my hands itch as though they were rough and chapped by some volcanic hot wind I'd spent three days in.

"Nothin' on thermal, Talk. But the gas is hot, so maybe it's messin' with the nods."

Tanner's voice was ragged with the burning gas, but he sounded like he was keeping it together much better than me. Then again, he is technically dead. What could poison gas do to him that death hasn't already done?

A moment later something tremendous hit the southeastern tower, on the other side of the gatehouse. Exploding ancient stone rocketed all across the kill zone. Grit and rock sprayed across our helmets and plate carriers like frag and spall from mortar fire too close at hand before disappearing into the mist. The gatehouse shook, and our own tower groaned as it literally shifted on its foundation.

The huge beast had either slammed into the southeastern tower, suddenly dropping out of the gas-shrouded night and ramming into the stout form with its massive bulk, or its huge claws had just grabbed a chunk of the parapet and pulled it away, trailing ruin and stone everywhere as it hauled itself off into the swirling night above our heads.

Later we'd find that the dragon had grabbed Dawson and carried him off. We never found him, and it's assumed he was eaten.

File that under things you didn't think would ever happen when you raised your right hand and swore your oath of enlistment back at the MEPs.

DUSTWUN. Duty Status Whereabouts Unknown. Eaten by dragon. Green dragon. Ten thousand years in the future.

But the sky lizard's attack against the tower, its huge leathery wings beating the gas, displaced some of the chemical fog around us, allowing us to get a brief glimpse of it as it heaved its huge, scaled bulk nightward again. Its giant leathery wings thrashing as it climbed to gain altitude quickly and avoid our sudden outgoing fire.

The team operating the Ma Deuce, or what the army officially calls the M2 machine gun, or Browning fifty-cal heavy machine gun, didn't hesitate to light up the departing dragon with a burst of outgoing hot fire. The Rangers weren't gonna let that opportunity pass. Fifty-caliber tracer rounds shot off into the night and raked the dragon's massive emerald flank. Whether the powerful heavy machine gun penetrated its armored scales or not, was unknown. The Rangers were ready to go full murder and excited to do so. I guess they thought the night watch would be boring, and here the Ruin had thrown them something to kill. Winner winner chicken dinner.

The dragon screeched and heaved its wings furiously, twisting and angling upward in some impossible spiraling, turning climb that thrust it into the dense gas above us, obscuring it from the tracking fire of the Ma Deuce. Thanks to the fancy and very cool lightweight tripods the Rangers had had the Forge crank out, they'd been able to get on target quickly even as the thing gained sudden altitude to escape our fire. But the flying dinosaur's amazing acrobatics had been just as quick. Unbelievably so, literally, or at least that's how I felt as I watched the whole thing go down.

Tanner felt the same way too and quoted *Jaws* in the blanket of sudden silence created by dense gas and absence of dragon roar and Ma Deuce fire.

"We're gonna need a bigger boat."

Later, PFC Kennedy, our nerd wizard who now out-ranks me, would tell us that, again according to a game he plays, green dragons are super-intelligent evil geniuses. They are not mindless animal brutes like some of the monsters we've fought here in the Ruin. Little more than animals. The green dragon is crafty, and it attacks by surprise and deceit.

But we'd get that class later.

Now as we watched it go, roaring titanically over the fortress, a cat-thing came over the wall, grabbed Tanner by the neck, and plunged a curved gleaming damascened dagger into his side, deftly inserting the blade where the plate carrier wasn't. Like it knew how to stick him and how to deal with our armor.

Cat-thing, you ask? Yeah. It was a humanoid cat. But dressed kind of like a ninja meets a Bedouin. It came over the parapet silently and I saw it clear the stone lip, and then I shouted, "Tanner!" and a lame, "Watch out!"

Truth be told, Tanner isn't as fast as he used to be now that he's some kind of undead and all. So the cat ninja, huge feline ears twitching, came over the parapet in one smooth motion, grabbed Tanner with its paws, and jammed a knife right in his ribs.

Tanner just laughed and smashed his FAST helmet in one savage downstroke right into the cat-thing's whiskers. The ninja cat yowled, and Tanner backed away, the carving knife still sticking in his ribs as his MK18 carbine came up and he double-tapped the thing in the chest with two doses of five-five-six. Despite the knife penetrating his lungs most likely.

The cat placed a paw over one wound, its wide cat eyes glowing green and vibrant in the dark and the night in stunned disbelief that its attack had failed so unexpectedly. Tanner raised his aim and splashed the thing's skull at near point-blank range, just to confirm the realization in its eyes that it was indeed good and dead. And that cats don't have nine lives.

The body of the cat-thing-ninja bent backward over the ancient stone of the parapet and just lay there.

"Hey, Talk..." said Tanner slowly, scanning what he could see of the fog. Rifle still out and watching. Then he ripped off his mask and NVGs. "Pull this knife outta me, would ya?"

I stood, didn't think too much about it, and just gave it one massive yank, telling myself that if you're gonna pull an assassin's knife out of your buddy's rib cage, you might as well get it done fast.

The dragon roared once more as it streaked over the fortress. Unseen and beating its wings, driving the gas into the towers, buildings, and down into the *Tumna Haudh* itself.

CHAPTER TWO

THE gas rushed past us, clearing the air around the towers now as a hurricane seemed to come out of nowhere. My guess, as I tried not to get blown right off the remaining tower at the front gate—the winds were that strong, approaching gale-force—was that this was some kind of attack also. The dragon was trying to force its noxious breath into every nook and cranny of the fortress and the vast dungeons and tombs beneath, as though it were the exterminator and we were just the rats that needed to be finally dealt with.

Rangers who were asleep would be the most vulnerable even though it seemed many were already out in the lanes of the fortress and moving to their fighting positions along the outer defenses. Suddenly getting the signal we were being attacked, and moving to defend without a full assessment of the situation. But if they rushed out into the fight we found ourselves in without their gas masks, they were going to have a hard time breathing for very long, much less fighting for an extended period of time.

It was total chaos in those first moments of the dragon's attack. The comm was alive and everyone sounded pretty worked up, or downright angry and ready to waste whoever had been dumb enough to stir up sleeping Rangers. It seemed that only Tanner was completely calm and collected. He stood like some Crytek gargoyle, one leg on the parapet, rifle pointed down into the mist flooding away from the fortress walls, firing at targets I couldn't see.

Within seconds the poison gas cleared from the fortress, forced down into the deeps beneath the crag. I was still on the MK47, watching what I could see of the kill zone out there in the dark beyond the walls. I had learned the lesson my extra duty had been for. I had been told to man the belt-fed, blowback-operated, air-cooled, crew-served, fully automatic grenade tosser and to watch the kill zone outside the walls… and I was gonna do just that. Regardless of the amazing spectacle now taking place within the fortress as the massive green dragon attacked in full. I wasn't gonna get busted again for not doing my job. Besides, I didn't have any more rank to lose.

"Whoa," grunted Tanner. "Talk… you gotta see this, man. I can see way better through the gas and fog and night. Like night vision but… on something… and everything's purple but it's like I can smell life out there and see it too."

Lately, Tanner had begun to say weird things like that.

"Cat hajis're comin' across the kill zone, Talk. Tryin' to get over the wall."

The dragon roared again, louder than anything so far. Like some challenge to anyone who would dare question its total domination and superiority over non-dragon beings. I turned and looked. Come on, how many chances have you had to see a real live dragon regardless of murderous cat hajis crossing the kill zone and coming over the wall?

What I saw when I chanced a look back at the fortress we were defending was incredibly amazing. It was absolutely, totally, and unbelievably… huge. But it was more than that, too. It was... and go with me here but these are the only words I can find to use to describe the dragon full revealed... and remember everyone calls me Talker because I talk so much... it was simply, malevolently, *beautiful* in all its horrible revelation as it towered over everything. It was the moment death and myth intersected, leaving you utterly mesmerized. I was seeing something no one from our time ever had, and I doubted few in the Ruin had lived to tell about.

Like I said, it was three city buses tall, or long. Or whatever. It was tall now because it had grabbed onto the *Barad Nulla*, the dark tower where we kept the Forge. Its huge claws grasped the stone parapets high above as its body rose up even taller, revealing golden scales like patterned armor along its belly. Its sides were layered with rows upon rows of massive vibrant green plates that were themselves like even larger armored scales, overlapping one another. If the fifty-cal had done any damage at all to it, I couldn't see it.

Its massive wings, leathery and bat-like, spread out over the entire fortress and even now seemed to beat slightly, barely moving, yet driving huge winds that tore across the fortress, sending debris everywhere, knocking Rangers coming out to battle to the ground, and even pulling away loose stone to career off into the avenues and alleys the Rangers were flooding out into, weapons ready to engage whatever had had the misfortune of bothering them tonight.

The leviathan of a flying serpent glared down at everyone, unconcerned that it had just turned over a nest of murder hornets armed with automatic weapons, high-ex, and pure Rip-It-fueled hate. Malevolently. There's that word again. But yes, that flying dinosaur was pure primordial malevolence. Endless malice. Not just hatred. But a sheer spite and contempt for us, and really... everything not it. For the scrambling little things it gazed down upon, it held little passion, little pity, and zero mercy. It hated everything.

Because everything... all of it... us and the Ruin... was beneath it. In more ways than one.

And it was honestly hard to dispute that as I stared up at it in utter stunned disbelief and amazement.

Its eyes were like huge glittering emeralds that burned with malice. Its snout was long, with yellow teeth and fangs larger than any prehistoric shark's, waiting there like savage executioners. Its head was triangular and massive and some sort of almost-grin spread across its leathery flesh as it glared down at us in pure alien contempt.

It roared a giant Godzilla-like screech once more, the blast thundering and echoing off into the deep canyons and sky that surrounded this place. And I kid you not... the tower shook underneath our feet at this tremendous sonic blast.

In response, the Rangers began to fire at it with their carbines, because Rangers gonna Ranger, Sky Lizard. Tracers glanced off its armor and shot off into the night, racing skyward into the broken glass of the universe.

Tanner shouted at me...

I snapped back to what I was supposed to be doing and saw dozens of cat hajis moving swiftly across the kill zone. The dragon's grand performance atop the *Barad Nulla*, the mysterious and ancient obsidian tower at the back of the fortress, had been an act designed to distract us from this next phase of the enemy assault coming at the front gate.

The cat hajis were going to overrun our walls.

"Light 'em up!" shouted Tanner as he dropped to one knee and began to feed the grenade launcher the belt of 40mm explosives. I took the safety off, leaned back, and depressed both triggers. A streak of grenades spat out and danced away in a sudden line across the kill zone. A wall of explosions blossomed, ruining the cat hajis out there in bursts of dirt and dust flying into the night. These explosive rounds will pierce armor two inches thick, kill enemies within five meters of point of impact, and wound anyone within fifteen meters.

I like to learn stuff.

Tanner was on the net and letting the Rangers know we had action at the front door, as he engaged the ones coming up along the wall.

That dragon roared behind me and later someone told me that was when the thing formed some sort of fireball close to what Kennedy could do and tossed it right into the *Tumna Haudh*. The broken tower the Shadow Elves had made their own was suddenly covered in living green flames.

"Firing ADM!" shouted Sergeant Kang beneath the tower, and a Carl Gustaf round lanced up into the night and exploded near the dragon, sending a thousand miniature steel darts spraying all across its armor and through its leathery wings.

Meanwhile… I started blasting.

I had no idea all this was going on behind me. I was switched to on and the kill zone in front of the fortress was my entire world as I started laying down as much 40mm explosive as the belt would feed the MK47. The kill zone was nothing but ruin everywhere I landed the grenades out there. If the cats and the dragon had thought their little diversion attack was gonna buy the ninja cats some room to get over the wall and start stabbing Rangers... well, to borrow from Brumm... MK47 don't care either.

I could do all this all day, I thought as more cats rushed the walls and just got blown to pieces by the 40mm grenades landing all over them. At the same time the fifty down at the gate opened up and worked the distant twisted trees over in short bursts, cutting down a large group of cat hajis coming out from there.

That was when the dragon used its breath weapon. Or at least that's what Kennedy later told us happened next. In his game, dragons got to use their breath weapon three times a day. So far, the flying dinosaur had already blanketed the fortress in poisonous fog with several blasts of its tremendous breath, but apparently that didn't count as its breath weapon, for what happened next was far more concentrated.

What happened next was, without a doubt, a breath weapon attack.

The dragon targeted a group of Rangers advancing on it from their tower barracks. These were the Third Platoon assaulters, attempting to flank the dragon and get close enough to use their M320s. The dragon must have thought them a threat, because it leaned its snake-like neck down, thrust its evil triangular snout into the fortress itself, and sucked in a huge breath of air. Some of the Rangers advancing on the dragon from other directions reported feeling something similar to the concussive air displacement felt with recoilless weapons like the Carl Gustaf. Then the dragon spat out a concentrated, almost gelatinous blast of its foul breath. It was more like a liquid than a gas as it splashed all over the street and barracks tower the Third Platoon assaulters were advancing from.

And it just... disintegrated them.

As in, dissolved their flesh and ate their bones as though they'd just been dipped in the strongest acid. Even the street was scarred and dissolved, along with one whole section of the small tower they were using as a barracks, the stone literally eaten away.

At that moment no one had any idea what had just happened. We had no idea we'd just lost eight Rangers to a single dragon breath attack.

But what some of us did know—not me, I was Captain Kill with the MK47 at the moment, one of the most satisfying experiences I'd ever had, raining down death on murder cats who'd just stabbed my dead friend—was that Sergeant Thor had deployed *Mjolnir* and had gone for a head shot on the dragon.

He succeeded in blowing off a chunk of one of its curving horns above its glaring malevolent eyes with a terrific shot from the epic anti-materiel rifle. That seemed to really torque the giant sky lizard off and it howled violently as it heaved itself off the *Barad Nulla*'s tall obsidian skyscraper, dragging falling stone as it went. Screeching into the night as the Rangers fired at it and the dragon climbed off into the now visible stars and darkness.

I took my thumbs off the Mark 47's trigger. There were no cats left to ruin out there in the kill zone.

And the dragon was gone just as suddenly as it had appeared.

Death had come for the Rangers. And now the Rangers would figure out how to pay it back in full... and then some.

CHAPTER THREE

THREE hours later, after my own personal raid on the sergeant major's kitchen to brew up some coffee, and yes, I must admit I gave our dwindling sacks of Portugon roast the once-over like any desperate addict adding up exactly how much stash he has left just for himself and himself alone, I got myself to the FOB's command post as the first birds of the dark morning began to go about their business despite the dragon's raid. The command post, or CP, was a small bunker of a building the captain had commandeered smack dab in the middle of the old fortress. Its ancient purpose within the fortress was unknown, and it was little more than just four stone walls and a door, but it was centrally located to all FOB operations, and this was the place where you could find the captain and all his maps. Or at least it was your best bet. Rumor was he PT'd with the various sections at least three times a day near their sectors. Constantly observed training wherever it was going on. And disappeared for much of the night, going out with the patrols that ranged around the fortress and down into the lands beneath the crag on a nightly basis. I suspected he had a secret coffee stash, but I wasn't stud enough to ever enter that inner circle like I had the sergeant major's.

It was all business here at the CP, this central hub from which the ground force commander ran the show, and the

Rangers treated it like a flat-out holy place. They would enter seeking wisdom and then emerge to go forth and cause much mayhem and vicious ruin upon their enemies. And over the last two weeks, while I'd been pulling extra duty as both punishment and learning opportunity, not to mention character development, much mayhem had indeed been wrought.

The nightly patrols had been given the opportunity to hunt monsters, or "big game," at least one night a week. There was a contest to see who could bring in the ugliest thing possible. That it was vicious and mean and dangerous were all givens, but the Rangers were obsessed with finding and slaying *freaks* of the Ruin. As of now, First Squad, Second Platoon's assaulters, had the winning trophy in the form of an ankheg's skull lying in the dirt near their place along the wall. They'd turned it into a firepit. What's an ankheg, you ask? Imagine a massive insect the size of a rhino that spits acid. They tracked it late one night and got permission to waste it on toward dawn. Problem was the thing took fire, and five-five-six just bounced. Then it sprayed acid as the MK48 super-SAW went to work. The Rangers have started carrying the improved squad automatic weapon that fires 7.62. The Forge model uses refined schematics—the older Rangers said the initial models were plagued with a failure to feed ammunition, but Special Forces operations worked out the wonkiness. Anyway the Beast, as the SAW gunners call it with a wistful gleam in their eyes, opened up and went full metal savage on the giant insect. The ankheg got the point and burrowed immediately. One of the Rangers told me the giant, many-legged, scorpion-clawed thing with freaky anatomy just burned through the dirt of the earth beneath it like the ground was little more than melted butter. In seconds it was flat-out gone.

Like that was gonna stop Rangers.

The patrol, not to be deterred, went in after it because, as Sergeant First Class Chris who was running the recce that night likes to say, "Rangers can do anything. That's what makes 'em Rangers. They realize this. Everyone else operates in the failure of thinking things can't be done. Rangers approach everything as though anything can be done. You just gotta decide to do it." He says stuff like that all the time and is basically the voice of wisdom over in Second Platoon. He ran pre-Ranger school back in the world that died ten thousand years ago before we came here on our one-way trip into Kennedy's game. Third Platoon has its own voice of wisdom in Staff Sergeant Domingues, who everyone calls Sergeant Joe when not directly addressing him. Every piece of survival gold he gives out and gets repeated is marked with "according to the Book of Joe" like outgoing artillery fire. Young Rangers repeat these sayings and phrases constantly. Learning them. Memorizing them. Becoming Joe. When I was first getting indoctrinated in the detachment, Tanner hit me with these about twenty times a day. Much of those days were a hazy blur, but I've found all of those nuggets to be true, and spot-on in a practical way I never heard at any big-brain university.

It is not uncommon to see Sergeant Chris and Sergeant Joe in the company of the sergeant major at some point in the day. They are basically his right-hand men. And they always seemed to be discussing something important. It is my observed opinion… that all things Ranger emanate from these three. They're like the high priests of a religion called RAH.

Rangers Acting Hostile.

Any time I got summoned to the CP I gave myself the once-over. It was that kind of place where you needed to show up in the right uniform, with the right tools, ready to work. Gear where it was supposed to be according to SOP. Rifle clean and ready to go. I was on everyone's list. I got it. They wanted to make a Ranger out of me. A better Ranger.

I was all in for that.

Whereas the sergeant major's kitchen was informal, Captain Knife Hand's CP was the opposite. This was as formal as it got. Formal as in *Ranger*. As in here was where Ranger culture lived and breathed. Standards, training, missions, living it and paying the rent on your space in the detachment. They say every day is selection in the Ranger battalions. That was true here. It was also here where I reported for extra duty every day. It was here my suffering commenced, my weakness purged from my disobedient soul. It was here I attended and knew wisdom. Approaching the CP during extra duty I'd chant to myself every day just before it began, "I'll quit tomorrow." Meaning I'd never quit. They'd have to kill me.

And they tried to.

Now, in the aftermath of the dragon's attack I found myself whispering my chant again and reminded myself I wasn't on extra duty now. But I whispered it three times more anyway. I was gonna help kill that dragon.

I'd seen what was left of the dead guys before going to make coffee. I think I went to make the coffee afterward because I felt numb and distant. It was a pretty horrible sight.

I was back as the linguist now, here to facilitate communication between an elf king, a dwarf king, an old wandering wizard, and the Rangers. It was still my job even though the locals were starting to get the hang of rudimentary language.

I'd seen Captain Knife Hand a couple of times during extra duty, and he'd never once acknowledged my presence as the guy getting punished. Once the charges had been made by Kurtz it was as though the commander had disappeared me in his mind. And I have to admit… that hurt on a level I hadn't expected. If only because I and everyone else respected him so much. And because I'd let him down by disobeying orders.

There was no getting around that.

So I wasn't gonna fail again. That's what you're really telling yourself when you're chanting whatever little *According to the Book of Joe* gets you through the suck you currently find yourself in. I wasn't gonna quit. The dragon would have to do that for me. And maybe it was the psionics I still hadn't quite figured out, or maybe it was just the echo of the flying dinosaur's roar in the last of the dark morning and the memories of the remains of Rangers who'd been eaten alive by chlorine acid, but I felt a cold shadow pass across my soul. That shiver you get sometimes for no reason. My mother told me that was when a goose walked over your grave in the future. I told her that was impossible. She told me about quantum entanglement. The future and the present. All knotted up.

In the aftermath of the dragon's attack, the captain called for a meeting to find out just what the hell had happened to us. In attendance were the platoon leaders and sergeants, the air force command team, pilot and co-pilot, Last of Autumn, Vandahar, the dwarf king and his two lieutenants, and Chief Rapp. And me. The captain and the sergeant major listened to reports of what exactly had gone down during the dragon's close air attack and supported raid on our FOB.

The Rangers listed their casualties and responses to the combat. Other than Thor's shot, little damage had been done to the dragon. It didn't like the ADM munitions once those started going off, but they hadn't killed it. The Rangers who'd pressed the attack close at hand had been the ones disintegrated by intense chlorine acid gel. Which meant they'd done *something* to torque it off, but no one was quite sure what they'd done exactly, seeing as they'd all been killed and couldn't tell us.

Sergeant Thor was for leading a team of snipers out there to lay some serious hate on the big lizard wherever they could find it. Immediately in fact. The master breachers wanted to find its hole and just drop some bottles of acetylene in and light the whole place on fire.

The sergeant major said he'd provide the lit cigarette.

Kurtz and Hardt said nothing. They didn't need to. I could tell those two were well past murder-thirty and ready to get their kill on, extremely so. They didn't need a Ranger batt to do it, either. I was pretty sure if the dragon could've been there to see the looks on their faces it would have at least been seriously concerned for its continued existence on the mortal plane. They were two guys you didn't want to mess with. They radiated hostile menace and violent intentions like I'd never seen them do before. I was glad they were on my side.

"I know all you Rangers wanna get your kill on with that giant flyin' iguana real bad," began the sergeant major in his slow Texas drawl in the aftermath of the sullen and grim promises of excessive violent death by Ranger. "So let's figure out what this thing did so we can know what we're gonna do to it when we all meet up again and suss this out."

The Ranger leadership ran through an AAR and basically broke down what had happened during the attack. The chemicals that had acted as camouflage. The hurricane. The breath weapon. Ranger response. Ranger failures. Ranger successes.

"It's important to note," said the normally quiet Sergeant Kang from the wall where he was leaning as the meeting wore on and the early summer morning began to break across the fortress walls, "that the dragon is working with indigs. We assessed at least thirty-two dead of some kind of new enemy we haven't encountered before, sir. Organized. Humanoid."

He paused.

Then, "Feline."

"Ah," exclaimed Vandahar from the shadows, softly nursing his pipe and sending smoke rings climbing into the low rough beams that formed the roof of the CP. "Those would be the Katari. They are guardians of the Valley of Tombs. The most sacred place of the Saur, apart from the Grand Pyramid itself. It is most unfortunate for us if they are in league with the dragon now."

"*Kat-tari?*" asked the sergeant major slowly when the old wizard failed to expand on the subject of our new enemies. "And what would they be exactly, Vandahar?"

The sergeant major's drawl made all three syllables of the wizard's name seem like separate words unto themselves.

"The Katari…" the old wizard spoke as though he were coming back from some distant place or memory. "Why…

they're the guardians of the temples and tombs of the Saur. Fierce predators with no equal. Save possibly for the Aslani of the deep jungles far to the south. What troubles me is, I have seldom, if ever, seen them north of the Land of Black Sleep. What they're doing here, in league with Ssruth the Cruel, creates far more questions than answers, I'm afraid to say. They are servants of the Saur pharaohs, exclusively, that is well known. The Katari's Order of Silent Death, that is. This is far, far from home for them. Yes, that worries me deeply."

Vandahar had given us a rough sketch of the world and had even produced an old map of how the world of Ruin looked now, ten thousand years after our departure. The Land of the Black Sleep was basically Egypt. So, since we were currently in southern France, or what our map called the Savage Lands, we were indeed far away from the Land of the Black Sleep. And the Great Inner Sea, or what we called the Med, was between us. So yeah… very far.

"Noted," said Captain Knife Hand tersely as the wizard seemed to conclude. "The Harvey's got support units. Vandahar, can we expect these assets, and these… Saur… you mention… can we expect them on the objective if we decide to hit the target?"

"The target?" asked the bewildered wizard, clearly having lost the thread of the conversation, unable to follow Ranger jargon. But that made two of us. I had no idea what a Harvey was and had yet to encounter one with the Rangers.

But because I love words, I was already excited. Plus, I had a hot thermos full of coffee. *Plus*, I was still wired from almost getting killed by that dragon and all. You know how ya are when a giant flying dinosaur that can create a hurricane and spit napalm acid attacks your home in the middle of the night? Like that.

If the Rangers were similarly wired, it didn't show. They were grimly determined, and at almost five in the morning local time, absolutely ready to get their kill on. So basically, it was Tuesday for Rangers.

"The dragon... that's our *target*, Vandahar," said Captain Knife Hand, that look of permanent indigestion already on his face.

The old wizard made an *Ah yes* face.

"Perhaps," he said. "Almost certainly. If the dragon is using the Katari to wage war against you Rangers then I would guess you will find the Saur close at hand. Closer than farther no doubt, I'll wage this old pipe on. And if that is so, then you must plan on foul treachery and the stench of a deeper necromancy than even mighty Toth-Azom was capable of. Or at least, *was* capable of before your... Sergeant Thor, you call that one... sent Toth's dusty old skull flying off into every which way. Dust in the wind, that one, as the old bardic lay goes. But I must remind you that the dead necromancer Toth-Azom was but a mere servant of Sût the Undying."

Perhaps seeing the increasing impatient look on Knife Hand's face, the old wizard sniffed and straightened.

"So yes. I would plan accordingly since all of you seem so desperate to go and confront the dragon right now. I must tell you though, that this would be most foolish. The green wyrms are the most cunning of all the great brood of Bethoc the Fallen. It concerns me he did not lay waste to more of you."

Silence.

"And where would we find this dragon? Where could we find it right now, Vandahar?" asked the sergeant major. "He got some kinda lair or something, a cave he makes his home? *Seer-uth*, you say his name is?"

The wizard laughed and set to stuffing his pipe with more of the fragrant weed he burned within.

"*Ssruth*, Sergeant Major. It is pronounced *Ssruth*. Cirth is one of the god witches of Caspia. Husband to Circe. Oh no. No such mean place as a cave or a hole for one so great as the Terror of the North, Ssruth the Cruel. Bane of the Dragon Elves. No. And everyone is well aware of where Ssruth the Cruel makes his dwelling. They go to great lengths to avoid that specific place because they are smart folk who want to go on living. Ssruth the Green Wyrm makes the ancient ruins of Tarragon his own. It is known. He has lived there since he destroyed the Dragon Elves of old and drove them out. And as some of your younger warriors like to say… *spoiler*, is it?… they *were* driven out. They were all killed because their pride and greed would not release them from the great treasures that became the dragon's hoard in the deep vaults below the Palace of Kings. It was then Ssruth's alliance with the dread Saur began and bore its poison fruit of which we have now been forced to partake."

He paused to coax his long-stemmed pipe to life once more. Satisfied, he continued.

"We of the council had thought in recent centuries there had been a great falling-out between them. The Great Wyrm and the Lord of Death deep within his midnight tomb, that is. As the dragon consolidated his stranglehold on the remains of the great lost kingdom of the Dragon Elves, the wyrm decided he had little interest in the further foreign adventures of the Saur. Their dreams of conquest and eternal life held no sway over the glittering ill-gotten gold he had already obtained through terror and murder. So, as I have noted, the times are indeed dark if those two terrors have reformed their old alliance once again. This, plus whispers coming from out of the Crow's March, lead one to believe something dark is forming against the last kingdoms of man. The Cities of Men are in grave danger, as Marhan the Wise once warned."

Last of Autumn's dark eyes darted toward me, holding mine for a second at the wizard's mention of the *Cities of Men*. Our boat. Her in the prow. Smiling because she was no longer queen of what remained of the Shadow Elves. And it was just us in that perfect fantasy. Their clan's obligation to destroy the dragon and free themselves of a curse either gone, forgotten, or disregarded. Other monkeys for other circuses. Not our problems anymore.

But I knew she'd never do that, no matter how badly she wanted to. She'd never escape and leave these problems and obligations to someone else. Even if that someone else was a contemptuous little brother who seemed to hate her. She understood duty. And if anything... she was the very essence of the word. Perhaps that was why the Rangers had accepted her so easily. She spoke their unspoken language.

It'll have to kill me, I whispered to myself. Knowing that the only way there was ever a chance at the dream of the boat, her in the prow, a lightness and freedom on her expression I'd never seen once, was if that dragon was dead.

Maybe I'd caught momentary glimpses of that happiness in her eyes. Maybe. And I wanted that happiness to be there again. I didn't need to be there even, in that fantasy we shared. If the dragon was dead and she was free... that was enough for me.

It'll have to kill me.

And once more the cold shadow of the dragon passed over my soul just as it had in the night and fog. Terror and destruction following in its wake.

"We'll get into the geopolitical implications down the road," said the captain. "The question I think I know the answer to is... why did this thing attack us?"

The wizard turned this over for a moment, adding more smoke rings to the ceiling.

"Well, the obvious reason is Triton, who has obviously gained some influence over the old termagant. He has convinced the wyrm it is in his best selfish interests to rid himself of you now rather than later. It would be easy for me to think that the injury you did Ssruth this night, and the last time you met in full battle, have made you a threat to his person. You Rangers are the most dangerous foe in current proximity to his... lair, if you will. The ruins of Tarragon. And if I understand the nature of your relationship with Triton... that he was one of you once... then he either wants revenge, or your... what do you Rangers call the magic bauble of endless wonders? A *taco machine,* is it? I have no idea what a taco is, but it does seem to make you powerful weapons of the Before I have only heard made mention of in the *Book of Skelos.* So that too may be the reason that lies at the heart of his attack. It's as old as war itself; you warriors know that. Someone else wants what you have. And they have come to take it."

As Vandahar's words faded, the sergeant major could be heard to mutter, "That SEAL weren't never one of us. Ever." The stoic Rangers all seemed to concur, if only by the sheer and solemn silence which convinced me that whether

McCluskey knew it or not, as far as the Rangers was concerned, he was a dead man walking. Vampire or not.

Eight Rangers had just died.

That was going to be answered for in full, with much murder and much gunfire. Probably explosives too. Correction—there *would* be explosions. The Rangers were already talking about acetylene. If there were any more coffee that I hadn't cornered left to corner on the Ranger black market, I'd bet heavy on dynamic explosions being in effect.

The captain stood and watched all of us for a long moment as we processed everything we'd heard. Getting a good idea of where we were going and where all this was ultimately heading.

"We start recons this morning," he said. "We develop the intel and the battlefield around the objective we are now designating *Lizard King*. We are going in. We are going to take out this target with extremely violent prejudice. The rogue naval special warfare operations asset is in play and is considered kill on confirmation. Or anyone who even looks or smells like that scumbag, Rangers. We need target capabilities. Scouts and snipers will depart, develop, and asses for collection."

He nodded at the Baroness and the Forge tech. "We will want the Forge cranking out weapons specific to inflict maximum harm to Lizard King. Sergeant Major is point on that. Rangers, we're going to kill it. We're going to go there, right where it lives, where it feels safe, and haul it out of its lair and skin it alive for the eight we lost tonight. I promise you that."

And of course, with each part of his speech, his Knife Hand was out and reinforcing the points he made. That made me feel good. Made the hairs on the back of my neck stand up at attention. It was pure RAH and the opposite of the cold shadow of the dragon.

RAH. Rangers Acting Hostile.

"We're gonna croak that squid good and dead, Rangers," growled the sergeant major in the silence that followed. "Some things ya just can't let pass."

CHAPTER FOUR

ALMOST six weeks later, on what we were guessing was a sweltering early July morning, the dragon came out to feed. It was a ceremony. It was a bribe. It was something savage and primal from an age I never thought I'd experience back in the ivory towers I'd fled to become a soldier. This was like something out of an elder age of savage sacrifice, pagan ceremony, and, well... flying dinosaur. In other words, it was more myth than real, except for the fact that we were watching it all through our sights as we crept into position, completely kill-thirsty at murder-o'clock high.

And even though me and one hundred of my best heavily armed friends were well past right of bang and more than ready to get our kill on, I'll say this to keep the record of events honest. And yeah, I know it's terrible, but what I saw that hot, sweaty morning as we silently moved to take our fighting positions was one of the most amazing, utterly terrifying, and beautiful sights I'd ever seen. And maybe ever will see.

But the Ruin is a strange place, and so maybe there will be other terrors and amazements to replace what we witnessed when a real live dragon came out to feed.

That is, if we live long enough to see those things.

Couple that with all the Ranger murder-in-waiting and... all I can say is, it was indescribable. Later the sergeant major told me that when he was young, he'd been in the jungles and had seen a quad fifty full of tracer rounds go off on a riverboat at night in the middle of all hell breaking lose with gun runs from little birds and air strikes from B52s. It was like that, he told me. Beyond description once you'd seen it.

Tanner put it a different way. He said it was like the first time he ever saw Desiree come on the main stage. Stripper Wife Numero Uno. "She coulda been a weather girl, or a model, or even a lawyer, Talk. But she went home with me that night and I thought, for just a little while before all the crazy I made 'em... I thought I was the King o' the World. You know? You know how women make you feel right then, Talk?"

I did.

I do.

Dead-dragon *Cities of Men*.

The next two minutes were gonna be a lotta broken glass to cross. But as the Rangers like to say, I was in it to win it.

Also, I know I have a tendency to digress and go off on tangents that are important to the story but not so much to the linear version of the narrative, and Tanner has read some of this account and he agrees with you.

"You're real wordy, Talk," he says.

And I know I talk about coffee a lot.

"You got a problem there, Talk."

I know that. So I'll try and cut down how much of the ink I'm putting on this page concerning my addiction. But even as I write this, I have perfected the perfect brew out of my dwindling supply of Portugon beans cold-brewed with cinnamon, cardamom, and this crazy sugar we found in the storage. It's crank off a gas station bathroom sink. It's not brown. It's golden. And it came in a teak box marked *Property Spice Lords of Kungaloor*. Maybe that has something to do with the buzz it gives you. You feel electric like you're some race dog racing for the finish line. But calm and all *Matrix* I-know-kung-fu.

Thai and Hindu. That's what the words are written in, on the teak box. Neither of which I speak. But the Forge was able to crank out a no-frills translation manual for me. Frills for linguists are things like dictionaries, language recordings, and flash cards. But no-frills was plenty to figure out the simple shipping marking stamped on the front.

Property Spice Lords of Kungaloor.

Interesting, 'cause I'm a linguist and all.

But mostly interesting because that crazy crank sugar makes my coffee all nitro.

And there. I just went off on a tangent and talked about coffee. I'll try harder.

But here's the deal. I have to tell you now about what went down in the space of about five minutes of dragon-slaying that took six weeks to plan. Because the Rangers are all about obsessive levels of planning. So... I'm gonna break it down for you in installments. Matching the actions on the objective with the planning and stories that happened along the way to get there. I'm going to tell you how I saw the knock-down drag-out fight with a real-life chlorine-napalm-breathing dragon go down, step by step. And then between each step I'll give you some detail about what went into that step to allow the Rangers to move on to the next step.

Why?

Because I know I go on and on about Rangers and how much I'm utterly in awe and stoked to get to work with them, and now that I'm not on extra duty or running and gunning for my life in hostile territory, or in the middle of a battle against orcs and the undead or whatever other craziness the Ruin has decided to throw at us that day, I get to go back and read what we've been through.

And I see that Tanner's right: I'm a little scattered. More than a little, if I'm being honest with myself. Which I try to be. But there's an organization there that I see, or at least, I can see the way my mind has organized this adventure we're all on, and what I don't want to do is make it seem like Rangers are *easy Superman*.

That's a Tanner phrase.

"We ain't *easy Superman*, Talk. Rangers train to pro athlete levels and they train hard to get there. All that started up during the GWOT. If you were back in the batts you got your own gym, trainers, and even therapists to work with you to get sharp enough to be the razor's edge of elite combat killer. You got what the average NFL player got, but also with weapons and explosives and enough training to waste a city or overthrow a country. We train like it's gonna be the Super Bowl of War every day. In a lotta ways. Like we can hotwire just about any vehicle. Sure, back in the sergeant major's day, all you had to do was PT like a beast, be a shooter, and work your radio. But now? Half these dudes could be scientists with all the training they get in cyber and all the other stuff that helps us track and eliminate Jackpots. DNA and the like. But like I was sayin'…"

I might take this opportunity to point out that Talker is a little scattered too. Maybe that's why we get along so well. So if even he says I ramble on too much… well, yeah. Point taken.

"Like I was sayin'… we ain't *easy Superman*. You know… like Superman is just Superman. Everything's easy to him because—because *he's Superman*. Yellow sun and all. Rangers, on the other hand, train, sweat, bleed, and develop every advantage they have to become Superman with guns and knives. Ain't nothin' easy about Rangerin', Talk. And when some screwup like me is tellin' you that… I don't know… I guess it means it's the real honest truth.

"Truth is I been barely hangin' on by my teeth in the batts. There wasn't one day I didn't expect them to come along and say, *Tanner, you're done, buddy*. Even now. If that can be done here, wherever the hell we are, I'm just waiting for Joe and Chris to come tell me to pack myself up and go over to the air force. And as much as I might be me… I ain't ready for that. So I train hard. Like I'm preparing for the Super Bowl but with guns and knives and probably a whole bunch of grenades and other things that go boom and knock the wind outta ya if you're lucky. Ain't no *easy Superman* in the Rangers, Talk."

So, as I'm beginning to tell you about how we went toe-to-toe with a real live, living, acid-breathing napalm flying dinosaur, I wanted you to know that yeah, Rangers are tough and squared away, but they ain't action movie stars. And I mean literally action movie stars who are just actors who have stunt men do crazy tricks and are just there to ruin and rail-kill all the extras and look good doing it. Rangers work hard to be Rangers. Being a Ranger is all about putting in the work to be one.

And so, I say all that to say this next part about why you're getting it this way. This account, what we got into that day, and believe me we were way in over our heads real quick, the Rangers prepped for it hard. They didn't just jock up with guns and explosives and hardcore little catchphrases. The first thing they did was apply their brains and skills to how they were gonna do the Lizard King. They fought the battle mentally before they ever fired a shot. They didn't just go the extra mile. They went a hundred extra miles to try and croak Ssruth.

And that's what I want this section of the account to show. Planning. Actions. Outcome. The Rangers that follow need to know what happened that day.

And this is what happened.

Almost six weeks later, on what we were guessing was a sweltering early July morning, the dragon came out to feed. It was a ceremony. It was a bribe. It was something savage and primal from an elder age of savage sacrifice and pagan ceremony. It was something I never thought I'd experience in my entire life. But there it was. Real.

We heard the thunder of the distant herd being driven in to feed the beast we were there to kill that morning. Legions of Saur and centaurs gathered with drums and thunder all across the strange ruins of the Dragon Elves' once-fantastic palace district. Chanting darkness. The drums beating *BOOM BOOM CLAP*. Crumbling monuments and sunken palaces turning green and gold in the morning light. Ivory marble covered in serpentine vines that would never let go until they had torn everything apart and made it all ruin once more.

Like I said… it was utterly beautiful, and totally mesmerizing. And it was surreal knowing what was about to happen and what we were about to face.

The centaurs, or Centauri as they are known to those in the know, servants of Sultria the Medusa of Atlantea, drove the cattle they'd taken from as far away as the high pastures below the lands of the Stone Giants. The half-horse, half-men came on shouting like cowboys riding herd and coming home at last. Cracking whips and waving cruel spears. Shining breastplates on their human torsos. Sneers on their thin lips. Their pointed goatees and ears almost demonic. They rode picket, driving the terrorized animals and other strange beasts that were like elk and deer, but more massive, into and through the ruins of Tarragon, coming down the fabled Ivory Road that led into the heart of the Palace of Kings, home to the Crimson Throne of the Dragon King who is no more. All this is where Paris once was.

And where Paris ain't anymore.

Paris as we knew it disappeared about two weeks after we left ten thousand years ago. But the River Seine, which is now called the Snake in High Tolkien, has turned much of the area into the disease-ridden, festering hot swamp it always was.

In lócë.

The Snake. Sometimes it's called the *Green Throat* like it's some fabled monster of old.

In Ezel Lanco.

I guess that's because it's where a lotta people disappear forever. And Green because the water is green and because Paris, and what they now call Tarragon, or the ruins thereof, was always a swamp even before the Ruin. A lot of capitals are and have been all along throughout human history. Go figure.

The Paris that was, and the Tarragon of the Dragon Elves that also was, is now a massive spreading ruin of mossy marble palaces, fractured morbid temples, creeping vine-overgrown monuments sinking into mud and lakes, and willow-laden tombs dipping into the swamp slowly year after year. And still, from what little we've seen of it—or at least the evidence of it—it was probably once pretty spectacular when the Dragon Elves ruled much of southern Europe. Even now it's apocalyptically fantastic—even if it is being slowly swallowed by the great green swamp spreading away in all directions like a sore that will never heal.

The Palace of Kings, where the dragon makes his home deep beneath the ruins of the old throne, is on a high hill near the river. And the palace, though crumbling and cracked, still stands in pieces that spread away in all directions. Impressive towers surround the central holy well where the dragon makes his home. Apparently, this was once a place of great ceremony for the extinct and ancient Dragon Elves. And the wide space before that sacred place is where the Centauri drive their prizes, their offering, their bribes, the stolen cattle and other forest beasts, for the dragon's feeding on this holiest, or most profane, of days.

Endë Lairë.

Midsommar. The longest day of the year.

Vandahar says, "The ancient agreements state it must be this day. Perhaps the Eld knew they could not defeat the dragon and so arranged a meeting between him and fate at some date in the future. Trusting that fate, or whomever, perhaps even the Hidden King himself, would provide one day and end Ssruth's cruel reign of terror over the Ruin."

The wizard had considered us all when he said this. We were on one of the long-range recons and he was downloading all his lore. Trying to tell us everything we'd need to kill the dragon. Not just the ways, but the *whys*. Resting at a halt, he told us this. His pipe lit. His demeanor peaceful in the afternoon shade we'd covered in. His careworn face studying each and every tired Ranger in the patrol. He was getting glares from Sergeant Hardt for smoking. But he was Vandahar and could do whatever he wanted.

Hard: We need to maintain stealth discipline, Vandahar. No pipe until we reach the patrol base. Even at the halts when we rest and try to maintain operational silence.

Vandahar: Oh yes of course. (Packing pipe.)

"And perhaps… that day has finally come," the wizard concluded in a whisper, gently puffing on his pipe.

And now that day had come, or at least we hoped it had, the drums rolling *BOOM BOOM CLAP* and the Centauri unaware that they were currently surrounded by one hundred Rangers ready to go full metal kill. To our parading enemies it was a special morning in which they were required to deliver Ssruth the Cruel's payment in meat for alliance, support, or destruction on demand. To us it was a special morning too—of a different kind.

That was the situation.

I was staged with First Platoon on the edge of the kill zone. We were part of the containment element. Kurtz's weapons team. We were located inside a tower, a square-shaped ivory-colored chunk of vine-covered marble. Kurtz and Brumm had just double-tapped the two Saurian guards in the interior of the tower shadows as we moved through the tall swamp grass and up out of the river we'd been waiting out the dawn in. Front sight forward to take the fighting position now. The Saurian guards, lizard men who wore kilts and helms and carried spears and daggers, were as surprised as anyone as Kurtz entered through a fissure in the tower wall the scouts had identified during their intensive recon over the course of the prior six weeks. We'd run this. Sand-tabled it. Even marked out a "glass house." First Kurtz. Then Brumm. Then killing. "Everyone gets cleaned," Kurtz had said. Captain Knife Hand wanted no mistakes. There was zero margin for error. This had to go perfectly first time through when it came to showtime.

As part of the containment element, it was our job to make sure that when the killing started, the big flying dinosaur we'd tagged as Lizard King didn't just boogie once things got hot. We knew, this far out and forward, we were gonna get this one shot to kill him in about the space of a minute and a half if we hit Lizard King with everything we had according to plan with as much violence of action as we could muster.

Speed, surprise, and extreme violence.

No fail.

No margin for error.

No *easy Superman*, as Tanner would say.

It was our job to contain the OBJ. In other words, create an inner ring that made sure Lizard King couldn't escape if he wanted to. Once we started killing him, we wanted to make sure it was done in one go. We'd pin him with extreme outgoing violence so the assaulters could work him over when he was wounded and retreating for his hole.

The two heavy weapons teams had different fields of fire on the dragon's potential exit inside the Court of Immortals that lay before the ruins of the Palace of Kings. As did three sniper overwatch teams who'd crept in one by one over the last twenty-four hours. Lying in brush and debris, looking like brush and debris that didn't move and didn't breathe. Well back in the shadows of a ruined temple to a strange god we'd never know, or tied to a swamp tree a thousand meters out with eyes on a key position. Another team of Rangers with a MANPADS anti-aircraft Stinger missile system coming up along the riverbank and ready to get into a building with roof access and good cover. Excellent field of fire, and the sky was their kill zone that day. And then three teams of two stationed around the inner containment circle with Carl G's and airburst munitions ready to rock and roll.

All these teams were moving into position now as the centaurs drove the herd and the drums rolled and went *BOOM BOOM CLAP*. Or had taken their position in and among the ruins of the Palace of Kings and the surrounding district of crumbling and toppled marble, that hot sweaty morning dark as we finally closed the noose about Lizard King's long scaled ancient neck.

Six weeks of hard work was about to pay back a debt acquired when the dragon disintegrated eight Rangers. And Dawson. Dawson made nine.

"Someone starts something, PFC," said the sergeant major one morning when he let me hit his blue percolator because he knew Sergeant Kang the Tasmanian Devil Shogun of the Ranger battalion was going to smoke me well and good, "you make sure they know you're gonna finish it."

He'd forgotten I'd been busted down to private. Or maybe he hadn't. But the look in his eyes was far away and full of deep dark hate. Smart hate, not stupid. You wanna know what a Ranger looks like when they're brooding over something? That's what they look like. And if they're quiet, you should be real concerned that something very bad is about to happen to someone. That was the only thing the sergeant major said that morning as I was off to get smoked.

And this was before the dragon hit the FOB. I think he just had the SEAL on his mind that morning. After the dragon, the sergeant major was nothing but vengeful silence. Like it was a promise to the universe that the hate it had earned was about to be laid in full.

"Carve it in granite, Talk," Tanner told me once. "That squid's a dead man walking far as the sergeant major's concerned. And he don't even know it's comin'. Which is the second-best way to have it. The best way is when they know, and they can't sleep because of it. Can't think. Can't eat. Nothin'. But they know we're coming for 'em. Back in Iran some o' them mullahs would just come out and surrender once they knew the Rangers had been given the green light to come for 'em."

Now we were taking the tower with speed, surprise, and extreme violence. We had walked this a dozen times in our training and set up for *the pump*. Or what Rangers call a mission. Glass house run-throughs for the taking of every position. We'd rehearsed it until we were doing it in our sleep. At least I was. I had dreams of trying to call Sidra but I couldn't dial the number and I had to do another run-through of our tasks. Plus, Sidra's long gone. Like ten thousand years gone.

In other words, we lived, breathed, and dreamed of assassinating the dragon. The undeclared grand-prize-winner HVT of all time.

It was mid-morning when I followed Kurtz and Brumm in through the fissure in the ancient tower wall and watched first Kurtz and then Brumm splash the alien skulls of the lizard men on guard there. *Sleestaks.* That's what some of the Rangers jokingly liked to call them. Some old show or something I've never seen, but PFC Kennedy gave me a brief sketch. Sounds like I didn't miss much.

"Time to stack some stak," Rangers said in the darkness as we made our final approach through the swamp to final positions. Dip and cold brew keeping us awake as everything finally came together to get our kill on.

I was third through the door on the breach of the guard tower we were taking. We knew there were always two in the bottom of every tower, two Saur lizard men that is, and two on the top of each of the five towers that surrounded the objective.

There was also a roving commander we'd identified. Except we could never pin down where he might be in all our planning. And as I left the morning light and entered the shadowy old crumbling tower, hearing the thunder of the approaching hoofbeats of the sacrificial herd, all those Centauri and driven prey for the feed, my MK18 was canned and ready to splash the commander if I got the chance. If he happened to be here, then I'd nail him with the silencer on to keep the noise down.

I pulled myself up and into the fissure—you had to grab crumbling stone in the tower's fracture and pull yourself up and in to get inside—and I heard the swift yet subdued eruptions from Kurtz and Brumm, who had already started the killing to clear the ground floor. I smelled cordite and saw the first two dead bad guys lying amid trash and debris. Kurtz was following his MK18 to the tower's missing door out onto the Ivory Way, the avenue that led into the Great Well of the Palace of Kings. Just as the plan called for and like we'd done a hundred times before to get here. Brumm one-handed dragging a stak corpse out of the way, the other hand holding a smoking M17 sidearm with a silencer.

Seconds later, Soprano was in with the two-forty bravo and little Jabba following, looking overloaded and forlorn more than any GI Joe dogface ever had. He was also carrying more cans of ammo than humanly possible. Tanner had finally found the chalk to write *Born to Gob* on the side of the dented FAST helmet that had been repurposed for the gob who'd basically become the weapons team's pet.

Tanner followed on rear security carrying the MK48 super SAW.

I tapped him as he entered, and he muttered, "Time to stack some stak, Talk."

They all thought that was hilarious.

Kurtz and Brumm were getting garrotes ready for the two on the top as Tanner took the fissure and Soprano and Jabba got ready to either lay hate from the missing door in the tower or shift to the roof once it was cleared.

Garrote kills are top of the Ranger bucket list in ways in which they want their enemies to die badly. In this situation they were called for, and not just for the bucket list. Taking down the two on top needed to be done silently, no carbines or sidearms, even canned. No knives because no one wanted a fight and screaming or hissing. So Kurtz and Brumm and the other Rangers taking out the rooftop sentries would go for the strangle kill. Cutting off the staks' ability to hiss and alert.

Kurtz shifted his wrist and checked his watch as we made ready to take the roof of the tower. Murder serious in full effect on his face as he gave us orders we already knew by heart in flat clipped whispered sentences.

"Two minutes to Lizard King. Net call says we're go for the hit. Soprano, on the front. Tanner, pick up downstairs once we shift to the roof. Talker, you're with us."

The next thirty seconds were pure adrenaline and I had to tell myself to move slow because slow was smooth and smooth was fast. Now the Rangers were actually depending on me. With both gunners watching downstairs and making sure that the roving commander didn't suddenly come waltzing into our assassination, Brumm and Kurtz were moving swiftly up the stone stairs that ran up along the inner walls of the old guard tower within the ruins. We needed to go three stories up to reach the guards on the roof. The stairs seemed solid enough, but anything non-stone in the old Dragon Elf watchtower was nothing but ruin. Tattered cloth that might once have been tapestries. Smashed and rotting wood that could've been fine furniture. Broken weapons. Smashed bones. A humanish skull except for the almond-shaped eye sockets. Probably Dragon Elf.

I was following Kurtz and Brumm up. Both had their strangling wire out and the dowels they'd made themselves in their fists ready to go. The plan called for them to enter the rooftop, stay low, and drag down the sentries there while strangling them. Controlling the takedown. I was along for two reasons. If the strangling didn't go as planned, I would put the tap on whoever didn't want to die according to plan. And if the strangling and dying *did* go according to plan, then I was to signal the two-forty to shift positions while Tanner maintained security on the lower level.

The top of the stone stairs that ran along the inner walls ended on a platform of rotting wood beneath an open trap door.

"NETCALL... eyes on Stak One." That was the call sign for the guard commander recon had identified. "He's on the road and moving toward the well. Lizard King coming out."

Brumm went for the first guard, moving fast, Kurtz on his heels. They knew right where the two lizard men would be. Staring at the massive herd being driven into the well area in the courtyard of the Palace of Kings. Brumm looped his wire around his stak in one swift motion, jerked it back savagely while placing his knee in the creature's upper back, and fell backward, rolling sideways and dragging the lizard man down onto the deck of the parapet where his impending death couldn't be witnessed from afar. His huge Saurian eyes were bulging in fear as I came onto the roof following my front sight, ready to meaningfully contribute, and its slender forked tongue darted wildly as it gasped for air it could not have. It struggled with its scrabbly scratching claws trying to reach Brumm, its weapons cast away, its lizard brain no doubt trying to figure out why it couldn't breathe anymore and never would again.

That one was good to go as far as my task and purpose here was concerned.

Following my holo-sight, I pivoted just like Chief Rapp of the Legendary SF Gunfighter School of Pro Stud Shooting had taught us. Economy of movement. Max focus. Maximum outgoing violence quickly.

"Kill them until they change shape or catch fire."

I picked up the lizard Kurtz had down on the ground and watched as Kurtz pulled so hard that two things happened at once. One, the wire bit clean through the weak scaly esophagus of the struggling strangled lizard man. And two, the stak just heaved itself out of Kurtz's clutch and control and broke the wire.

As the lizard man stumbled to his knees, scaly arms flailing wildly like he wanted to shout for help or was reaching for the tribal animal horn on its hip to sound the warning, Kurtz hissed, "Do him now, Talker."

So I did. One shot to the back of his smooth scaly skull and the stak just flopped forward and died on his knees, green blood drooling out through his ragged torn throat and onto the dusty surface of the crumbling guard tower.

Kurtz was up fast and low. Looking around to see if we'd screwed everything by firing. He made no excuses about his wire busting, but I could tell the look of rage and murder on his face was, for once, directed entirely inward.

He turned to me.

"Get the gun up here now!"

I moved to the stairwell, signaled Jabba, and seconds later Soprano and the goblin were hustling up the stone steps to make the parapet of the ruined tower of ivory stone. Overgrown with swamp vines.

The dragon roared out there and I felt my blood go suddenly cold. The ground shook. Either from the thunder of the meal being driven to it, or because of its massive claws and bulk thrusting itself up out of the ancient well in the courtyard of the Palace of Kings that was today's kill zone. It howled like some mighty T-Rex smelling blood and prey.

I moved to the edge of the parapet, right of Brumm, who was ready with his SAW.

"Lookee that," muttered the gunner.

And I did. The *BOOM BOOM CLAP* echoed off the crumbling stones of this long-ago sanctuary of the Dragon Elves as I stepped forward and looked out on all the garlanded Saur who had come out to see their ally come forth to feed. There were hundreds of them out there on the field. Like it was a parade, or a holy festival. They hissed and cried in high-pitched shrieks I would have thought them incapable of because they were reptiles. They stamped their clawed feet and beat large ceremonial drums on the *BOOM BOOMs* of their noise. Clapped sticks and spears on the *CLAP*.

Their tribute to the great beast in full, coming out now. First Ssruth's massive, triangular, scaly and horned head erupted out of the well, and the strange congress hissed with ecstatic joy at his mighty appearance. Then came his long serpentine neck. An evil grin revealed great yellow fangs as the terrified animals were driven toward him in the final seconds of their existence. His terrible huge claws reached forward and dragged his endless and massive bulk out of the hole he came from, and the ground shook and rumbled, ancient stone collapsing from the nearest buildings.

Then his wings emerged, opening up like two great leathery sails on the biggest warship of the lost ages of naval warfare that ever was. They blotted out the morning light, opening wider than I thought possible, and only then did I realize just how huge he was.

But I also spotted the horn that Sergeant Thor had blown off the tip of. And that gave me comfort. Courage even. We could do this.

BOOM BOOM CLAP.

"All elements in position," announced Captain Knife Hand over the net.

BOOM BOOM CLAP.

The Rangers had wiped out several Saurian guard positions or crept into their shooting locations. Snipers. Air defense. Weapons teams. All was ready. All teams go for the hit on Lizard King.

Assaulter elements, using the new XM25s the Forge had cranked out, had threaded the ruins of the palace, cutting right through the throne room itself, and were now stacked and ready to cut the lizard off from any chance to make for the hole once the shooting started in full. Behind the assaulters, the master breachers and the demo teams were ready with all the explosives they'd brought to play.

"Reaper on station," said the cute ponytailed air force co-pilot over the net. "Target acquired and broadcasting one hell of a heat signature. Weapons free…"

The dragon rose up onto its hind legs and snatched at two of the shaggy cattle being driven into its greedy grasp. Impaling each with a fantastic and gigantic claw.

We're really gonna do this, I thought as it all began to happen.

The dragon roared with ferocious delight and devoured both animals at once.

"All elements…"

It was Captain Knife Hand. We knew this was coming. We'd trained for everything. It was all by the numbers now. Waiting for the opportunities that intense violence would present. Watching for the failures that would surely come with that also. Plans and contingencies for everything. The Rangers had come ready to take their shot. That's all they asked to avenge the eight. Plus Dawson.

"Go to masks, all elements. Firing demo thirty seconds…"

CHAPTER FIVE

"FIRING demo in thirty seconds…"

Destroying the tower, or as it was known in High El-ven Tolkien, *Mindon Elen*, roughly translated as *The High Tower of Stars*, was critical to Captain Knife Hand's plan for putting the hit on Ssruth the Cruel. The high-ex surprise the dragon was about to get kicked off the entire attack phase of the operation now that the Rangers had a perime-ter established, or an inner cordon secured, which ensured the enemy was kept out and anything within the kill zone was kept in.

Where it could get good and killed by the Rangers.

Mortars were plotted and ready to drop all over the dragon thirty seconds after the demo sent the tower crash-ing down onto the flying dinosaur. Carl G teams with an-ti-air munitions were ready to do the big lizard if that thing even thought about trying to get airborne and start doing gun runs, or gas runs as it was, all over us. Then there was the Stinger team ready to put the hurt on the dragon's heat sig if it turned all fast mover. All of the anti-air units were outside the inner ring. Everything that composed the inner ring was oriented inward and ready to lay some serious ki-netic hate on call sign Lizard King who had just come out to feed.

But Captain Knife Hand had wanted dynamic explosives to do much of our work before the shooting started in earnest. The main problem that faced the Ranger planning, which was extensive, was that the area the dragon was coming out in, according to scout recon, was the most inaccessible part of the kill zone we needed to access.

Dragon. Saur ground troops. Centaur heavy cav. And the ruins were rife with all kinds of denizens that were either in league with Ssruth on some level, or just mindless killers whose lairs were death traps just waiting for prey to come waltzing in.

Luckily the Rangers didn't waltz. And they were pretty fierce predators in their own right. The entire swampy ruins of the once fantastic capital of the ancient dragon elves was a very dangerous place to be on any given Sunday, but right now, with heavily armed Rangers full of bad intentions and high explosives, well, it was downright fatal.

The scouts had identified something useful from their first patrols closer and closer to the ruined city of Tarragon. The Tower of Stars had been identified as being of possible use in the opening moments of the ambush on Lizard King. And in that, the captain saw the potential to drop some serious hammer on the killer lizard that could breathe chlorine napalm on you if you gave it half a chance.

The Rangers were intent on not giving Lizard King anything close to half a chance.

The trick was not to give it any opportunity. To starting hitting it and keep hitting it from multiple directions until the dragon decided to crawl right back into the trap the Rangers had laid for it. Where it thought it would be safe. Where the Rangers were going to kill it once and for all because that was the place that it would be the *least* safe. And the tower was the Ranger's opening throat punch.

"The *Mindon Elen*," Vandahar had whispered almost reverently when Chief Rapp's indig unit linked up with the Ranger scouts at the patrol base a few miles south of the ruins. The old wizard stood staring for a long while at the ruined tower through the yellowy jungle haze that surrounded the city.

Hard to believe this was all the City of Lights ten thousand years ago. But then again, a lot of things were hard to believe here in the Ruin of now. And some of those things were trying to kill you.

Embrace the fantasy, I told myself as I studied the tall, slender, forlorn tower rising in the distance over the swamp and the ruins.

The Ranger patrol base was nothing more than a small muddy island lying along the Seine, or the Snake as they called it here. And I mean small. We could all barely fit on it. But it had great cover and you disappeared inside the clump of swamp vegetation once you crossed the muddy, moss-laden waters to get to it. Never mind the local poisonous killers swimming here and there. The swamp was thickest here. The waters alive with deadly snakes and other creatures we'd caught sight of that might have been very large crocodiles, or something far worse. Sergeant Hardt had decided this was the most inaccessible part of the swamp within reach of the vast ruined city, so it was here he'd decided to operate his stalk-and-chalk patrols from.

Two elements out each night. Marking enemies. Exploring outer sections of the ruins. Taking out potential enemies that weren't directly associated with the dragon's power structure and that could be dispensed with to facilitate operations. Laying the groundwork for the ambush on Lizard King.

The Rangers were currently betting who could kill the biggest crocodile river monster while they were out and about crawling and swimming through the swamps, avoiding Saurian patrols and other potential allies of Lizard King. The rules of Ranger Big Croc Hunt were that it had to be done with hand weapons. No explosives or gunfire. The Rangers moved incredibly silently here, using nothing above a whisper for days on end. Their voices back at the patrol base had become almost unused to being used and were now scratchy and little accustomed to talking at normal levels. Things a linguist notices. There was also that vague sense of constant chlorine in the yellow haze and mist. So that had to account for some of the vocal damage.

Back at the FOB the command team was busy training and supervising special weapons cranking at the Forge. Out here close to Objective Lizard King, it was Sergeant Hardt's show to run. And everything wrapped around the constant patrol. Which meant I was constantly reminded by every NCO that Ranger school was nothing but a death march of endless patrolling in which you swapped leadership positions and learned mission-critical skills that made you Ranger-qualified.

"Patrols are essential, Talker," Kurtz lectured me as we got ready to link up with Chief Rapp's indig element. "This is where you're weak."

He didn't say this with his usual bitter critical assessment of weakness on my part. He said it as though it was just a statement of fact and he needed to make sure I was aware of it. Which it was. Which I was. My RASP had been abbreviated. I was not an infantryman. I am a linguist. In

Basic Training, a patrol to me had meant little more than a long walk.

Now Kurtz was telling me the truth because I needed to know it. We were going downrange and getting close to the dragon. There would be no walls to hide behind. The weapons we carried as we went well beyond the walls, wire, and perimeter, would be all we had to defend ourselves against it should the giant gas-breathing sky lizard decide to come out and play with us before we were ready to shoot it in the head.

"Can it like… smell us? *Sergente?*" asked Soprano. Jabba, the small two-forty bravo gunner's constant companion, put his large flappy claws over his eyes at the mere mention of the dragon. Anytime and every time.

"Jabba no like. Jabba big bigga no like, dray-gunnn."

"Kennedy says affirm on smell," Kurtz replied. "Baroness is working on something that may help there."

Then he turned back to me.

"Survival on the battlefield, Talker, means we use stealth, dispersion, and security as we move. Constantly. At all times. We live it and breathe it and there is no excuse for it not to be practically applied at all times. That's how we patrol. We use five things to accomplish this. Principles, Talker. Planning, recon, security, control, and common sense. You're gonna learn those on the move with Chief Rapp's indig force. The weapons team is there to protect them and help train. You'll be learning along with the indigs."

"This-a gonna count for Ranger school, *Sergente?*" asked Soprano as he got into the front leaning rest position before Kurtz could start smoking him as usual.

Kurtz shot the gunner a hate-filled look and told him to elevate his feet on the tree. Soprano knew the drill and started repping out inclined pushups. He could do them all day now.

The scouts had already been out there a week, sneaking around the ruins and trying to develop as much ground intel as they could before it was time to do this. And once the first maps had come back—using our rough internet, which consisted of extremely high overflights by the drone to pick up email packets and then return south to the FOB with updated intel from on-scene—Vandahar had been able to identify key features that might play into the captain's battle plans. One of those features was the *Mindon Elen*. The Tower of Stars.

"It is an old tower," the wizard said by the sergeant major's hearth one afternoon. He had taken to swinging by to get coffee in the afternoon, as he'd acquired a taste for it.

So, I hated him for that.

I also made sure to swing by if I could because he was regular like clockwork, and if I approached the sergeant major's command center and smelled pipe smoke then I knew the blue percolator was brewing my particular brand of addiction. Timing was everything. So sayeth all junkies since time began. One afternoon I heard him talk about the tower.

"Studying your captain's maps and seeing his plans to nail the spike into old Ssruth's black heart," began the wizard over a cup of my coffee, "it occurs to me that if you could get some of your fantastic... explosives, I believe you Rangers call them... if you could make it fall in a certain direction, then as the wyrm came out of his lair for the Midsommar feast, then perhaps... you could bring the tower down right on top of him. That would give the old scoundrel quite a surprise, and perhaps there would be some advantage in that for you."

The sergeant major blew on the hot dark coffee in his canteen cup and muttered.

"We can make that thing fall anywhere we want, Vandahar."

I had coffee too. But I didn't say anything cool and all action hero like the sergeant major had just said. I was too busy sipping.

Less talking and more coffee is always the pro move. I'd been busy interfacing between the Shadow Elves and the Rangers, and the dwarves and the Rangers, making sure all communications were clear. The dwarves were all about improving our walls regardless of automatic grenade launchers and Ma Deuce fields of fire.

"There is just one... problem," mused the wizard as he began to talk with his pipe, holding the old coffee cup in one hand and pointing the stem at concepts only he saw. "Sultria."

Silence. That eagle who'd been soaring out there ever since we'd arrived was out there that afternoon, drifting on the heat hazy currents. Summer was really beginning to come on. This place was breathtakingly beautiful in almost every way.

"What's a Sultria?" asked the senior-most Ranger NCO. Then he drank more coffee and waited for the story to unfold.

"Sultria is... a medusa, Sergeant Major Stone. Do you know what those are?"

The wizard always used everyone's full rank and name. Except for me. Just plain old *Talker* seemed to work for me.

Like he sensed my rank and station were always in flux and always would be. Best to keep it simple with me. You never knew if my stock was up or down with the Rangers. Side note... sometimes I'd catch Vandahar studying me when he thought I wasn't looking. And if I looked up and caught him, he'd just smile in his friendly old man's way and then look off like he was daydreaming about something important or long ago.

"Yeah," muttered the sergeant major. "Medusas are in mythology. Greek mythology. An ugly woman with snakes for hair that could turn you to stone if you looked at her or she looked at you. Never could quite figure out which it was because I never thought about it much. Never thought I'd need to. But now... it occurs to me... I guess you had to look at her to get turned into a statue and all. That right, Vandahar?"

The wizard nodded and released a giant smoke ring that smelled of lavender and sandalwood. His smoke rings were quite pleasant, and considering the impending absence of these Portugon beans, we were down to two sacks, and the fact that all of us were now no longer getting *black market* items off the Forge, Penderly was being watched like a hawk by the command team, I'd considered learning how to smoke a pipe in the very likely doomsday scenario of coffee going all *bye-bye*.

NOOOOOOOoooooooooooooooooooooooo...

I had too much pride to brew up nettles and leaves and pretend it was an Arabica pour-over. Way too much pride. I was sick. But not that sick.

"Pride goeth before the fall," Tanner had remarked when I confessed my fears of impending-no-coffee-ahead late one night on watch. Like I was Lightoller seeing that most famous of icebergs late one night last century plus ten thousand years in the middle of the Atlantic. I thought that was an odd thing for my friend to say. He was still Tanner, and then sometimes... he wasn't.

"The ruin reveals," Autumn told me later when I mentioned it. "He's becoming now."

And I didn't have the courage to delve. I didn't want to know the answer. I didn't want to lose my friend again. I need someone to tell me how to Ranger.

And I need my friend. We all do.

Believe me, I was never that guy. Friends weren't big for me. I had them. But really words and phrases in strange languages were my best friends.

The army changed me that way. And it was probably for the best.

But back to the sergeant major and Vandahar and how I ended up getting to do intel work deep inside the belly of the beast. Yeah. That sounds cool. Almost got me killed. I was scared every second. And again, I thought I was just here to do languages and maybe pick the lock on the occasional classified file cabinet in some foreign embassy.

But here I was... being all I can be.

"Yes and no, Sergeant Major," the wizard began once his drifting smoke ring had left the small ancient kitchen of the sergeant major's command post. Left and gone out to play in the steep canyon with the eagle out there on the summer thermals. Eagles don't care about Rangers or dragons. Eagles gonna eagle. "You have it right in that the medusa turns you to stone if you gaze upon her, Sergeant Major Stone. But you're mistaken in that she's ugly. Sultria's beauty is rumored to be quite legendary. I am told she is... well, she has some spectacular features that men... do enjoy. A shame about the serpents that will bite you to death and paralyze you should you make the mistake of being entranced enough by her form to get close enough for the stone gaze to take effect. But her beauty has always been quite legendary. Only the undead are immune to her fatal charms."

The sergeant major asked a question then. He wanted to know how Vandahar, or anyone for that matter, could know what this medusa looked like, seeing as anyone who looked at her turned to stone. An insightful question, or so I thought, and Vandahar acknowledged the same.

"That knowledge is thanks to an unlikely source: Scarpa of Accadios, a famous painter who once dealt in necromancy. He had skeletons recovered from near her fortress in the blue shadows of the Atlantean Mountains in that ruined desert wasteland beyond the known, and he used shadow speakers to extract from these skeletons some rather extensive descriptions of her person. I've seen his painting in the Grand Passage of the Emperor's tower. It is... well..."

Vandahar seemed uncomfortable for a moment. He took a sip of coffee and sat back, working at his pipe.

"Well... let's just say she's quite beautiful if the dead can be trusted and... odd thing for me to say... for the most part they can be. Let's just leave that at that, Sergeant Major. No hag she. Quite the opposite."

The sergeant major refilled his cup. Then mine.

Small victories.

"And how is this Sultria, who lives way off in the Atlantean Mountains, which near as I can tell is what we would have once called the Atlas Mountains, which puts her in the vicinity of Morocco and Algeria, how is she a problem?"

The wizard cleared his throat and adjusted himself. Working on another fragrant smoke ring.

"Ah yes, Sergeant Major Stone... when the stars fell... that caused the ruin there along the accursed coast where once there was great and mysterious civilization. Sultria is a powerful force within this world, but a minor player in the grand scheme of things taking shape. The Cities of Men shun her diplomacies because she is... well, she is a monster after all. And she's done much to prove that. She is quite given over to evil, even if she tends to keep herself off at the ends of the world down there along the Lost Coast. A place few ever go, and fewer ever return from. But because of her inclinations, and the bounties placed on her by the Emperors of Accadios, she makes a natural ally for the Saur, and is rumored to have even tried her hand at making forays of alliance into the regions of Umnoth, sending her best champions to seek audience with the Nether Sorcerer himself. But of course, the Witches of Caspia would not have any of that. And I'm very sure she's up to something in the Crow's March if the ravens are to be believed of late. All this is too much to be merest coincidence. The great dark legions..."

The wizard seemed to catch himself. Realizing he'd gotten lost in other conversations that seemed so much more than what we were about that summer. Pulling a hit on Lizard King. Bringing down the Tower of Stars in our opening move to waste the dragon.

"Sultria's strange court consists of two sister medusas. Both powerful, filled with guile, and quite dangerous to everyone, including each other. She, Sultria, is queen ruling from behind the walls of the Circle. Nemesi and Alluria, her sisters, are banished to other realms in service to their sister. In service to their very cunning sibling and whatever macabre machinations she is about. It is rumored that the more dangerous one to Sultria, Nemesi, is little more than a court prisoner to the Lich Pharaohs deep in the Land of the Black Sleep. But Alluria… she has proven herself a capable ally to her sister, and has acted as chief envoy to dangerous and very powerful creatures within the Savage Lands and the Dire Frost, if the tales are to be believed. The centaurs currently finding Ssruth's Midsommar meal, ranging far and wide over the savage lands to plunder and steal what cattle they can, they are in service to Lady Alluria. And Alluria makes that ancient tower, *Mindon Elen*, a relic of the earliest days of the Dragon Elves, her own. She desires close proximity to our common foe, for she is an ally to the great dragon. Or rather, her sister is. Supposedly. But we of the council have long suspected Alluria of whispering treachery to the old wyrm. As foolish as that would be. Dragons are master manipulators. And the green tarragons are the worst, if the *Book of Skelos* is to be taken seriously."

For a long while the wizard was lost in thought as he chewed over information it seemed he had not thought about for some time. Nodding to himself as the sergeant major picked up his Kindle, read a page for a moment, then put it down before speaking again.

"I'm guessing getting into Alluria's tower, Vandahar, with her in there… that would be a challenge."

"That is correct, Sergeant Major. Medusas are crafty and suspicious. Jealous really. It is their nature. Getting your… high explosives in there… a difficult challenge to say the least. Though I'm quite keen to see it happen. Or rather the effects."

"You look at her..." began the sergeant major. Over-riding the wizard's imagined explosions and destructions of Ranger explosives well placed. One of the smoke rings exploded like a Death Star in the air above us and it was clear there was some psychokinetic link between the gossamer rings and the wizard's dreams. But the sergeant major was too busy chasing the thread a Ranger lives for: killing. Killing his enemies. Payback for the eight dead Rangers. And Dawson. Settling up with McCluskey. "You look at her, then you're a statue until the end of days. But as long as you don't look... you're okay. You can still talk to her. That right, Vandahar?"

The wizard nodded once. Gravely.

"And supposing you were doing that. Talking to her. This medusa," the sergeant major said. "What language would the two of you be speaking?"

And now he was looking at me. And so was the wizard.

I'm not stupid. I knew where this was headed. Or at least, I did now. I can't honestly say that, in my years of studying languages, it ever once occurred to me that the skills I was developing might one day lead me, ten thousand years in the future, to an actual face-to-face sit-down with a living, breathing, snakes-for-hair, turn-you-to-stone medusa.

Life takes some funny turns.

Two hours later I was joining Chief Rapp's indig force, along with Kurtz's weapons team who'd be going along to help train and pull security along the patrol to the objective and the Ranger patrol base. We were going forward to link up with the scouts and figure out how to bring the tower down on Ssruth's head.

And I had a feeling I'd be doing a little more than just speaking languages and returning fire with forty of my most heavily armed friends.

CHAPTER SIX

THE two-week march up to the Ranger patrol base located deep in the swamps south of the ruins of Tarragon was long and hard. From the get-go, Chief Rapp and Kurtz made it clear this wasn't just an operation... it was also a teaching experience. The indigs, as they were known among the Rangers, were going along to learn to do things as Rangers did things.

We had two separate groups of indigs. *Separate* was putting it mildly. The Lost Boys, Shadow Elven males of the dwindling tribe, ranging from their teens on down, were the first group. The second was the dwarves. Age indeterminate. But think Amish biker gang and you'll get the picture real fast. To anyone reading this in the future, *Amish* and *biker gang* might not be familiar terms to you. So let's just say they were a rough and heavily armed lot that had strange traditions and a plainspoken manner reminiscent of some separatist religious sect. They were nice and polite, but it was clear they could kill you about six different ways in the space of a sentence.

This was where Chief Rapp came into his own as the lone Green Beret among the Rangers. Most people have a lot of ideas about SF. Some of those ideas are true. They are indeed highly competent killers who pull all kinds of high-speed low-drag missions in foreign and very extreme situations. They differ from the Rangers in that they work in smaller, highly specialized groups, and they are primarily teachers.

The classic old-school SF mission is Green Berets going to work with untrained or barely trained rebels in foreign countries and teaching them the basics of fighting as an effective military unit. Weapons, marksmanship, first aid, planning, and communication. Other stuff too. Then, fighting alongside that newly trained force and leading them, ultimately, into combat, usually facing overwhelming odds and superior military equipment. The Green Berets are the guerillas of SF. They are trained to the highest levels. Whereas Rangers are savage Viking killers, the Green Berets are more Warrior Poet Kings. Your mileage may vary. That is just my observation.

Here's something true about both of them, however. Rangers and Green Berets. If either of them is up late at night thinking about how to settle you... you'd best get religion and leave town. I've been around them long enough to know they get real focused and real inventive about killing you if they've decided to get that done.

Free advice. But you will be billed for advice not taken.

Chief Rapp had been assigned to our flight when we left Area 51 because he was to assist the ground force commander in tactical planning and warfare doctrine when we arrived two to five years in the future. Which was the plan. Two to five, that is. Not ten thousand, which is what happened. That was Chief Rapp's other specialty besides being a medic. SF generally have two specialties they crossover train in when they get assigned to the operational detachment teams. ODA teams. A-Teams. Chief Rapp was both a medic, basically a field surgeon, and he also did doctrinal warfare planning and training. He could make you an army out of some barely trained and heavily dissatisfied people whose backs were to the wall as far as their worldview was concerned.

Now that the Ranger fortress had locals—indigs, indigenous peoples—it was time to train them as a fighting force the Rangers could work with for mutual defense and extended operations.

And also, learn from them.

Already the Rangers had acquired much from the Lost Boys. The savage little murderous elf children's knowledge of the local flora and fauna was absolutely invaluable. Southern France still had the Mistral and tranquil countryside, but it was rife with dangerous monsters full of poison and magical abilities that did things like turn you to stone, shoot lighting and/or fireballs, and even make you old like Sims who everyone now just called Old Man even though he was technically still only twenty-three. And their tracking, the Lost Boys that is, and their stalking ability, was on par with that of the Rangers. But much of that was due to the fact that the young Shadow Elven males wore no footwear of any kind, seldom bathed unless they just happened to be crossing water, and despite being half-naked adorned themselves with all kinds of found leaves and sticks they found meaning in, which acted as camouflage on some level. They were masters of this and took great pride in becoming invisible. They enjoyed playing tricks on the Rangers, and given twenty meters they could utterly disappear into a forest that even the best Ranger snipers could not spot them in. Until they switched to thermal sights.

Then Sergeant Thor would mutter, "Bang. You're dead, little guy."

Where they suffered was in the area of patrol communications. They used forest calls and natural sounds that had become too easy to identify for the Rangers. Almost musical and verging on war cries. Chief Rapp theorized they used these to terrify and drive their prey into pre-determined kill zones. But it gave away their positions, and that was antithetical to what the Rangers wanted when they moved. Which was silence and utter invisibility. The elves had no usage of hand signals. They had no understanding of how to account for even their own personnel on patrols. It was not uncommon for Carver, their leader and Last of Autumn's brother, to have missing boys at each rest. Sometimes they would be found having gone to sleep somewhere, or they'd spontaneously decided to fish, or they'd gorged themselves on blood berries and fallen far behind.

They were also obsessed with killing a manticore. That was their current goal in life and they sought to track one everywhere they went despite the task or mission at hand.

In short, they lacked discipline.

Kurtz glared at them. Shouted at them. And had to restrain himself from violence at almost every turn as he attempted to train them according to Chief Rapp's plan to forge them into an effective scouting and light assault force. When Kurtz instructed Carver what they'd missed on patrol that day, each and every word from the Ranger NCO was a MOAB on the kid's face as he was humiliated in front of his people. People he'd one day rule over.

It took three days to figure out that Kurtz was too Kurtz to work with the arrogant Shadow Elven leader in any way possible. Chief Rapp managed to make a game of it in the end, and perhaps the SF operator had known all along during the first three days of patrol that this was where it was going. Watching Kurtz grow more and more frustrated with the Lost Boys' lack of discipline and inability to meet standard on tasks of accountability and patrol communication... I think that was all part of Chief Rapp's plan in the end. The day Kurtz fired Carver as platoon leader, which is standard in Ranger training with peer assessment and constantly swapping out leadership roles, was the final straw for the boys. The Shadow Elf indigs disappeared ten minutes later, fleeing into the forest in every direction.

Not all at once. But every time you turned your back, another one was suddenly gone. Until there were only two left. Last of Autumn, who'd come along to supervise them. And Stubby.

Stubby was the only fat Shadow Elf Lost Boy I had seen. He was always eating. And that was probably the only reason he hadn't fled, as the dwarves were sharing their ironcakes with him and he had no intention of leaving that easy food source.

Ironcakes are bars of tasteless *whatever* that give you incredible endurance and energy. Think flour-flavored Adderall. Eating one feels like you just ate all the carbs Olive Garden could do that day and had to call three other Olive Gardens to get all the endless breadsticks and pasta bowls they had in order to satisfy your insatiable dwarven appetite.

I finished half of one once and vowed to starve to death before I ever ate another. The dwarves eat three a day. Smiling and drinking their beer from the drinking horns they wear on their weapons belts as they do. Each of them keeps a small cask on top of his pack. These casks are never not full. Though no one has any idea where the beer comes from or how they brew it up. They're very secretive about that. And no... they don't share their beer. Something about it being religious to them and we are unbelievers. They make this face that says, *No. That is not done.* I suspect they're lying and merely don't want to share.

I can relate.

After Last of Autumn recovered the AWOL Lost Boys from the forest and ordered them, as their queen, speaking slowly and full of Shadow Elven menace in High Tolkien, Chief Rapp took over, understanding that Carver, as their leader and future king, was the key to their working relationship, operationally speaking. If Carver gave the orders, they got it done. If Carver understood the training, he taught it, and the rest of the motley murderous lot listened. The truth was... the future king had already trained a formidable fighting force. They killed stuff constantly. They had no fear. Zero. They got up in the tall trees and did crazy stuff. There wasn't a river they wouldn't swim in. Monsters and all. They knew how to move through the forest like they were merely another part of it. They just needed some refinements in order to accomplish what the Rangers wanted them to do.

Chief Rapp, not a Ranger, and the gentle but strong opposite of Kurtz, made him more acceptable as a teacher and informer to them. His manner was easygoing for such a massive man. He was six-six, and even his muscles had muscles. Soon, as the march progressed toward Tarragon, whenever he was doing something, there would be a clutch of Lost Boys standing over or around his shoulder, silently watching everything he did like it was the most interesting thing in the world. In time they began to give him bits of their camouflage. The chief wore it proudly and could tell you from whom each piece came.

"You get tired of that?" I asked him one night as the two of us took watch after a long day's haul toward the swamps south of the objective. "Them following you everywhere?"

"Intended. Plus, Talker... they jes' kids. I always liked kids. Reminds me o' myself when I was that age. I was jes' like them when I was young. Never wore shoes unless I was on the football field. You know how it is when you're that age in summer... you gone all day until supper. Them are the best days you wanna remember forever. You understand?"

I did not. But also I did.

Kurtz was shifted to the dwarves, and the dwarves found some kind of long-lost brother or spirit in the angry NCO that had come to train them in the arts of Ranger warfare and extreme violence. They spoke Kurtz so well that in time Kurtz wasn't Kurtz anymore. If anything, he'd become one of them. Speaking in their low hushed manner as he taught them how to Ranger along the way toward Tarragon.

Kurtz's frustration was evident with the dwarves in only two situations. One happened sometimes. The other, every night when the dwarves tried to build overly extensive defenses wherever we stopped for the night after establishing our objective rally point. But the sometimes one was river crossings. These made the dwarves weird. Where the Lost Boys excelled, the dwarves turned into a clutch of old women who were overcautious to the extreme. It was their king who got them moving the first time they needed to cross a Ranger rope bridge. They pretended their massive packs or many weapons gave them pause and had them dithering. But it was really the swift water, and they were loath to cross it to the point of unreasonable fear.

The Lost Boys had already crossed and had far-side security locked down. It was taking so long to get the dwarves to even start their crossing that some of the boys were returning to swim in the river, or fish. Kurtz was steaming and finally the dwarven king bellowed, "Wulfhard Ravenslayer did not fail before the orc host at Sturm's Door, and I will not let a little stream bring me into low esteem here and now in front of the animal elven boys!"

He was saying all this in German and so I was the only one who understood. Perhaps Autumn did also, due to her hybrid *Grau Sprache*, or Gray Speech of the Crow's March, in which she and I had first learned to communicate.

Then the powerfully built dwarf, loaded down with his impossible pack and at least three weapons I could count, they all had several on them and were always producing one I'd never seen before to try its edge and see if it needed a quick sharpening, made his way toward the water's edge and the rope bridge that Tanner and Brumm were teaching them to use. Jabba and Soprano were on the far side with Chief Rapp. They made it, but a week later the dwarves were even more unhappy when we found ourselves chest-deep in the foul swamps of Tarragon. They suffered it, but the looks on their faces made it clear they would not willingly do this if it were not of such "grave import," as Vandahar had put it to them.

"The slaying of the wyrm will send a message, Wulfhard Ravenslayer," the old wizard said. "The Nether Sorcerer will know he can no longer count on the great serpent to harass the Stone Kings and your hardy people. This could change the war against the orcs. It is best we do what we can, now that we have such formidable allies as these... Rangers."

The grim dwarf king stared into the fire in response, listening to the wizard telling us of the grand struggle that was going on across the Ruin. Then: "They are no longer my people." The dwarven king whispered this to the smoke and flames. "That has been made clear now."

The fire popped and cracked. The smoke rising into the night. We were not into the swamps yet.

"As if that were ever true, old friend," said the wizard softly. "As if you could ever stop being their true king."

The dwarf turned to the wizard, his dark eyes watching the old man. Asking a question. As if to say, *And where exactly do we find ourselves now?*

The wizard chuckled to himself and lit his pipe, puffing it to life.

"Today does not mean tomorrow won't be different in some new and possibly horrible way," he said. "Be faithful, King of Stone, as your grandfather was when we made battle at the Gates of No Return. Hold the line that is true. That can be counted on even in these shadowy days when the forces of darkness finally gather under the Nether Sorceror's gaze."

The fire popped and crackled some more, and a long silence passed before the dwarven king spoke again.

"Different does not always mean better, Wanderer," he muttered.

A week later of trekking through a seemingly endless swamp and getting our own training course in Ranger swamp operations found us arriving at the Ranger patrol base. Sergeant Hardt and Sergeant Thor were running patrols every night all over the ruins of Tarragon. Studying every aspect of the city sinking into the swamps, noting every trail and route into the kill zone. Putting together exactly how the Rangers could hit the wyrm from every direction when it came feasting day.

"The tower..." Sergeant Hardt said, noting a big stick that was used to mark the *Mindon Elen*, the Tower of Stars, on the sand table the Rangers were developing, "is accessible through this district. Lots of crumbling stone buildings here and the streets are overgrown with swamp grass and small streams. Good cover. Excellent concealment. Many of the structures are filled with swamp water. We can use that and we can get a team of shooters with eyes on the tower's front door *here*." The Ranger's lead scout pointed as he spoke. "They'll have to go through the swamp *here*. Very deep. And then come out where this old building is sinking into the swamp water that's made its way across the city *here*. The second level is accessible from the water and they can move through there. There was a thing in there called a shambling mound, PFC Kennedy told us that was what it was. It was actually down in the water, under the surface feeding on vegetation and some of the big crocasaurs, that's what we call them, but if we can get the target to come out of her tower... to come out and look around... we can smoke her from there."

"She won't come out," noted Vandahar. "How did you dispose of the Ruin that Walks?" That was his translation for the shambling mound.

"We saw how it worked, watched it devour crocs. It's pretty horrible to see something that big, a crocodile that's easily twenty-seven to thirty feet, just get dragged into something that looks like a giant walking compost pile. It was coming up out of the water and just dragging them into it with tentacles that appeared out of nowhere inside its mass. We knew we couldn't use gunfire or explosives to maintain operational integrity and stealth, but we had a spear gun we keep for these kinds of operations, and we attached an explosive and went spear-fishing for it. Got it in there under the water—thing moves real slow—and got ourselves out of the water. Then we detonated in the morning when the birds are the loudest. At dawn. It only hunted at night, so we knew it was under the water. That concealed the explosion. Recon dive after that and saw it was scattered all over in every direction. Lake's clear, even the crocs were mostly ruined by that thing."

"It will come back in time," noted Vandahar. "But for now, we are safe."

Come back in time, I thought.

"She has centaurs, but none of them will come down close enough to the river for us to take them without using our carbines," continued Hardt, referring to the medusa who occupied the *Mindon Elen.* "If we could get one, we could get some intel off it on what's inside the tower and how we might get explosives inside to bring it down when we need to. Needs to be here…"

He pointed toward the side of the stick that indicated the tower closest to where the dragon would come out in the great Court of Immortals. The rough map made of sticks and stones, MRE packages, and plastic spoons, was pretty impressive. If you squinted and knew what Paris had once looked like, it was a pretty fair representation. Whoever the Dragon Elves were, they had pretty much rebuilt Paris the way Paris had been. But on a much grander and more savage imperial fashion of crumbling wizards' towers and fantastic statues and monuments. And that was saying something for Paris.

"Oh," mused Vandahar, standing back as he studied the map and stroked his beard, "I don't think that will be too much of a problem. Alluria is as greedy as she is beautiful. Her lust for power to rival her sister's will give us access if she senses advantage. Her vanity will place the explosives you require to effect the destruction of the great tower. There will be much loss in that, for it is a place of powerful and ancient sorceries that should have aided us much in the great battles I fear are coming soon in the east. But those battles will not be unless the wyrm is destroyed here and now, and so we must... as you Rangers say... do the tower."

"And how do we do that?" asked Sergeant Hardt after a moment.

Vandahar puffed his pipe.

"Guile, Ranger. We shall use guile. Send for the one among you who has become a minotaur. Tell him to run and not take two weeks to get here. We have much to do. In the meantime, Talker, I shall need to train your gift so you are as blind as a bat."

Okay... I'm partial to seeing.

"Without eyes you won't be able to look upon Alluria. That way she won't be able to turn you to stone when you bring her the little gift we'll place a very explosive surprise in."

If an old wizard could giggle, then Vandahar did. But it wasn't a giggle. It was more of an asthmatic coughing fit with some tears he had to wipe away with a tanned hand across his worn and lined old face.

"I should really stop smoking this stuff..." he said, shaking his long-stemmed pipe as tears of laughter ran.

CHAPTER SEVEN

"FIRING. Firing. Firing."

Sergeant Kang, located with the assaulters and Ranger master breachers, all of them carrying all the demo they could do, fired the special present we'd delivered to the medusa known as Alluria, who was apparently some kind of neighbor to Ssruth the Annoying, or whatever, and soon to be lizard steaks as far as the Rangers were concerned.

Yeah… the Rangers were going there. They were gonna get their 'Q on after this fight. Promises about who was the best grill master had been made. Challenges accepted.

Sergeant Kang fired the det and I had feelings about that somewhere in the back of my mind bothering me, because I had actually talked with her about as up close and personal as anyone can get with something that can turn you to stone just by looking at you. But right now, watching the great green terrible dragon that seemed easily eight stories tall as it reared up on its powerful haunches and began to feed, all of its mythic primordial beauty both frightening and savage, I was riveted on what was about to happen next. As soon as Sergeant Kang's terse Korean-accented American faded from the net call for the runway denial munitions det, there was a sudden savage *BOOOOM* and *CRACK*. Two 155mm artillery shells, both of them inside a golden idol of the "god" we'd made to fool the medusa, and had left with her for safekeeping and alliance. Those two one-five-fives blew out the back wall of the high tower known in Tolkien High Elvish as the *Mindon Elen*, the Tower of Stars. The explosives cratered about eight thousand square feet of tower foundation, crumbling under-dungeon, and the section of the district that abutted the grand passage and well where the dragon was being adored during its centaur-provided feeding frenzy.

Stone and earth shot away in the first second of the blast just after the shock wave pulsed through our fighting positions.

"Damn," someone swore as comm suddenly squealed and went high and haywire.

Most of us were already covered and concealed. Chemical masks donned and hunkered for the blast wave that swept the district as the tower began to fall toward the dragon while stone fragments arced out over the ruins of Tarragon, like some F-15 pilot back from the world that was had just streaked in and dropped a bunker buster on our collective behalf.

We'd estimated the tower to be somewhere on the order of twenty tons. The dwarves had explained to us why that would be accurate as far as they were concerned. They were masters of stone and estimating structures. They also told us which structures on the battlefield would survive a blast of that magnitude once Sergeant Kang and Sergeant Chris explained to them how big of a blast they were going to make.

The dwarves had gone in with one scout team for two nights and surveyed many of the potential fighting positions we could access before the battle. Even going so far as to delve into the catacombs beneath the city, fighting a roper they found in an abandoned passage and hauling away its collected treasures from what looked to be several years of feasting on unsuspecting explorers and Saur warriors who'd managed to get lost down there.

"Ve are quite at home in ze down below, Talker," explained the dwarven warrior named Max. "Ve know its dangers and seldom mind zhem." That was how Max talked. Max the Hammer. He seemed to be the personal champion of the king. There was no fight he would not pass up even though his manner was genial and almost playfully friendly compared to most of the rest of the grim lot of stone warriors. I'd seen him swing that awesome hammer of his in battle, and he was someone you didn't want to mess with in that kind of scrap. He crushed skulls, broke bones, and hammered souls into the afterlife with an ease I found sociopathic despite his friendliness. Violence with this strange playfulness and quiet humility mixed together for a fight that was both disturbing and fascinating. Honestly, have you ever seen two dudes go at it with hand weapons like axes, hammers, and swords? It's something you can't *not* watch even if you wanted to.

Max was the one who'd spotted the roper's suddenly fierce eye glaring at the Rangers and dwarves as they explored a tight stalagmite-filled passage down below the temple districts of the ruined city. The monster's trap ready to be sprung as tentacles suddenly flashed and struck from the darkness. Max reacted quickly as the wicked thing lashed out with its ropy tentacles and took hold of his fabled hammer. The dwarves' champion let go of his weapon, grabbed at his belt knife, and dove in at the thing, slashing and tearing, puncturing its hate-filled single red eye as he jackhammered it to death with his small blade. In the end, the dwarves and Ranger scouts walked away from that bizarre fight with a fantastic bronze chest filled with fine gems and an ancient Thracian shield that had been an artifact of some renown according to Vandahar.

"It perhaps possesses magical properties, as Thracia was a Lost Coast city known for such things," said the wizard.

The dwarves discussed what they'd found upon their return to the Ranger patrol base, and after some heated and very strange debate, determined which of ruined Tarragon's ancient structures could survive the blast from the runway denial munitions detonation the Rangers were planning on using. There were a few spots within the ruined city the Rangers had identified as perfect for the inner security ring to use as fighting positions. Those possible positions, according to the dwarves—one in particular with a good field of fire on the kill zone, a grand and ornate cathedral of rotting ancient scrolls and strange murals depicting the height of the Dragon Elves' power and conquests against the ogres to the south—would have gone down instantly, according to the stonemason dwarves. Killing the Rangers inside.

Now, as the munitions inside the idol were detonated in the opening moments of the battle against the dragon, the blast wave swept across the kill zone and the Royal District that lay in front of the great burial monument of the Dragon Elven kings. Several buildings went down instantly to our rear and across the dead city, massive stone facades turning into waterfalls of rotten granite, crumbling in great avalanches into long-silent streets where once there had been trade, triumphs, and life.

Bets were being won and lost as the Rangers had gambled on how many and which structures and monuments would collapse. The city's colossus, which was as high as the Arc de Triomphe of Paris had once been, a statue of an unknown armored elven king riding what Kennedy told us was a war basilisk, a giant lizard that turned you to stone, broke down on two of its six legs and the long-forgotten king went over in the tomb district it guarded behind the deserted and overgrown palace gardens. Crashing down in a sudden tumble and causing clouds of dust and rubble to blossom into the sky and across the streets there.

This happened in a sudden air-getting-punched-and-sucked-out-of-your-lungs-at-the-same-time moment despite the MOPP masks we had on. At almost the same time two things began to happen at once. The Tower of Stars began to come over just as planned, falling straight toward the giant feasting green dragon and the gaping fracture in the palace district it had emerged from. The dragon, still clutching two half-eaten mammoth shaggy cattle, whipped its serpentine neck about to see the tower's high fall coming down upon it. Flying stone from the explosion of the tower rammed into the dragon's emerald and armored hide. Ssruth's first instinct was to get airborne fast to escape the destruction—the problem was, the dragon weighed several tons, and was too huge to move quickly. You could see, as flying grit streaked past your vision in the tremendous blast wave and stone debris shooting out in every direction, that it wasn't going anywhere near fast enough to get out of the way of the toppling *Mindon Elen* falling toward it.

This was better than any CGI mega-blockbuster ever conceived in long-dead Hollywood. You just had to ignore the flying stone and screeching dragon that could kill you if things went that way. Chances were high, anything was possible in the next two minutes. Things were now about to get as fatal as they could possibly get.

I watched the tower fall in almost slow motion and wondered if the medusa was in there. Alluria was her name. Of course she was. Phobos the blind slave she loved on her mind as she fed gold coins to the idol we had given her and desperately asked it questions like it was some carnival arcade machine that guessed your weight or told your fortune. I wondered in the last moments where she was, but I knew the answer. In her inner sanctum, gazing at the fantastic thing we'd given her, hoping it would help her murder her sister and give her all the wealth and power of the Medusa Throne. Or just the possession of blind Phobos who loved her despite her being her. Dreaming her dreams and plotting her schemes like some young lovestruck girl who would do whatever it took to have everything the way it was supposed to be, as she saw it. Wishing she was something… else. Wishing just to be looked upon.

That last part was me. My takeaway from the encounter. Your mileage may vary.

Was she blown to bits, disintegrating in an instant, as the runway denial munitions erupted at thousands of feet per second, expending suddenly violent dynamic joules of energy? Or was she staring at the morning as it became the day the Rangers had decided to slay the dragon and pay back the SEAL? Thinking perhaps today of all days… perhaps things could be different?

If just for her.

It was a beautiful morning. And some people, and creatures, die anyway. She chose the wrong side. Not everything is right. And there are prices for the things you do in this life. Anyone who tells you different is lying to you.

I remember my dad telling me that once when we sat on the porch and watched the Arizona desert night sky and all the stars that could be seen by man with that fantastic instrument called the naked eye.

The two-forty teams opened up on the two ceremonial legions of Saur that had come out and assembled to witness the feeding of the great green dragon Ssruth the Cruel, last of the terrible wyrms. As the smoky destruction blossomed away from the base of the tower, billowing out in slow motion, erupting away from the *Mindon Elen* and where it had stood for something like six thousand years, I alone of the Rangers knew what had just happened. And Alluria who loved Phobos wasn't important to anyone. The Rangers were here to kill. The stories that got tangled up in the payback weren't important to any one of them.

All that history was gone, I thought. All that art, treasure, and golden fantastic wonder she had gathered within the tower, saved and collected from the ruins of Tarragon, first of the great kingdoms of the Ruin, gone. Civilization after everything we ever knew had disintegrated and the New Dark Ages had begun. All those stories. All those words that were scribed on scrolls and marked down in dusty old flesh-clad books. All of it gone.

War is hard, and Rangers are merciless because it's the only way to win. They will use everything to kill you. This is the way it had to be. This was what *in it to win it* means to them. But still...

High-speed fast-moving seven-six-two slammed into lizard scales and beaten armor shaped for aliens that were once us if I understood the Ruin and how everything had become the way it would. Revealed. The Ranger weapons teams operating the two-forty bravos opened up on the Saur legions that had been standing at attention on the parade field before the dragon and the feeding ceremony. Now they were either ripped to shreds by the blast, or stumbling around clutching bleeding eardrums if that's what they had. Some were just knocked senseless. Shields meant for hand-to-hand warfare on the burning sands along the Nile, or what was known in the Ruin as the River of Night, were fractured and dented, or were holed completely as the devastating fire of the Ranger gunners opened up and slaughtered them with little mercy and much precision. Traversing fire mixed with plunging fire is absolutely devastating. Saurian warriors were cut to shreds in a sudden single instant of incredible outgoing violence.

Yeah, we were fighting a huge, flying dinosaur that apparently possessed super-genius intelligence and could breathe chlorine napalm at you like it was a fire hose on crack, but there was a bigger conflict going on down there. The Rangers had been doing a fight for survival. Now they were taking it to the enemy. Doing what they do. Showing up where you didn't want them to be and saying, "Surprise, losers!"

Something much bigger was happening, and that's what it felt like. We were getting involved. And whether the Rangers knew it or not… they'd just gotten involved in the greatest struggle between light and darkness, the oppressor and oppressed, that the Ruin, and maybe history, had to offer. Autumn had tried to tell me this in her own halting way. I didn't know it then, but I know it now. The killing of the dragon was just the beginning.

The high crumbling tower crashed down onto one of Ssruth's great leathery green wings, breaking crumbling stone all across his mighty scaled body.

And I didn't need to wonder what had happened to Alluria as the ambush began in full. She had died within all the smoky destruction expanding out across the kill zone. Where the *Mindon Elen* had been. Where now there was a giant smoking crater belching smoke like an angry demon's chest heaving.

Ranger gunfire rattling destruction and promised payback.

CHAPTER EIGHT

CORPORAL Monroe was an assaulter from Third Platoon. Sergeant Chris's kingdom and subjects. He was now, after a long and painful fever that verged on some kind of worst flu ever, an eight-foot-tall minotaur complete with razor-sharp bull horns and a hairy hide. His lower half was still humanoid—though unhumanly hairy—but his upper half was now a perfect inverted triangle of bulging muscles and then his bull's face. He made it to the Ranger patrol base via Last of Autumn's horse, who knew the way and knew how to move fast. The Ranger who had become a beast of a minotaur just held on for dear life and got off when the horse needed a rest. When it was time to ride again the horse would lower its head and Corporal Monroe would climb aboard and off they'd go. The Forge had cranked out a special plate carrier for him and even an actual old-school M60E3 machine gun Special Forces had developed for CQB. Collapsible stock, foregrip, ultra-lightweight barrel, and a high-powered red targeting laser because Corporal Monroe's new anatomy made it harder for him to achieve gunsight with the iron sights. The targeting laser told him where the rounds he was spraying would land. Also, the trigger had needed modification to fit his now massive fingers.

Three days' hard riding and the big minotaur was whipped upon arrival at the patrol base deep in the swamp. Autumn's horse looked pretty whipped too. The dappled gray was covered in mud from where it had made its way through the swamp to close the last miles.

"Ain't never seen no horse clear a swamp before," said Brumm as Autumn went to stroke and feed her mount and friend. Brumm had arrived with a collapsible bucket of water from the nearby spring the Rangers had located. He was helping us clean the horse.

"He is… no… not…" she struggled for the right word as she tried to improve her English to communicate better with the Rangers.

"… *senya*," she said, not knowing the word she needed in English and instead retreating back to Tolkien High Elven.

"Common," I translated as I brushed mud off the flanks of the horse.

She nodded, her porcelain face blushing pink for a moment.

"He is… *special*."

And when she said *special* she looked at me, as if to ask, as people learning a new language do, if the right word was being used in the right way. I'm used to that with foreign-language speakers. But now, as I write this, I don't think that's what she was doing. I think she was using the word *special* to indicate both her horse, who was more like a person to her, and me, who was like something more than just a friend. *Special.*

Maybe that's just a trick of memory. But there was a look, a flick of the eyes. That thing women do when they want you to understand something important, something unspoken.

Something *special.*

I spoke the word *valdëa.* In High Tolkien that means *special.*

She nodded, working on her horse. Head bowed. Shy now.

Later the wizard walked us through his plan once again, mainly for Corporal Monroe's sake as he was a newcomer to the Ranger patrol base, and the plan we had developed to infiltrate the *Mindon Elen.* Monroe had carried the idol Vandahar had requested be made from the Forge to conceal the explosives. Working with Ranger master breachers, the old wizard had communicated to the Rangers this special item the Forge would need to construct for our deception to take effect. Vandahar knew what would get us in the front door, and the explosives experts had needed to figure out the rest of the plan—which consisted of the two artillery rounds, secondary explosives, and a WiFi trigger mechanism that could be installed and relied upon because the Rangers had managed to get a signal booster near the tower that gave a good broadcast strength reading.

"No problem for us," said Sergeant Chris back at the FOB. "That's just Tuesday for Rangers. Tell us when you want something hard."

The Forge had the idol and components cranked out, and it was Tanner who added the final gimmick that made the thing utterly genius.

"It'd be cool if it could like... you know... answer questions or predict the future like some Chinese fortune cookie... or hey... like that Magic 8-Ball toy we had as kids. These primitives would think that's pure dark magic and all. They'd fall for anything it told 'em."

Now, around the sand table at the patrol base, we studied what the Forge had produced: a four-foot-tall grinning idol that looked a lot like a demonic version of a Navy SEAL. Specifically Chief McCluskey. They'd even made it so the demon, sitting in a weird lotus position with a flat bowl between its legs, wore armor that looked strangely like scuba gear.

No one from the Ruin would know what that was.

"What do... the runes... mean?" asked Last of Autumn as she pointed at what the Rangers had made sure was stamped on the SEAL's chest.

"It's a specific insult," I told her.

"And... that looks like... on his face... they drew something with one of your... *markers*? Is that the right word?"

She traced the outline of an obscene feature of the male anatomy that had been drawn on the McCluskey idol's forehead.

Vandahar harrumphed indignantly. "Well, this isn't a game. I wish they'd taken this more seriously." Then: "We will tell the medusa it's an idol of... ahem... fertility, as it were. Such savage cults do this. She will see it as legitimate."

Someone back at the Forge had gotten carried away with the gold-plated idol that shone in the firelit darkness around the sand table. Rangers have a very dark sense of humor. As I have said before, it's not uncommon for people to switch seats on an airplane after a few moments' conversation with a Ranger. Most people don't prefer that level of bluntness. Funny stories about loading your pants during combat the first time or laughing because someone couldn't feel his toes anymore now that they'd been blown off didn't entertain normal people the way they entertained Rangers.

"Yeah… still it's pretty funny," said Tanner, staring at the Ranger insults cleverly disguised on the idol.

"Sure," said Kurtz soberly. "But what if this chick has comm or an actual relationship with our secondary target? He sees that and he's gonna get suspicious something's up."

We still, for all the scouting, had no eyes on Chief Mc-Cluskey around Objective Lizard King, and the command team was now getting ready to move forward with all the weapons and supplies for the attack. We were beginning to question whether McCluskey was even part of the operation and on site so the Rangers could ice him. He was tagged for the remaining weeks of stalk and chalk, or ground recon, as a high-priority target to locate in order for the Rangers to make sure he was dead when they got through with him. There was gonna be some real disappointment if the dragon and the SEAL had a falling out and the wyrm ate him before we got there. The sniper teams were arriving and already getting close, doing long-range observation from within some of the more isolated ruins that lay near and around the palace district of ruined Tarragon. If the SEAL was out and about, they'd spot him. Then a special team led by the sergeant major was gonna get their reap on.

"It seems," began Vandahar, "that we have all we need now to conduct our plan. I have taught, as much as I can, young Talker here regarding the nature of the medusas he will be dealing with. Their world and concerns, and a new skill he might apply to his powers that *may* protect him from her, shall we say, stony gaze."

May?

He had told me it *absolutely would*.

I reminded Vandahar he'd said that.

"It should, my boy. Don't worry. A lot depends on how focused you can be when you are in her fatal presence."

Should.

Don't worry.

Depends.

Great. Really building up my confidence here.

"Lose your concentration," the old wizard continued, "and switch back to what would be normal vision... and you will be... well, how shall we say this... you will be susceptible. So..."

He didn't finish. Because we all knew what that part of the plan was. Fail and I got turned into a statue.

Good times with the Rangers.

Since the preparations for the plan had been set in motion, it was true Vandahar had spent an inordinate amount of time with me. Getting me ready for the role I'd need to play for infiltration. We came up with a cover. And yes, I did get a long master class in the nature of medusas. There are no male medusas. There was one, a long time ago, and he actually fought against the Saur as a mercenary in service to the Kings of the Waste. His name was Gaulio and he was a pirate of some sort, apparently with a blind war galley crew. He harassed Saur shipping in and out of their main ports along the entrance to the Nile, or rather the River of Night. He went upriver on a daring raid and fought several engagements against the Saurian slave galleys and forts. Even going ashore to sack the temple cities and fantastic monument tombs in the Valley of Kings and Priests. He brought back much spoil to Parvaim and died an old medusa warlord with a harem of a thousand blind women from various races.

Or so the legend goes, according to the old wizard.

But the medusa gene does not pass through the male. Apparently. The females mate with prisoners they blind and then bear offspring. Usually just one. If it's a girl, they keep it. A boy and they turn it into a slave. Sultria and her three sisters are considered quite rare because they are medusa triplets born at the same time.

Medusas are very long-lived because they drink the blood of their victims and feast on a certain gland extracted from their terror-struck slaves that gives them the ability to concoct a magical potion they learned from the Saur. The medusa does not drink the potion for long life, which is the concoction's intended effect, but for an unintended side effect: beauty. Apparently they're vain and murderously jealous.

Also they're fun at parties, said no one ever.

A hundred years ago, Sultria rose to power, taking an ancient Atlantean fortress in what we would have called North Africa. The Atlanteans apparently rivaled the Dragon Elves long ago, but little is known of their fantastic civilization as the ruins are considered to lie beyond the edge of the known world where the warring tribes of giant orcs are considered some of the most ferocious and brutal of the Ruin.

"Few dare those cursed sands and fractured mountains, Talker," Vandahar told me.

The three medusa sisters were, in reality, enemies, but an alliance existed between them because medusas are considered kill-on-sight by almost everyone in the Ruin. Such it was that Alluria, as I have said, was banished to the Savage Lands with a mission to secure alliances that might help Sultria. It was rumored, and I would soon learn that the rumors were true, that Alluria had a lover, a slave she'd grown fond of, but that this slave was kept captive by Sultria deep in her dungeons beneath the old Atlantean fortress she watched the shadows from.

"Sultria's alliance with Ssruth and the Saur is what troubles the council most," noted Vandahar.

I asked him what the council actually was. He had referenced it several times, but I'd never delved into the subject. I probably needed to for the command team's benefit. I mean, who knew? Maybe Vandahar was actually Christopher Lee from *The Lord of the Rings* and his council was some kind of axis of evil we were now in league with.

In league with. I was hanging around Vandahar way too much.

"Ah... the council. The council is nothing so grand as you might imagine, young Talker," said the wizard, once more lighting his pipe. We'd moved on to him teaching me my new psionics trick I'd need for the infiltration of the Tower of Stars. We were taking a break and he'd asked me to "brew up some of that dark potion you call... coffee. I'm rather fond of it now."

As he worked at packing his long-stemmed pipe, I thought about holding his head under the moss-laden pond we'd stopped near as he trained me. That was the addiction talking. Believe me. I just work here. He'd probably zap me with a lightning bolt anyway.

Once he'd had some of my coffee, emphasis on *my*, he began to tell me of the organization he'd referred to often. Way out here away from the precious few sacks of coffee left, I mentally added up how much I could afford to share.

"The Council of Undómë," began Vandahar, "was once a great and powerful order that has roots going all the way back to the times when the Ruin began. We helped establish the great Cities of Men where we could, when we could. The world in those days was much overrun with the forces of darkness and evil. Monsters abounded and ruled the lands. Man was little more than a hunted savage in those dark times. The most terrible of the monsters established the first Savage Kingdoms even before the elves considered doing so. That is little known in these days even by those who consider themselves much learned. But trust me, Talker, those times were dire and most savage indeed. The light of humanity was almost fully extinguished by what it had become. Strange that... but it was so in those terrible long years.

"The council was formed to help humanity survive when it looked like they most certainly would not. As the Saur began to reveal themselves in the southern sands for what they truly were, the Spider Queen's appalling work was fully wrought now on their twisted visages. The council dedicated themselves not only to defeating the Saur, but to the impossible task of recovering the lost pages of the *Book of Skelos* so that record of what the Saur truly are... would be known to men, one day. And that in the terrible knowledge of that truth, the Cities of Men might, like the last light of a flickering candle in a world descending into madness, might know what they were fighting against. And more importantly... what they were fighting for.

"We were there when elves and men first formed their battle lines against the Saur on the eastern banks of the River of Night. Legions of warriors as far as the eye could see standing against a horde of darkness the Ruin would shudder to think of if they'd seen it that day. In the good golden years that followed, many of the council helped bring about the Golden Age in the Eastern Wastes. But when the stars fell and the Nether Sorcerer arrived from whatever dark place gave him being in time and space, we were hunted and slain. And now... now, young Talker... the council is just..."

The old man that was the wizard looked around suddenly as he stopped his story, as though only realizing where he was now, and not in the then-long-ago deeds and wonders of his tale. He studied the soft afternoon light in the trees, smiling wanly in the uncomfortable swampy silence, and for a moment I thought he'd forgotten the question of who the council was as he held the steaming cup of my coffee forgotten, and his wisping pipe, also forgotten.

Then he swallowed thickly and stroked his beard contemplatively. "Me. I am the last of the Council of Undómë, Talker. They are all... gone."

He seemed smaller and lost in that moment of his confession. I sat down next to him. And we drank coffee in silence. Some lonely swamp bird called out forlornly as the afternoon turned toward its last.

Undómë, in Tolkien High Elven, means twilight. The Council of Twilight. I can make some guesses as to why they called it that. What their mission was. What the stakes are now. And why this old wizard has made an alliance with a bunch of lost Rangers hoping somehow the inevitable can be avoided. That the mission can be fulfilled even though the hour is getting late. What had he said?

The light of humanity was almost fully extinguished by what it had become.

I'm guessing that's still a possibility. Or maybe things are even more desperate than we think. Maybe it's already a reality. And maybe the sergeant major was right after we took the fortress and the Forge. Maybe someone in the Ruin threw up a prayer to the universe, and the universe decided to send Rangers.

"I'm alone now," whispered Vandahar to the gently moving trees. "I have been for a very long time. I just kept them all alive in my mind, saying *we* and the *council* because... well because I needed to go on and finish this business. I needed to finish the work we started long ago. You do that sometimes, Talker. You keep the truth alive even if no one believes in it anymore. If just only to remind yourself that you do. That you still believe it. Because you forget, Talker. Sometimes... you forget when you are alone."

CHAPTER NINE

SO, what they see when they see me rollin'…

LOL. People reading this in the future that is the Ruin will have no idea what that means. *When they see me rollin'.* But trust me… that was pretty funny back in the day. I woulda killed on the internet if there still was an internet to kill on. If a picture of me in my mysterious stranger costume was a meme and all. Maybe. Then I woulda killed.

Also, I get that you have no idea what a meme is. Trust me, they were lit. Seriously. The Rangers made me appreciate them more. Especially the ones about the air force.

But what the two centaur guards standing at the entrance to the fantastic tower see when they see me rollin' up on them is me dressed as, let's call my role that of a *mysterious stranger*. Like I'm some dark Jedi or something. Dark robes and a giant hood that covers my face and hangs down over my head. I keep my hands inside the huge sleeves, clasping them together. Still wearing my assault gloves because maybe if I need to, I can knock one of them out with an uppercut to the jaw. There's a knife in each sleeve I can pull if I need to. My sidearm is in the combat pants I'm wearing underneath my robe. Tattered and torn Cryotech fatigues with a leg holster. All this is obscured by the long-hooded robe of the mysterious stranger dark Jedi I'm playing to effect an infiltration on the medusa's tower.

All that the centaurs see, as I approach, is a robed and hooded stranger moving in an almost prayerful walk up and out of the swamp and misty night that surround the ruins of the ancient city of Tarragon. Lair of the green dragon Ssruth the Cruel. No doubt I am thinking deep and brooding thoughts as I make my way over uneven sinking ground. I am followed by a minotaur carrying a large chest over one shoulder and a rough spear in the other. And behind this, shadowy and almost menacing like some dark forest rogue who robs people along the trails, in a black leather outfit straight from the Chief McCluskey Ren Faire tragedian line, is Tanner.

The centaurs see us coming out of the forest and snort as they trot and stamp the ground, raising their spears as though they'll chuck their weapons without the slightest hesitation. If it looks like they're going to, the two sniper scouts hidden nearby are going to vape their skulls from the sunken building's roof down near the scum-laden water. That's the contingency plan. Where the Rangers killed the shambling mound—or as Vandahar put it, the Ruin that Walks—the snipers are in place and ready to go live with suppressed weapons.

I stop and broadcast now before things can go off the rails. That's what I call it. Broadcasting. Vandahar tells me it's like focusing. But he doesn't actually possess the gift, as he calls it, that I do. Psionics. But to me, now that I'm getting more familiar with it thanks to some hints he's given me, it feels more like broadcasting. Like I'm a radio station. Broadcasting a signal.

In that moment within the swampy forest darkness that's heavy and still, with the murderous and wild armored centaurs ready to panic and turn everything into a mess at the slightest provocation… I begin to broadcast.

I think of a hot stove. Boiling water. I remember one time when I knocked over a pan of boiling water that was on the stove. I was little. My mother screaming and scooping me up. Except it wasn't me who knocked over the pan. It was her. I remember her scooping me up to make sure none of the hot water she was boiling managed to scald me for life. I was screaming. Maybe crying. But I remember her being practically hysterical. Hysterical that I might not be perfect anymore. And that it would somehow be her fault.

I remember, even though I had to be little more than a toddler and it was just the two of us, I remember hearing her almost pray.

She never prayed. She wasn't religious. But in that moment when I had been made imperfect, she had suddenly become so. Some British lady told me that once. *Sometimes you pray even when you don't believe.*

Later, my frightened mother would teach me that stoves were dangerous. Boiling water scalded. Grease fires melted flesh. After that she never cooked much. We ate out or ordered in often. I guess it was good she came from a rich family. But what she imbued me with from then on, on that day of terror and the end of everything good as far as any parent is ever concerned, was a sense of caution. Caution around stoves. Around dangerous animals. Vans near playgrounds. Anything that could ever ruin you. Because then you wouldn't be you anymore.

It was a primal memory for me, and it was exactly what I needed right now to stop everything from going completely sideways before the entrance to the medusa's tower.

Whenever I saw a stove, I knew to be cautious. It could hurt you badly. Scar you for life. Mar you. Make you imperfect forever. Vandahar had taught me that with psionics I could broadcast these primal memories as emotions for a short period of time and thus influence people, or monsters, actions and attitudes, with my starkest memories.

Psionics.

And right now, I needed those two centaurs to be real cautious and not get their heads blown off by hidden Rangers before I got two artillery shells armed with remote signal triggers inside the tower and ready to explode, come the day we went and laid some hate on Lizard King.

So, there in the hot still darkness, I pictured a stove and a pan of furiously boiling water. Remembering my mother's hysterical sobs thinking she had ruined me forever. And knowing she could never live with herself if she had. I pictured that and like a radio station I broadcasted the signal of my powerful memories turned into contagious emotions… letting them emanate from me in quiet menace.

The centaurs hesitated. Their silver spears held back and trembling as I stood there in the dark with the minotaur slave and the dangerous assassin behind me. That's what they saw. I was not someone to be trifled with. I was dangerous. Best use caution with me.

Are you picking up my signal, horsey-men?

I heard Corporal Monroe snort like a bull sensing danger. Brief and gruff like a bull before it's about to charge. And Tanner hissed in that grave whisper that came out of him every so often when he seemed *other* than himself.

"That you doing that, Talk?" he whispered in the dark as we made our approach.

I nodded slightly.

As we got close I spoke to the centaur guards at the entrance to the *Mindon Elen*. The Tower of Stars. "I seek audience with your mistress," I said in French. Apparently, according to Vandahar, that was my best chance at communicating with them. I watched their eyes like linguists do. Waiting for that spark of recognition that the sounds I'm making are doing something. That I am being heard. That we are communicating.

"I am Spock," I said aloud in the hot still darkness of the early night. "Emissary of King Conan, Ruler of Bro. And I bring a great gift for your fabled mistress."

Now it was time to see if our gamble would pay off and get us inside so we could lay an IED on them.

CHAPTER TEN

THE emotion of caution I broadcasted did something to the centaur guards. It made them take a hard look at us instead of calling for the rest of their troop to come flooding out of their tower and do us in with spears and swords. It stopped them and gave them enough pause to go ahead and look at what we were trying to convince them they were seeing...

A mysterious stranger, who was probably some kind of wizard and/or wise man. And his manservant monster minotaur, carrying an item of some worth protected by a costly and ornate chest.

I didn't have to do much convincing when it came to Corporal Monroe. He was now mostly monster and not so much man anymore. He had huge horns, a tough and hairy hide, and even his eyes had changed from brown to green like a cat's, glowing in the darkness.

"Do you have... like, powers now?" Tanner had asked him as we made ready to put on our show.

Monroe snorted. "Nah. I'm stronger though. They used to call me the Squat King back at batt. I could put up nine hundred easy. But now if the Forge could crank out a rack and some weights, I bet I could beat that easy. And these horns? Not sure what to do with 'em, but I got some soft-grain sandpaper and I'm trying to get 'em real sharp.

Hurt like hell when they were comin' in though. Thought I was cracking my skull open."

That was probably the most Ranger thing I'd ever heard. Here, let me use my deformity as a weapon to kill my enemies with.

Later I asked Autumn why the Ruin had turned Corporal Monroe into a minotaur. Or the captain into a were-tiger. She didn't know. All she said was, "The Ruin reveals, Talker. The Ruin reveals."

"So I'm stronger, at least two feet taller, and I got horns," Monroe said to Tanner. "Sounds like a T-shirt, don't it? You know... went ten thousand years in the future and all I got were these lousy horns."

Monroe laughed at his joke and Tanner chuckled dryly. Slower than he used to.

Then, "I can see at night," said Tanner. "I can see weird things like people's living essence and sometimes ghosts who are just passing by and ain't even interested in us. I hear the voices of dead things around certain places and... things."

Tanner looked at me.

"That don't seem right, does it, Talk?"

I said it was cool because what else are you gonna say? I could shoot some kind of force out of my eyes when I was real pissed. In other words... we're freaks.

"Maybe that's why the wizard wants us to go in," said Tanner. "'Cause we're the Freak Squad. We're the monsters."

"Probably," I said, wondering if my freak power had just made the other freak use the word *freak* to describe us freaks.

"But we're still Rangers, Talk. We're still that."

Now, as the centaurs realized I was something probably important and valuable as the three of us freaks of the Ranger detachment stood there in the swampy twilight, guttering torches burning along the path that led up to the high tower that was the *Mindon Elen*, one of them clopped off to get their commander.

A moment later the biggest centaur I'd ever seen, wearing a hammered gold breastplate and carrying a huge iron-banded club, his only badge of office other than his brutish size and haughty manner, a laurel of leaves in his short hacky chopped hair, came out to sneer at us.

"Why come you to the Tower of the Serpent Maiden, intruders?" he barked in Ruin-French. His nasals were horrible. Centaur French sounds much more harsh than actual French. Like a German-speaking dog barking at you in French. How the Ruin managed to effect that change linguistically I would never know. But it was painful to listen to.

Linguistically speaking.

"Do you speak for your mistress, horse man?"

That was Vandahar's coaching on my opening move once I got someone in charge to come out and deal with us. "That's what I'll do once I'm Karen-ing their manager?" I said to the wizard. Vandahar looked at me like I'd suddenly gone insane and started gibbering Jabba nonsense. He told me centaurs were generally rude and boorish and that it was best to come right back at them with the same traits. They only respected what they feared. Like any horse you had to show them who was boss before you could get to know each other.

I took two steps forward and raised one hand from my cloaked sleeves. A signal to the hidden Rangers.

"Let me see who exactly dares to stand between the King of Bro's emissary and his task at hand."

From back in the swamp the Rangers fired a flare overheard and bathed all of us there before the tower, freaks and centaurs, in red light. The flare creating dancing light and shifting shadows in the tangle of swamp and night.

The armed centaurs who'd come out whinnied in terror. Some of them stamping their hooves and making short charges back and forth as I "caused" hell's light to show me their faces.

We were hoping this would bother them on some level.

The giant brute held up his club and waved at the rest to be still with a giant ham of a fist. He swelled his chest and trotted before me, stamping the soft ground.

"A sorcerer from Bro? A kingdom I have never heard of?" he barked harshly. "The mistress is not so easily gained by vagabonds wandering out of the swamp in the dead of night."

I didn't have unlimited psionics. The broadcast had left me depleted for the moment. So… it was now all on me and my skill as an actor. I'd never taken an acting class. But being an interpreter has a little bit of performance in it. The plan called either for us to get into the tower's entrance within two minutes… or pull back. And if the centaurs didn't let us go easily then the Rangers would start doing them with suppressed fire and we'd try to clean the place and not jeopardize the mission. The scouts were ready to assault over open ground with Vandahar providing some supporting fireworks to let them take the entrance. Then we'd hold the tower until the ambush and blow it when the time came.

Not the best option. But an option if everything went pear-shaped right now.

And that depended on me.

The demoted linguist.

I inclined my cowled head to one side, playing some part I'd never known I could actually play. The dangerous guy who spoke softly.

"'Tis good," I whispered low and in what I thought was a menacing tone. "'Tis good that the future ally of King Conan has such a fine warrior to guard her. Wealth and riches beyond imagining are to be had for those who are so shrewd, horse man. That has been noted."

One of the things John who wasn't John taught me back in my two-week off-books practical intel course on the shady side of the Vegas-that-was, is you catch more flies with honey than vinegar. Interrogation and influence get done a lot quicker if you find what people want and make it seem like it's gonna happen for them. Vandahar had instructed us that centaurs are greedy and mercenary by nature. So I introduced that possibility. The chance at big prizes. Why threaten when you can persuade, am I right?

Spoiler: I was right. We were taken right into the looming tower, passing through an arch where once there had been a massive door. The giant shape of the door looking like some mouth now forever screaming in horror.

"We in it now," remarked Tanner under his breath as the centaur guard ranged about us, ushering us into the tower's darkness.

Corporal Monroe snorted and held his spear tighter. "Say the word, Private Talker, and I'll kill our way right out of here real quick."

RAH.

Rangers Acting Hostile.

CHAPTER ELEVEN

WE climbed a vast stone stair, covered in cracked and broken glyphs and writing I recognized as Dragon Elven. Monroe and Tanner followed me, centaurs staying at the bottom as a blind slave had been summoned to lead us up into the high reaches of the tower for our audience with Alluria, sister of Sultria, queen of the medusas. We climbed through levels that were distorted by flickering candles that barely illuminated the dark areas there. Shadowy figures moved silently about strange tasks in the brief glimpses we got of them. These precincts felt abandoned, or that whoever was in them was waiting and hiding. Ready to drag us into other darknesses from which we would never return.

"I'm guessing they're all blind in there. That's why they don't need much light," hissed Tanner as he came close to me. He moved quietly. Almost supernaturally quiet. "You'd need to not be able to see if you were gonna work for somethin'… y'know."

The air getting cold around him was a new thing that had started manifesting itself. It wasn't always like that. But I had noticed the change in temperature around Tanner on patrols, and during the dragon's attack. Noticed later and after the fact. Perhaps it was some kind of defensive feature he was developing.

But who knew?

The Ruin reveals.

He was still Tanner as far as I was concerned. That was enough for me.

Corporal Monroe as the minotaur simply snorted, his bootsteps heavier than ours and making a definite *thump* up each step as we climbed higher and higher into the darkness of the upper reaches of the Tower of Stars. Five or six stories up began the statues. Except they weren't really statues. They were victims. Turned to stone forever. The first levels were just monsters. Orcs like we'd fought but each special in some way. A war chief frozen in savage rage. A creeping cloaked assassin. A high orcish priest so demonic it was like nothing Dante ever conceived. A massive ogre with a huge battle axe, leaf-bladed centaur spears sticking out of its back. Strange serpent-like men, but these had the cowled hoods of cobras ready to spit deadly venom. A lizard man Saur here and there. Dull-eyed hunters. All of them placed now as though they were works of art rather than what they had once been. In their lives before stone.

These were trophies of the medusa's hunts, or warnings to enemies that had come to slay her either by outright combat or cunning deception. The message was clear. *Don't mess with the medusa. The same fate as these awaits you if you're so dumb as to try.*

They had tried. Then they had died. She had turned them to stone at some point in the past. And it was a strange stone they were turned into. Green. Vandahar later told me each medusa turns their victim into a different type of stone, even different colors of stone. The medusa of Shadiz, he said, turned men into a beautiful rose-colored marble. Sometimes reckless adventurers were sent deep into the Eastern Wastes where demons whisper among the haunted and lonely sands, where mighty djinn guard her buried temple, to retrieve the stone-gazed statues for works of art to be held and admired in Accadios, greatest city of the Cities of Men.

Not my circus. Not my monkeys. Hopefully I never need the money that badly.

Here, in the half light of these shadowy levels of the *Mindon Elen*, the Tower of Stars, guttering candles were arrayed about each statue as though they too were works of art to be admired or worshipped. But really to warn. The stone was green. The Baroness would later tell us, when we described the stone to her, it was most likely epidote or some other pre-Cambrian stone. As learned as I was, I had no idea what any of that meant. All I knew was as we got closer, the stone seemed more alive in its immobile deadness, lines of white mixed with the softer and deeper greens. The stone was rough and unpolished, but the features of the monsters that had been turned to stone were perfect. As though someone had photographed them... then turned them to stone. Forever.

The red wax candles dripped along the floor like running blood, and the beautiful yet utterly horrific carved images watched it as though it were their own. It left all of us uneasy. It was too real. This was a thing that could happen to the Freak Squad if we messed up in there. I said that, and like Rangers they both replied, "Then don't mess up." Up until now it had all been an exercise. It's one thing to go up against hajis, be they orc, cat, or what the Rangers had faced back in the world. But this was something worse.

"This is jacked up," huffed Monroe, whose voice was getting huskier and deeper by the day. I was glad he was strapping the M60E3 under a canvas sack slung down across the back of his shoulder, the belt wound around it. If it was go time he'd have it out, belt free around his other massive hairy arm, and we could at least blast our way out of here. Maybe.

"Ain't nothin' but a thang, Corporal. Kinda beautiful, though," whisper-hissed Tanner. "The whole place is. Pretty sure I can see a lot more than you guys since I'm all undead Batman now. This place has artwork and books. Lotta strange stuff hidden in piles outside the firelight we're just passing by. There's an old ghost here too. Sounds like a woman singing… but no one can hear her. It's really beautiful though."

Freak Squad is right. Eenie meenie miney moe and we are it. Embrace the fantasy, Talker. Embrace it.

I began to whistle "Shoot to Thrill" in my head as we climbed higher and higher into the dark and gloomy tower. Things felt Cloudy with a Chance of Extreme Violence.

The servant led us up along the remains of a dusty level to reach the next cyclopean stair that had to be near the upper heights of the tower where intensive sniper observation had at times shown us bare ghostly lights moving about late in the night. Planning had always indicated this was where we'd get our interview with the medusa. The Ranger snipers had eyes on all windows, but the apertures were great for firing solutions. Even the drone piloted by the pretty ponytailed air force co-pilot was overhead. Just in case two ground-to-air missiles were going to improve our odds any. The sergeant major and the captain were eyes on Kill TV. For whatever good that would do.

But just thinking about everyone having our backs gave me a little more gas in the tank for what was about to happen.

Two huge braziers lit the stair here, each made of some impossibly huge, beaten copper discs. Small flames guttered within the huge plates but suddenly bloomed to menacing life as we approached.

"That's weird," huffed Monroe, and switched the heavy chest to his other broad shoulder.

In the ominous distance, among the shadows near the flaming braziers, I thought I saw a woman kneeling by the foot of the stairs, but when we got close it was clear it was another statue. Frozen in time forever. Another warning. Another promise to Freak Squad if we didn't get this right in one go.

"Here she is…" Tanner hiss-whispered. "She's the one who's been singin'."

"Who?" asked Monroe in a low rumble.

"Ghost," said Tanner. "She's near the statue. Right there. I can see her plain as day. Same position as the statue. I can understand her. She's crying and says this is where she found out her man died in battle. Says she can't ever leave. Loves him too much. That the song she's singin', Talk, I can hear it… I think it was his favorite. 'Girls, Girls, Girls' by the Crue was what I told Desiree I wanted her to dance to if I ever bought it over in the sandbox some way. Told her she was free of me after that. To dance one more time for me and then go find someone else who wouldn't be bad to her."

I couldn't hear a song. But because I do languages, something occurred to me as the blind servant leading us indicated it was time we should put on the eye wraps the brutish centaur had given us to protect us from his mistress's gaze.

"Is it speaking English?" I asked Tanner. "Or any language you know?"

Tanner thought about that for a second. His breath papery and raspy now. A soft imitation of the dead we'd fought when Toth-Azom came for our Forge, or for some other reason we still had not discovered.

"Now that you mention it, Talk... no. Ain't no language I ever heard before. But I can understand her fine. Understand her pain. I know the story. She loved him a lot. Real bad, 'cause he was good to her. She's a real looker too. But it was more than just that. Sucks to be that guy. She's a good one."

At that point either my latent psionics ability flared up on some level, or I made a mental connection about the situation that science can't figure out and just calls *intuition*. Still not sure what my *gift*, as Vandahar calls it, really does. But when I used to spend time with my dad in the southwest, when he was training horses, something happened one time. And I was right there in that long-ago memory looking at it like it was a photograph that had just popped up in my psionics mental app. One hot afternoon one of the stallions broke its leg and had to be destroyed. That was a bad day. But that stallion had a mare that just died inside when it happened. She was carrying his foal, and when she delivered the foal a few weeks later, it was the spitting image of the big stallion that was gone. Except the mare wouldn't have nothing to do with it. Just kept standing near where the stallion had died. Not eating. Not taking care of the foal. Just dying day by day. Slowly. My dad went out there one day when it looked like much couldn't be done, talking to her softly and taking an apple in one hand. He got close and leaned next to the mare, put his head down on her neck, and just began to whisper to her. Patting her long neck and stroking her for the better part of an hour. I asked my grandfather what he was doing.

My grandfather was an old, old cowboy. Real old. Rumor was he'd been a Texas Ranger when he was young. But he never said much about that.

"He's tellin' her it's okay to let her stallion go." We were both watching from the fence of the corral. "Sometimes you got to do that," he told me. He was silent for a moment. Then, "Sometimes... and this sumpthin' you best remember if you ever have a loved one that's fightin' real hard, some disease, and they're just a-hangin' on through the pain 'cause they don't want ya to be sad if they got to leave soon... you tell 'em it's okay. Then they'll go to where they got to get off to. It'll be okay for them. You unnerstan' that, boy? You got that?"

I did.

I told it to my dad when he was dying of cancer and it was real bad two years later. That worst summer of all summers I wish had never happened to us. He patted me as he lay on his worn-out couch and croaked, "Ain't done... yet, kiddo. But thanks all the same."

He didn't want to take any of the doctor's pain pills. Wanted to be all there with me that summer. Even though it was about as tough as I've ever seen a thing be.

When it was time, he just went. But I made sure he knew it was okay to go. Especially after the doctor started hospice. And then one hot afternoon...

Well, that's a story for some other book not this one.

The psionics, I think, recalled that specific memory from my past as we stood there at the foot of the shadowy stairs leading up to the medusa that was our objective. Not the emotions of that day. Those were powerful for me. Still. But the memory of watching my dad lean his head down on the grief-struck mare and just tell her it was okay to let her mate go. She had work to do. Her foal needed her now. I'll never not remember that moment. And if I do, well, then I guess I won't be me anymore. Nor would I want to.

But there was something else. I had a feeling the memory was prompting me to use it to figure out some key to the Ruin that was going on at this moment, and it had nothing to do with why we were here. It was just psionics doing psionics because psionics gonna psionics. The Ruin revealing. That was all I could tell about what was happening here at the moment. I felt like I was on a kind of autopilot when I told Tanner what to do next for no reason I can adequately put down here and now.

"Tell the ghost... she can let him go now."

I would tell you I had no idea what I was doing, and I also had a suspicion of what would happen next. That's psionics. Like there's another brain that is me, seeing the invisible connections, and giving me puzzles to solve for big prizes. I knew. And then I didn't know. At the same moment. Weird stuff. Really weird stuff.

"Okay..." said Tanner uncertainly.

Then he began to speak. Speaking in the language of the dead. Which was simply amazeballs. For me. But of course I'm a language nerd. So obviously. The air definitely got colder as it started. Something like an autumn wind full of dead leaves, dry and cool, could be felt in the air and on the skin. But also, it wasn't there.

This was a real supernatural phenomenon that seemed very different from the weirdness of the Ruin. Which was saying something.

What I could understand of the language of the dead sounded like Latin, but with soft blended Arabic pronunciation. It was freaky and it sent chills up my spine to hear Tanner hiss-whispering this to nothing we could see. To the unseen spirit world all around us.

It was very *Otherly*.

He finished, then backed up a step, turned toward the stairs, and seemed to watch something leave us. The air for a moment becoming warm, more well-lit, soft dust motes that weren't there suddenly appearing as dying comets moving through the air like barely seen fireflies on childhood summer nights long ago.

Then it was over, and the gloom returned.

"She's gone now." He paused. "Where do you think she went, Talk?"

"Home, Tanner. She went wherever that guy she loved went. She went there. She was just anchored in her grief. It was time to let go."

Like that mare.

So Tanner is a Dead Whisperer.

CHAPTER TWELVE

"WE bring a gift…" And just at the moment the medusa asked why we had dared disturb her, I forgot the story we'd constructed to get here. Just for a moment. Thankfully we'd used terms and names from our world. Not made-up names we would be unfamiliar with, names that would suddenly become hard to remember when things got tense. Names from our time that sounded weird but that were keys in our hard drive to how to tell the whole story over and over again. Without flaw.

Who am I, I thought quickly as her rattling tail hissed in the darkness we were surrounded by. Her presence was deeply unsettling. She radiated danger and menace and there was no empty threat in that. Vandahar had warned us she was one of the most dangerous creatures of the Ruin. And also a Medusa.

Spock. I'm Spock.

Spock of… Bro. That's right, *King Conan of Bro*. That's who I supposedly work for.

"From our…"

Find the right word, I shouted at my brain. I'd almost started off in English I was so rattled. The medusa spoke both French and Greek. I was better at French than Greek. But she seemed to speak a lot of Greek with Farsi slang and bastardizations mixed in. Ten thousand years was bound to play havoc with some of the more active trade languages. "Sovereign… King Conan of Bro."

We were standing in self-imposed darkness, but I could hear torches guttering in the vast room we'd been led into. We'd been made to wear blindfolds for our own safety. But technically Tanner was supposedly immune to being turned to stone because he was undead. How that made sense I didn't know… but that was Vandahar's contention. Even though it felt more like a guess than a hypothesis and certainly not science. Sergeant Hardt hadn't been too keen on Tanner testing that theory out unless absolutely needed, so even Tanner the undead guy was currently blindfolded. Monroe also of course. Minotaurs had no natural immunity to being suddenly turned to stone. I wasn't immune either, but I had a trick I could try, where I could see the medusa and prevent being turned to stone at the same time. Vandahar had taught me to do this. Pretty cool. If it worked.

If it didn't…

But right now, as I heard her rattling tail and the soft chorus of hissing that was supposedly the snakes in her hair, I really *wanted* to see. And also I didn't. The fear was palpable in her presence. Like you needed to see what was going on because you were afraid. And also, you didn't want to because it sounded pretty bad all the same.

"Are you bothered… by me?" she purred, coming close. I could tell by the hissing of the snakes she was hovering nearby.

I took a deep breath and went with what Vandahar had told me might be a safe bet for manipulating her.

"Yes, Lady Alluria. Very. The Court of Bro has heard of your fabulous beauty. Who would not be... nervous... in your legendary presence. Having traveled many..."

I stalled. Do they use miles here? In Tolkien it was leagues. I had no idea.

"... through, uh... many lands."

Yeah, that's a safe bet.

"With the tales from travelers and caravans in my ears. Tales of your... great... charms. One is tempted to see if the tales are... true."

"Oh," she sighed seductively. "They're so true. Very true. Why don't you take off your blindfold and have... a look... for yourself?"

Because then I'd get turned to stone, I didn't say aloud.

She was close. I could smell her perfume. It was heavy with the scent of flowers. Overly sweet. But actually a nice change as the Ruin and the monsters in it didn't always smell great. At least it was better than Taco Bell Bag of Death Island back on Ranger Alamo.

"I have never heard of your king, Sock of Bro. Strange, that... don't you think?"

She was testing me to see if I remembered my own made-up name.

"Spock. A humble servant of my liege."

She purred like a cat who had a mouse cornered. Now she was slithering around the three of us. Constantly moving. Constantly rattling like the deadliest of rattlesnakes. And then there was the soft hissing of the snakes in her hair.

"This present... Is it perhaps... just your minotaur? He's rather... *quite* strapping, in fact."

"Nay, Lady."

Did I just say *Nay, Lady*? I did. Calling all discount Ren Faire tragedians. We have a cleanup on the overacting aisle. Man, was I in character, or what? Of course, the *or what* was what I was afraid of. This could go real wrong real fast.

"Our king has sent you a gift at the behest of his great sage, Obi-Wan Kenobi," I began, getting down to business just to get some hand in this conversation. "Obi-Wan has informed my king that if his invasion of the Savage Lands is to be successful then he must have you as an ally. It was a prophecy. Foretold... and all," I stumbled.

That last part didn't sound *Mysterious Stranger* in the least. I must have winced audibly, if that was possible. But that's what it felt like.

I quickly vowed to clean that up and be better at ad lib acting or whatever it was called. Otherwise... here we have a statue of Talker.

"Our holy god has created an oracle that will answer all questions truthfully," I continued. "To prove to you that we seek an alliance with one so powerful, and beautiful, as Alluria the medusa whose fabled beauty is rumored to be the rival of even that of her great sister to the south, we have brought it... unto... you."

Unto?

I used beauty too much also, or—

"What do you know of my sister!" she snapped savagely. "She is a hag and a whore!"

I'd brought her sister into the conversation, and that was apparently a sore spot.

The medusa was close, and so were the snakes in her hair. She hissed and shook, and it felt more dangerous than any enemy we'd faced yet in the Ruin. Maybe even the dragon, or perhaps I'd just forgotten how serious that had been. I felt my skin crawl and wondered two things at once because I'm steady like that. Also… I could go for a hit off my cold-brew with some magic Kungaloorian sugar right now. But you knew that was coming. Here's what I wondered both at the same time.

Was one of her snakes about to bite me, or were the two Rangers with me suddenly going to just go all Ranger Acting Hostile and try to kill her regardless of being blindfolded once they felt in sufficient danger to justify the act? Each had several weapons not counting themselves on them. Tanner had the best chance. In that he could see and not get turned to stone. Plus, he was flat-out hillbilly in a fight. He did not know when to quit. But Monroe could just whip off the canvas cover on the M60 and go instantly kinetic on her. He'd have to do it blind and that could be bad for everyone, basically turning the entire room into spray and pray with a weapon that spat out a lot of ammo fast. But good also because there was some chance I wouldn't get killed by the blind fire spray of 7.62. Some.

Or, worst-case scenario, in the heat of the moment he could whip off his blindfold—and that would be very bad for him if he made eye contact with her before or during get-some-thirty.

Vandahar had told us that if Tanner and Monroe did need to fight, or if I suddenly lost my trick the wizard had taught me, it was best to keep our eyes lowered to the floor and fight by not looking at her directly. Keep our eyes on the ground and her tail. But hey… good luck with all that, the wizard had practically said in his ornamental Vandaharian way of speaking. *May the Fates of Ner guide you from death's embrace*, or something like that.

I mentally scrambled and kicked my brain in the butt as I shifted my mouth into *Do Something*.

"We know nothing of your sister, Lady. Only that we were told by the ancient prophecies to come and find the most fabled beauty in all the Ruin, medusa or not, and then give her the sacred idol that talks. We have come. We have found. And now we must ask would she be an ally to us, as King Conan's armies will soon sweep across the lands, ruining the dark forces of the Black Prince, the Cities of Men, and even the Halls of the Stone Lords themselves? Would that the beautiful ally might profit much and have the desire of her heart given to her even if King Conan had to burn the Ruin to make this happen in payment and alliance."

I restrained myself from adding the Greek version of *forsoothly* and other ornate verbal uselessness.

If they gave out really sweet medals to linguists for doing above and beyond linguist stuff, I was pretty sure I'd be getting one for this. But they don't so no one cares. Work harder.

Vandahar's plan had been to exploit the rivalry between the medusa Alluria and her sister Sultria. If the medusa, according to Vandahar, could be convinced there was a way her sister could be defeated, then perhaps she, being Sultria's greatest rival for the Medusa Throne, would be inclined to take the offer of alliance.

"And what is this... idol?" she said disdainfully. Sniffing the air as she rattled her tail softly. Like some kind of weirdly seductive samba.

"It is an artifact of great power recovered from the mall..." I lied.

"I know not of Mall," she said petulantly. "Where is this Mall?"

Stay in there, Talker.

"Mall was once a vast wonder unlike anything the Ruin has ever seen," I said, telling the truth. "It existed ten thousand years ago when the seas ran with blood..." and a lot of other overheated nonsense I could think of as I channeled my inner Vandahar.

At the end of it she merely rattled and murmured, "Interesting..."

Then a quick demand.

"Let me see it now."

I told Corporal Monroe to set the chest down, open it, and step back, accidentally adding *Corporal* because it felt wrong for me, Talker, a private and a linguist, to be giving orders to a Ranger corporal who was a bonified stud lifetaker. That was a mistake on my part. And it suddenly exposed me for a moment. Made me sound unsure as I caught myself in this verbal fencing duel the dangerous medusa and I were currently having.

"What is *Corporal?*" she asked in Greek Farsi. "Is that his name?" She'd snatched on my hesitation, not understanding the English we were exchanging in.

"Uh... uh..." I stuttered. Why not. "Yes. My servant's name is Corporal."

She slithered about, circling us once more. Murmuring to herself and slightly more agitated. Snakes hissing. Have I mentioned all of this was really fun being unable to see and all? One star. Would not recommend. Highly.

Monroe put the chest down and opened it. Then something we hadn't planned for happened.

"Take it out of the chest," she barked, almost like a sergeant. "Do you take me for a fool? It could be trapped! I'm not reaching in there!"

It was clear she had slithered close for a look, but she was too cautious to be sticking her hands in a box for something that was clearly meant to entice the eyes with all its gleaming golden glamour. The problem was, Monroe had set the chest down, opened it, and then stepped back. That had been the plan as we'd rehearsed it on the little island at the Ranger patrol base.

"Corporal Monroe," I said, "I need you to get it out and lay it on the floor in front of our host."

"Get what out?"

"The idol. Out of the box."

Monroe took two heavy steps forward and I heard him bend down, his M60 slung in a canvas bag behind his back connecting with the stone floor. Then...

"I don't know what happened," he said. "Can't find the chest, Talker, because I can't see. I might have turned a little and lost it. I don't want to move around much just in case..."

Blindfolded, he couldn't find the chest.

"I can take off my—"

"Don't," I snapped. "I got this."

Meanwhile the medusa, slithering and rattling, snakes hissing in her hair, purred coyly, sensing our unease and difficulty.

"Is there a problem, Spock of Bro?"

I cleared my throat, straightened my back, closed my eyes, and removed the blindfold.

I heard her catch her breath.

"Careful..." she whispered.

The trick Vandahar had taught me was to see with my eyes turned off.

"Your gift allows you to see things with your mind, young Talker," Vandahar had told me during the training. "Connections in the universe. Emotional resonances. Thoughts, even. It's hard to say what you can actually do. But many of your kind… have the ability to concentrate very well, and then see in… darkness. I would suspect that in dealing with one such as a medusa, this would be quite helpful."

He had then taught me how to focus my breath, clear my mind, turn off my eyes… and see while blind. We had tried this blindfolded, and for some reason it didn't work. It was like I needed a leap of faith or something to trust that the trick was working. I had a suspicion that what I was doing was actually looking into other people's minds and seeing what they saw and then my brain was somewhere making sense of it.

But that was just a hunch.

Whatever it was… with practice I could do it. For about two minutes. Then it would shut off and I'd feel pretty punchy for a while. Like my mind was foggy. Then I'd get a big headache and the only thing that seemed to make that better was some sleep.

But right now, doing the trick I'd been taught, I could see better than I could with my eyes. For a moment, as I moved toward the chest, I could see the room the medusa called her inner sanctum. All of it. From almost an overhead glass house view if I chose to. Like I was seeing through the eyes of a spider up there in the shadows. Hijacking its brain for a look. It was a large room. It must have taken up this whole level of the tower. Where we were at, getting an audience from her, there were huge, scalloped columns, but at the far end of the room there was a dais, a raised area, and lush, richly woven carpets. An old campaign table was there too, loaded with yellowing maps. And stacks of books. Old books. Ancient books. Books like the sorcerer's spellbook we'd recovered during my first Reaper mission. Books like the *Book of the Dead* the crow thing had brought itself back to life with. And then given himself, or itself, access to my mind with, until the Rangers ventilated him on the objective.

The dry husky laugh of the crow thing shaman had finally ceased. And that was for the best.

I picked up the Chief McCluskey monkey scuba idol with obscene Ranger scrawls on it and set it down on the floor, directly in front of the Medusa's scaly tail, forgetting I shouldn't look at her even as I stood up straight and stared her right in the face with my unseeing eyes.

'Cause I'm a pro like that.

In my defense… I had a lot on my plate. Dangerous monster. Murder Rangers just ready and waiting to… murder.

Oh no, I thought. *This is probably the last thing I'll ever see*, knowing I was most likely about to turn to stone.

But she was utterly… beautiful. I know… I'm sick. But I'd hit that. That was my first thought. She had huge perfect breasts that were barely contained within a diaphanous silk see-through gown. A heart-shaped face that was stunning despite the soft green glow of her perfect skin. Large almond eyes that had been made even more so by cat's-eye makeup and huge lashes. Her waist was tiny and then became a rather sensuous serpent's tail. She wore a diadem in hair that was really hair, black and lustrous to the point of being blue, never mind the snakes undulating and hissing within their nest. She was classically, otherworldly… *beautiful.*

Truly.

She caught her breath as I looked right at her with my mind and my unseeing eyes… and didn't turn to stone.

"You have…" She hesitated as she slithered away from me, almost twisting away to avert her eyes. Hiding behind her own naked and narrow shoulders. There was something innocent about that. Something truly seductive that she hadn't contrived. "… beautiful blue… eyes."

I took a deep breath. My unseeing open eyes still blocked the stone-turning effect. But the psionic trick was still in effect and so my brain was seeing that way and my optical nerves were totally shut down for the moment. Whatever had just happened… I hadn't turned to stone. But I had less than a minute before my brain couldn't take it anymore and the trick would shut off and my eyes took over. At which point I *would* turn to stone, most likely.

"How come you have not turned to… stone?" she asked. Like a frightened child. The imperious manner gone. A soft scared little girl's voice.

"It's a gift I have," I said as my heart thundered in my chest with fear. "Just for a moment I can… see with my mind. Not my eyes. That is why…"

My voice was trembling.

I was shaking. Shaking because I'd accidentally almost turned myself into stone. And that probably meant death despite the Ruin and magic. I didn't see how any magic was gonna get you back from being turned to stone. Heart. Blood. Everything just stone now. Like those statues down on the stairs.

"Oh…" she said softly. Her perfect mouth and lips making the soft little sound of *Oh*. Even the snakes had stopped hissing and were just watching me as though they too were in a trance. Or like some jury trying to see how guilty I truly was.

I took the eye wrap blindfold and made ready to tie it over my eyes again.

"No," she said, holding up a delicate yet cold hand to my face. Stroking my cheek as she stared into my eyes. "Just a bit longer. I won't turn you…"

She slithered close. The beautiful dark eyes watching me like the first moment when lovers love.

"Do you know what…" she said haltingly, "… someone like me wants…"

She was close. Getting closer. I steadied myself. The snakes were getting closer too. And time was running out. But… if this was gonna get the IED in place… then it was time to embrace the suck.

She just watched me for a few seconds. I could feel the clock burning and I didn't like it. If I messed up, I was gonna be a statue for a really, really long time. Really.

"… what a girl like me really wants… do you know?"

She said this as though she too was in a trance.

"Any girl, really…"

So close, our lips were almost touching. I had just a few seconds more. My brain was throbbing.

"It is to be seen, Spock. That is all. I would trade everything… just to be seen. Even if…"

She faltered, and I watched a crystal tear run down her perfect skin.

"Even if I wasn't beautiful. I would just want to be seen. But for someone like me… that isn't possible."

She turned away and slithered into the darkness near what I took to be her throne on the dais.

"You may blindfold yourself again," she said, once again the Queen of All Things Imperious.

Fingers trembling, I did this quickly. Never so grateful to comply.

Then she was back. Coming at us and interrogating fast. All business.

"What does it do—this idol?"

Her voice was haughty. The rattle of her tail dangerous and deadly. The hissing snakes not helping any.

I fell back into my role as Spock the Mysterious Stranger.

"If you place a coin in its hand, it will answer a question for the lady."

The Forge had cranked out an animatronic device that was sheathed in Forge-created gold. A small computer would basically tell the thing to speak. Its lips didn't move—it wasn't that high-tech—but one of the Rangers had recorded the answers in Greek because the wizard had told us that was the language the medusas preferred.

Then the Magic 8-Ball algorithm was downloaded and coded in, a very simple and easy one according to Penderly, to spit out an answer.

"Any question?" she asked. Slithering close and dangerous around it. Nervous. "The truth?" she asked, and I felt there was more to this question than just the obvious. Something important to her.

I nodded. And added, "It is so, my lady."

She stopped, cold and silent, and though the psionic trick was done now, I could feel the weight of her stare on me. Silence.

She slithered quickly off to another part of the room and was back a moment later.

"She's getting a coin, I think," whisper-hissed Tanner.

"We shall see…" she said like some Karen who wanted to see my manager. Like she didn't want to believe anything good could ever happen to her. "Perhaps you are just charlatans come to sell me something false."

She was close and dangerous despite our prior moment. Desperate for something…

I heard the coin land on Mini Monkey McCluskey's outstretched golden idol hand.

"Is Spock a liar?" she snapped.

The Ranger who had recorded the idol's vocal pronouncements, probably not understanding the Greek he was using, spoke.

"Very Doubtful."

His pronunciation wasn't great. But he got it.

And that's me, being a language snob when it adds absolutely no value. When I'm standing in front of a real live monster that could turn me to stone if it wanted to. I am a sick and shallow man.

She didn't know what to do with that. Her tail rattled nervously. The snakes hissed and seethed.

"Is it night right now?" she asked for her second question.

I really hoped this thing stuck the landing. That was what I was thinking even as I prepared to answer for it if it gave some Magic 8-Ball nonsense like *No* or *Very Doubtful*. Technically, Alluria, I'd say, it's day somewhere on the other side of the world because hey the world is actually round, and I don't know if you know this here in the Ruin ten thousand years after we used to science and all, but it really is. Now don't turn us all to stone and please here accept two one-five-five artillery shells that are going to crater your tower on the day we decide to whack your neighbor the dragon that's been giving everyone a hard time.

"Yes," she said softly once the Magic 8-Ball McCluskey idol had said the same thing. Almost to herself again.

I let out a breath I hoped she didn't see. I heard Monroe shuffle and I wondered if the big minotaur was about to ventilate her with high doses of seven-six-two at very close range.

She placed another coin in Monkey McCluskey's hand.

"Does... Phobos... live?" she asked, her voice papery and trembling.

The Ranger who'd recorded the random phrase spoke, and once again I was holding my breath as my mind did the translating work of what we were gonna hear. Randomly. No one had anticipated she would actually ask it questions. Or do so like her life and very existence were on the line. And ours too. Because that was what it felt like right now.

Close and dangerous.

Signs Point to Yes, announced the Ranger-recorded voice. Randomly. Or maybe not. Maybe the universe that answered prayers and sent Rangers didn't mind tilting the machine occasionally.

And then she was weeping. Weeping like a woman in love. Weeping like someone who was drowning and could not breathe. Who'd been holding their breath for longer than they could remember. For a very long, long, long time. Weeping like that spirit.

No. Not like that.

Like someone who had hope now. Hope where there had been none. None at all.

CHAPTER THIRTEEN

NOW, as I watched where the Tower of Stars, the *Mindon Elen*, had been, the smoke of its sudden catastrophic destruction rising into the early morning air as the battle against the raging dragon got underway, the first Carl G gunners opened fire from all quarters.

Streaking 84mm murder hornets went *CRACK* and sped away at the momentarily stunned sky lizard as the echoes of the blasts resounded off and into the spreading ruins of the city. Strange yet beautiful swamp birds took flight in great swarms at violence's imminent call to action.

We had three teams of recoilless rifle gunners spread out across the inner ring security cordon the Rangers were determined to keep the dragon within. Each team got the green light from Captain Knife Hand as the blasts faded out over the ancient and ruined city. Rangers moved out from cover and into position to fire. Rear security super SAW gunners scanned the rubble for bad guys who might try to push in these early moments. All of the Carl teams had been close, hiding within scout-identified abandoned structures throughout the palace district, ready to pop up and go live fire on command. Now they were rushing out into the rubble-strewn streets to get their kill on.

And at the same time, the weapons team got the signal to shift fire off the dragon and take care of the *In and Out*.

The In and Out was a structure that lay along the Ivory Way, the royal road that ran through the city and into the palace district of the ruins. It was most likely some long-forgotten temple of the ancient Dragon Elves to an unknown god no one worshipped anymore. And hadn't for a long time. To me it looked like a bank from New York City. One of the old ones with the high marble steps and the crouching lions out front. But maybe I was thinking of the public library.

Why would I have ever been at a bank? C'mon, me.

Sergeant Hardt had tagged this structure the In and Out because the Saur were always going in and out of it. The high volume of traffic made it clear we couldn't get close to it without risking detection. So the Rangers had reconned from distance through observation and studied it to find out what they could about its current use. What they learned was that the Saurian priests, who had accompanied the infantry here to the Ruins of Tarragon to serve the dragon, seemed to be on some kind of permanent station. The In and Out was their headquarters. And it was well guarded in all its forlorn and savage glory. The Rangers thought about placing high-ex near it, just to go ahead and bring it down in the first moments of the ambush, but that operation was too risky given the level of activity around the area.

The front of the temple was covered in sacred totems that looked vaguely like Egyptian sphinxes and didn't seem to be part of the original Dragon Elven architecture. There were other various gods of that neo-Egyptian pantheon that seemed disturbingly familiar if you stared at them too long. In front of each sacrificial idol was a huge bonfire that burned nightly. During these times, from deep within the cavern of the massive temple beyond its columned portico came dark, almost drum-like chanting and, believe it or not, choral singing that seemed almost human.

"That is the way of their dark religion," Vandahar had said, providing intel. "They worship their pharaohs as gods who have defeated death long ago. They view the Ruin of those long-lost days as their beginning and becoming. The songs are the songs of the deathless, and to hear them and not be Saurian is considered a great blasphemy. And a death sentence… when they can enforce it."

The Rangers were listening in the twilight that night we first heard it. Deep in the shadows and leafy green swamp, war faces on and invisible for all intents and purposes.

"Well, I guess I can cross death cult choir off my concert bucket list," Sergeant Kurtz muttered in the quiet, exhibiting a previously unrevealed dry sense of humor. Tanner almost lost it when he heard that, and Kurtz gave him a look of pure murder that seemed to indicate the PFC was not to ever expect repeat performances of the comedy stylings of the detachment's most hardcore Ranger.

Though Kurtz didn't realize it, I had the feeling the dwarves were lightening him up a bit. It was like they were brothers from another mother. And ten thousand years or so apart.

We knew the Saurian version of a QRF, quick reaction force, would come from the In and Out once the battle started. If the tower exploding and falling into the now roaring and screeching dragon hadn't gotten the priests' and their holy guards' attention within the temple, then the sudden automatic weapons fire would, from the medium two-forty bravo weapons teams that had now begun to murder the devastated and stunned-by-the-blast Saurian legions on the field out there.

For historical note, a legion is four thousand infantry soldiers. The Rangers, who are for the most part all fascinated by history, as there are lots of old and interesting ways you can learn to kill people from it, told me this.

They're not prideful by nature. They don't boast or brag. But they were rather proud of their historical knowledge, and almost all of them had studied some facet of it on some level. If only to kill better.

I had no idea what a legion was before I joined and no idea it was four thousand of you and your best friends draining swamps, building roads, and going Roman on anyone that got uppity.

And yeah, right now, arrayed across the Ivory Way and the Well of the Palace of the Kings were about eight thousand Saurian troopers. They were dead already even though their commanders were trying to get them into something that looked like a rough series of phalanxes and set up a defense. They were on open ground, and opposing them were three professional Ranger weapons team two-forty gunners traversing for maximum murder and a full field of view with almost no obstructions. The lizards were scrambling but they were dying in large numbers, torn to shreds by violent gunfire. Shortly, the two-forty gunners were "talking the guns" and working over each phalanx as soon as it managed to orient itself to incoming fire from a new direction.

It was clear on some level they'd been informed by the SEAL Chief McCluskey we used modern weapons and there would be problems with Saurian Bronze Age tech versus modern warfare. For them. Some of their heavier shields were standing up to gunfire, but the almost frag-

ile-looking Saur wielding them were ending up with shattered arms, or just knocked down flat trying to deflect the
incoming fire. Then they were shot a bunch.

The Saur, the SEAL, and the dragon had not expected
the Rangers to be where they were this morning on this
morning of all mornings.

Of course, that's where the Rangers were going to be.

"He shoulda known this was gonna happen. Shoulda
know'd this was coming." The sergeant major had muttered
that to me the night before the attack. We were both brewing up cold brews for the attack and drinking a lot of coffee
because it was going to be a long slow night of creeping
and scout elimination to get into position before we moved
into the ruined city to make the final hit on Lizard King.

Kurtz was running the gunners working over the phalanxes on the field that were getting cut to shreds, when the
captain gave the order for Weapons Team Alpha to shift fire
on the In and Out.

"Affirmative!" shouted Kurtz atop the battlement of the
squat tower we'd commandeered. "Soprano, shift gun to
second position target and open fire."

"*Sì, Sergente!*" said Soprano as he stood, grabbed the
gun and tripod despite his small stature, and brought it
forty-five degrees across the rooftop to set up with a firing
window on the temple the Saur were now flooding around.
"C'mon, little monkey, bring the belts right now."

Right now, we had almost no incoming and it was
nothing more than a free-for-all shooting gallery. I could've
seen some get carried away with the killing. Not the Rangers. It was all business and economy. They were making
sure every sector got worked thoroughly, as the Carl teams

shifted position and shot rounds at the dragon in the center of the action.

That was when Lizard King went for a breath attack. This was the dragon's most powerful attack, and the Rangers had AAR'd this situation to death because in the end there had been almost nothing anyone could do to defeat it. But at least the Rangers all knew that when the dragon inhaled, as it had atop the tower, and shot its neck forward, that the powerful chemical attack was coming your way.

"Team Three *Rhino Rhino Rhino!*" shouted Sergeant Huxton.

Rhino was the net call referencing a combat jump the Rangers had done in Afghanistan. It was code that the gunners were under direct threat and needed to shift position for immediate cover. The three-man gunner team ran for their lives heading for a building the Rangers had identified as being able to protect the exposed Carl Gustav gunners from the dragon's blast.

The other teams were to pick up the slack and get the dragon's attention off the Rangers' jump to cover. They did that now, over-cycling on the dragon, dumping everything they had at it. One Carl round streaked across the battlefield, missed Lizard King and smashed into a thousands-of-years-old building. Stone rocketed out the back of the building, devastating the Saur who were covering there.

Jabba shifted the belts, shrieking the entire time that the dragon was gonna *"Big bigga biggie Die!"* He seemed to have gotten stuck in this loop and couldn't stop repeating this obvious truth over and over as the dragon took fire from another Carl Gustav ADM round. Area defense munitions, streaking in to explode.

"Talker!" shouted Kurtz. "Make those bastards over there dead now." Kurtz was pointing at one of the phalanxes that was fighting its way toward a pile of collapsed stone to get some cover from our medium machine guns currently leaving dead Saur everywhere they chose to lay hate.

The dragon's tail suddenly whiplashed in pain as the incoming ADM round's airburst sent brutal steel flechettes all through its leathery wings. Half this group of Saurian infantry was crushed instantly, smeared across the dirty ancient stone of the once-royal Ivory Way.

"Keep them off us!" shouted Kurtz as I stood there dumbfounded watching lizard men get tossed all over the rubble and stone while their comrades raced for cover.

Then I was working the carbine and putting fire into them. These weren't like the orcs or the undead. These went down when you hit them with the MK18. Their armor couldn't stand up to five-five-six green tip.

Another ADM round nailed the dragon directly and sent more steel darts through its wing and massive forearm, causing the titanic beast to howl in sudden pain. The air was beginning to get thick with chlorine gas as I got busy shooting down lizard men. I missed the last guy as the Carl G round cracked and exploded, sending shrapnel across the battlefield in every direction, some of it even skittering across the tower we were fighting from. When I scanned the field to pick up a target, my eyes locked onto one of the lizard men who'd been holed straight through his yellowish belly by one of the flechettes.

The third round that was gonna hit the dragon failed as the huge emerald beast roared and swiped its other giant forepaw, or forearm, or foreleg, or whatever you wanna call it, across its front and a shimmering shield of stardust magic suddenly went up. The 84mm ADM round slammed into this invisible barrier and exploded backward in the direction it had come, sending shrapnel tumbling back toward the ring of our defenses on that side of the ambush.

"NETCALL NETCALL NETCALL... Lizard King using his shield... Feelgood drop your iron."

Kennedy had given us a master class in dragon fighting, as far as his game of pens and paper and strange-shaped dice was concerned. Besides being able to attack you with their claws, their teeth, and their huge wings, they could cast spells at you too. Also don't forget their napalm chlorine breath that can basically eat you alive.

Now with the dragon's most recent blast of its breath weapon, and the Rangers running out the back of the ancient stone structure that was disintegrating from acid hurl, the air was getting thick and caustic with chlorine.

If the dragon's shield worked like it did in Kennedy's game, then a certain amount of damage would knock it down. Problem was, we had no idea what that amount of damage was, or if the rules of a game meant anything in the here and now of the Ruin. So the plan was to drop some serious steel on it once it went there.

Vandahar with Kennedy as his apprentice was able to contribute somewhat to solving our problem.

"Ssruth is a master wizard. His shield will be quite formidable to take down. The spell is known to me, but of course mine is a much weaker version of his. He does not need to concentrate while it's up, and he can attack us regardless of it. His sorcery is very effective against his enemies, or else he would not be so long-lived of course. If he can get up into the sky, pull back or escape, he can then make his attacks from the air. And that would be very bad for you Rangers despite your formidable prowess at causing mayhem and destruction."

During the final briefing before the attack, the captain had stressed this and emphasized why the opening moments of the attack were all about denying the dragon the ability to use his wings. We could not let him get there.

Two ADM rounds had struck, but was that enough to render his wings useless?

We had no idea. But the plan was for the Ranger 120mm mortar teams, designated as Doctor Feelgood, stationed throughout the more isolated areas surrounding the palace district, to start dropping rounds all over the dragon the moment the dragon's shield went up.

Why Doctor Feelgood? Indirect fire is a drug for Rangers. They love it and it gets the job done.

"Doc Feelgood incoming!" shouted Kurtz.

We ducked and covered. Two mortar teams were using antipersonnel rounds for their opening salvos. One team was firing M935 precision-guided mortar munitions. The antipersonnel rounds were going to explode everywhere. The Saur on the field who hadn't been murdered yet and weren't covering were about to be good and finally dead.

Within seconds, the first antipersonnel strikes came whistling in from overhead and slammed into the objective area. Falling all over Lizard King and his ridiculous shield.

A moment later, the team firing the advanced round nailed the dragon directly with an M935. One of the snipers was using a laser designator and keeping it right on the dragon so as to direct the shot on target. The smart-guided munition nailed the dragon—and so did the next three.

We had no idea at what moment the shield went down but the dragon was going airborne regardless, its huge, shredded, and holed-in-dozens-of-places wings heaving themselves to ruined glory. The last round managed to land right on the dragon's back and exploded, blowing away bloody armored emerald scales and chunks of dragon flesh.

The titan howled as its wings, unbelievably and impossibly giant, dragged the badly wounded dragon skyward and away from our killing field.

The mortars ceased fire at the same moment the Carl G gunners fired their next round of ADMs to deny its escape. Brutal flechettes exploded across the sky as the machine gun teams resumed fire and raked the temple and Saur coming out of it.

That was when the Stinger missile was fired from a high tower the Rangers had taken in an adjacent district. The dragon was barely flying, attempting to circle the palace that was our cordon in one wonky half circle. Planning had indicated that the dragon at this phase of the operation would either try to head back into the well at the base of the palace steps, where the Ivory Way ended, or make for its secondary entrance the Rangers had discovered and mined with explosives just in case. Because of course Rangers would do that. Four clicks to the east was a large canal the Dragon Elves had set up for some long-ago purpose that made little sense now that the swamp had flooded most of the ruined city. The Rangers scouting and marking everything had found the abandoned mud-filled tunnel the dragon had broken up to make an entrance back into the palace district where it made its home. Sergeant Thor had actually gone in alone and scouted the tunnel, confirming the dragon's location and possible use of the tunnel as an exit.

That the dragon would go for that secondary secret entrance had been considered, and thus the Ranger master breachers, before moving in with the assaulters to final position, had mined the exit late last night. If the dragon went there now, he was going to get ruined by about three hundred pounds of C4 and a lot of fast-moving shrapnel they'd put together. Plus they were going to crater the tunnel from the street above and bring it down on him, burying Ssruth alive.

In other words... they weren't playing around.

"Will that kill Lizard King?" Captain Knife Hand had asked.

"If it don't... then I don't know what will, sir," replied Sergeant Chris.

Right now, watching the dragon lumber through the air as the machine-gun teams cut down the Saur on the field in front of the ruins of the ancient Dragon Elven palace, I couldn't help but feel that if the Lizard King *did* go for the secondary tunnel, that would make things a lot easier.

But as Kennedy had told us, "Green dragons are highly intelligent, guys. Like... supergenius-level intelligence. If he senses he's under attack and it's an ambush, then he'll quickly do the math and figure out his opponents have done the work to scout him and figure out what he's gonna do and what his options are. But, again—"

"We know," one of the Rangers interrupted. "*It might not be like your game.*"

Kennedy had given this warning so much, it was now a common refrain for many situations that had nothing to do with how dangerous the Ruin could be in comparison to his game of Dungeons and Dragons. While opening an MRE the Forge had cranked out—which were hit or miss, as in either better than back ten thousand years ago MREs or somehow impossibly worse—a Ranger might say, "This might not be like your game," as some kind of prayer or *well-here-goes-nothing* before knifing into the meal ready-to-eat.

Now the Stinger streaked in and the dragon, as gravely wounded as he was, breathed all over the incoming missile with a huge jet of chlorine napalm acid, spitting it out in a wide spray and intercepting the lethal ground-to-air explosive. The missile detonated, rocking the dragon back in the air because the missile had been so danger close when it exploded due to suddenly getting covered in fantasy flying lizard spit, that the blast had displaced the dragon's flight and caused it to suddenly stall midair.

A second later the dragon crashed into the roof of the temple the Saur had been using, plowing straight down through the massive building and doing something no one had foreseen in the planning. Managing to avoid the constant murder the Rangers had planned for it by crashing into an object the Rangers had not anticipated it crashing into and thus giving itself cover and concealment.

But the Rangers had a plan for the unforeseen also.

CHAPTER FOURTEEN

"EYES on Lizard King. Repeat, does anyone have eyes on Lizard King at this time?"

It was Captain Knife Hand over the net in the sudden pause of the battle. Gunfire rang out as the Rangers finished off the last of the Saur who had come out to parade for the dragon just moments before all hell broke loose. The ground force commander was with the assaulters, the Rangers looking for something to kill.

Negatives came back from all section leaders. It was clear the dragon had lost the ability to fly and had somehow angled itself to smash through the Saurian temple. The question was whether it had died in the crash, or whether it was being cunning, as Kennedy had indicated it might, and lying low, waiting for us to come in and get it.

Thoughts were running through my head, and I'm sure they were running through every Ranger's head at that moment. All of us going back over Kennedy's brief, as no doubt the command team was going through what we were going to do if the dragon managed to stay within the cordon yet evade us.

"We have to consider that possibility, sir," the sergeant major had said during planning. "If he stays airborne the Stinger is eventually going to get him. He figures that out and he's as smart as PFC Kennedy here says he might just be, then he may be trying to go to ground within the district and cover from our fire. Get us to come at him one by one in some kinda bottleneck. I would strongly advise against that, sir."

There was a long pause during the briefing as the Rangers studied the sand table and especially the map of the palace district where we'd be fighting. There were actually a lot of buildings and ruined streets, both within and outside the security cordon, that the dragon could get into if it got desperate enough and managed to survive not getting killed in the first two minutes. That became the problem for the Rangers to figure out.

Why?

The captain explained it to us.

"If Lizard King does go to ground, we have a serious problem, Rangers. All teams will be spread out over the inner ring. He has the potential to get in here…"

The captain used a stick to point at a series of collapsed buildings that must have once been some serious minor palaces for the city's ruling elite. "These are all big enough for him to cover in or behind. Are we sure there are no obvious entrances here?"

Sergeant Thor answered for the snipers and scouts.

"Affirmative, sir. We've scouted the entire area and there's no sign the dragon has ever used those buildings. Or anything besides its two identified routes into its lair."

Kennedy spoke up, holding the dragon-headed staff like it was some kind of badge of office. And who were we kidding, it was. What he could do gave him a certain cachet among the Rangers now. Like it or not.

I thought it was pretty cool and so did a lot of the other Ranger lower enlisted. Many were hoping now to get some kind of "Ruin Reveals" magic powers, or find a magic weapon of some sort to go all Conan on the staks with.

"Um... sir," said the fledgling wizard Ranger hesitantly. "If the dragon is a... a... wizard... of some sort... well then, he could... shrink himself, sir."

"Shrink himself with what, PFC?"

"A spell, sir. They can do that, sir."

Captain Knife Hand rubbed the bridge of his nose as a new variable entered his kill-equation, solve for dead Lizard King. That permanent look of indigestion on his face was there too. I could see what he was seeing and was concerned about as we all studied the sand table. The Rangers could end up getting picked off one by one if they sensed the dragon on the run and decided to react to wherever he'd gone to ground. Basically, getting overconfident and sucked into his killing trap. The Rangers' best shot at bringing Ssruth down came from working together. But if the flying dinosaur managed to change the game and get the Rangers to rush him at a chokepoint he controlled, then we got picked off one by one and the plan came apart.

That wasn't good.

Now, adding the possibility of a spell into the mix that could shrink the dragon down to, say, the size of a mouse... well, then there were probably a million ways back down into his lair for him.

The Rangers needed a plan for that too.

So they made one. But it was a doomsday plan, and it involved a lot of casualties if it was going to be done right.

"We go down there, sir," the sergeant major said. "We're in his world now, sir. And this thing is supposedly, what, thousands of years old? It didn't get that old being dumb."

Vandahar sensed his moment to speak up.

"More, perhaps. Dragons are not of the Ruin. They came before the Nether Sorcerer, but they did come from somewhere... *other*. It never pays to underestimate them. Captain."

Well, that's just downright weird. Somewhere... *other*. The Ruin never fails to surprise me on some new, weirder level. I did not look forward to the day when it really pulled a lethal fast one on me.

"And perhaps there is something in that," murmured the wizard as he settled into being forgotten about once more.

The captain cleared his throat.

"Listen, we can't do anything about his... spells. But let's say he does manage to evade fire and cover. As far as we know, according to Sergeant Thor's recon, he only has two access points back into his... lair below the city. Chances are, if we understand the psych brief as provided by PFC Kennedy, and the more clinical one provided by our scientist on narcissistic sociopath personality disorders, then it stands to reason Lizard King may want to control access to where he guards his wealth. If he's smart enough that in the first moments of the ambush he knows he's surrounded and getting outgunned, even if he doesn't understand the tech, then he may not make for the primary entrance back into his lair. He could go into any one of these buildings, or move through these side streets, hoping to get us to react. But the plan we've made still holds. We control access to his escape routes. Since he's smart, we can anticipate he'll know we've set up a denial at the secondary. His only hope at continued survival is to just fly away. If we've denied him *that* ability also, then he only has one option for continued survival... he tries to go home.

"He's smart and he's guessed he can't use the secret door he's made over in the canal. During the fight, the assaulters have covered the demo teams and we've set up the explosives all over the well. If he goes down in there, manages to fight his way in, then we drop the acetylene bottles in and blow the whole place. But of course, we understand we'll have to do that fast to catch him close to the surface. And there will be casualties if we can't get clear fast enough. Still, he'll probably be expecting this. Avoiding the trap. One more option denied to him.

"And that's the plan: denial. If he goes to ground on the surface, we force him to go for the primary hole by denying him cover anywhere else he chooses to fight from. We control the space… and we wait."

CHAPTER FIFTEEN

AT the same moment Captain Knife Hand was calling in a fire mission to drop high-explosive bunker-busting rounds all over the Saurian temple the dragon had gone down in, we heard the drums-and-sticks calls coming from around the ruined capital.

BOOM BOOM CLAP. BOOM BOOM CLAP. BOOM BOOM CLAP.

The temple was now littered with wrecked and torn lizard men bodies all over the cracked and crumbling marble steps. The whole place didn't look so much like a battlefield but more like a massacre. The two-forty teams had savaged the Saur who'd come out from the In and Out. Priests and temple warriors were now separated from the legions only by the crimson sashes and headgear they wore. Plumed Bronze Age helmets with cheek guards and bronze breastplates for the warriors and captains.

"Them dead staks are better than them other dead staks," said Brumm as we stared out at the carnage all over the field. The summer morning getting hotter. Noting the differences between the Saur legionnaires and the temple guards.

That was when the *BOOM BOOM CLAP* started up again.

"Sar'nt, we got movement to the rear of the tower… They're coming at us now," said Tanner, who was watching the bottom level of the tower we'd fought the battle from so far. I checked my watch. It had been two minutes. Just a little more than that since the fight with the dragon had started.

It felt like a week. A very long week.

I took a huge pull of cold brew and stowed it. The day had just got longer. Brumm spat dip and muttered, "Looks like we got someone else to play with."

Two minutes from when the dragon had begun to feed, and I'd double-tapped the guard on top that Kurtz had failed to garrote. Probably close to many thousand dead out there. One devastated dragon hiding in the smoking temple across the way, hoping we'd come in and get him now that he wasn't airborne.

The Rangers had craftily and hastily gone to work repositioning their assets according to plan. The Stinger was ready to go, as was the drone just in case the chlorine-breathing turkey was playing possum and could actually still fly.

But it was becoming clearer by the second, the dragon was most likely badly wounded and turtling inside the temple. Just waiting for us to assault and then maybe it could kill a bunch of us, destabilize the attack, and bulldoze its way back to its hole.

The Carl Gustaf gunners had repositioned with HE rounds ready to go. Now that the dragon was less mobile, it was time to punch some serious holes in Ssruth the Whatever.

The captain gave the order to move the acetylene bottles into the well and have them on remote arming triggers.

If the dragon managed to detonate the explosives on the well then there was still a chance we could cook him below.

"Eyes on bad guys. Lots of 'em coming through the weeds," updated Tanner. "More Saur and more cat hajis in the streets north of our position. They're moving to surround, Sar'nt."

The Rangers were not surprised by this development. There were a lot more Saur throughout the city and they had a tendency to lie low during the night, coming out only during the daylight hours. The cat hajis, on the other hand, had been out at night. The Rangers had watched both groups patiently from the shadows of long-abandoned places and determined that most of these assets were in alliance with the dragon but headquartered away from the legions. Numbers were hard to estimate but now that they were moving into the palace district to respond to the attack on the dragon, the Rangers' inner security plan went into effect.

The drone feed was updating the battle boards of the team commanders and showing three groups staging beyond the cracked and broken palace walls that guarded this district.

The weapons team got the call to, "Stand by to shift to Highway One."

There were three "highways" into the district that the Rangers guessed the cat hajis and auxiliary Saur troops would attempt to use to relieve the dragon: Highways One, Two, and Three. These were really just main thoroughfares through the old city, wide avenues among the crumbling ruins, that we'd seen the bad guys using to arrive at the Saurian temple at various times. The Rangers had hidden MPIMs all over these routes, and some of the smaller, less-used access points into the kill zone were now either over-watched by sniper teams or mined with smart claymores. Camera feeds alerted the demo experts responsible for that sector that there was movement, so the explosives could be detonated at just the right moment. And now Kurtz's weapons team was being shifted to cover Highway One, which was about to turn into an ambush as the main force of Saur and hajis moved down that avenue of approach to relieve the dragon.

Behind us, the mortars began to slam into the temple now that fire had been adjusted to land all over it. The captain was attempting to bring it down on the dragon with indirect fire.

It took three minutes to reach the position at Highway One and we made it just in time. The hajis could be seen coming down the dusty streets where buildings had collapsed out into the paving stones that lined the thousands-of-years-old road, and where grass came up through the cracks.

The next minute was pure hell as the hajis pushed us to get inside the cordon.

Pure hell for both sides.

CHAPTER SIXTEEN

BRUMM triggered the MPIMs from the left side of the street, devastating what looked to be a company-sized element of the Saur moving up. The explosion was sudden and brutal as the first chain of mines in the string went off, rippling like rolling thunder down along that side of the street. Sending flying building material and projectiles into the crowd of strange warriors. One of the lizard men was hit so hard he was tossed across the street, landed halfway up a building, and got impaled on some old piece of perfectly jagged stone that had survived thousands of years of slow destruction.

"Look at that stak fly!" shouted Soprano from behind the long-ago fallen pillar the two-forty was using as a fighting position. Jabba was down in a ball, huge claws clasped over his comically gigantic flappy and pointed ears. "You miss-a the show, monkey," lectured Soprano as he bent close to the two-forty sights and prepared to start firing.

The mortars stopped to our rear.

So far everything was going according to plan. Calls over the net were indicating the temple was collapsing and the dragon was either going to get crushed in there or he'd have to come out. The Rangers had cached extra belts for the gun here and boxes of frags nearby in a building that looked like it must have been some kind of ancient food service place once and long ago when the Dragon Elves were a people. There were old pots and pans there and cooking areas that looked like they were made for woks to be held over fires. I'm sure they called them something other than woks, something different, but it seemed like that's what had gone on here. We'd stored the ammunition and explosives here in a dark crack we'd covered over with debris.

Brumm and I were sent to get the cache and get it back to the fighting position at the Highway One chokepoint. By the time we got back, the two-forty was already dealing out slow murder on the cat hajis and Saur pushing up the street. Brass and linkage were spitting away in short bursts as Soprano fired and Jabba fed the belt. Kurtz was hunkered just behind the top of a nearby pile of collapsed rubble, spotting enemies and directing the fire of his gun while using the M320 grenade launcher to drop rounds farther down the street where the enemy was covering in clusters.

Tanner was on rear security. I was just laying the belts out next to Jabba, who despite his fear was steadily managing the belts and spent brass into small piles.

That's what we were doing when the dragon made its move and erupted from the temple behind us. We could see it farther down the street, through an old ceremonial arch that opened out onto the Ivory Way and then across the palace grounds. It was distant, but not distant enough for how monstrous and enraged the thing was. And at the very moment the dragon erupted from the temple façade like a raging bull coming out of the chute, it shot a line of steaming acidic chlorine napalm at another team of Rangers. "Rhino Rhino Rhino!" was going off over the net as the

Rangers started firing everything they had at the suddenly attacking giant lizard.

The combined haji-Saur force seized the moment and pushed us hard. Teams of them moving down the street, getting wrecked by Soprano's fire and Kurtz's indirect rounds, suddenly turned into a flood and just came mass wave down the street on top of us.

"Here they come," said Brumm as he opened up with the SAW. Saur got cut to shreds as they got close to the line of rubble we were fighting from, Brumm walking and dosing the approaching enemy with lethal amounts of fast-moving armor-piercing lead. The closing force lobbed spears and flung sling stones at us. The pathetic response seemed almost comical until one of those spears smashed into Brumm and knocked him flat in the dust.

Tanner was up on his left, covering from the wall and shouting at the staks, telling them what they could do with themselves.

The cat hajis on the other hand moved like lightning over the rubble. Several had recurve bows and moved as they fired. And they fired a lot. Arrows were suddenly raining down on our position.

I mag dumped on a bunch of lizards getting close to Kurtz that he couldn't see from the other side of the pile of rubble, and when I covered to get a new mag in, staring back down the avenue, I saw the serpentine head of the dragon racing across the Ivory Way to our rear, screeching and shooting more chlorine napalm at unseen Rangers.

Then the booby-trapped alley off on our left flank went off. Meaning someone had tried to flank us there and tripped the tripwire, detonating the mines there. Smoke and disintegrating brick erupted into the narrow courtyard off to my left like a sudden flood of dirty smoke and dry dust.

That was when I noticed Brumm had been hit by a spear and was down on all fours, coughing and trying to get air into his lungs.

He might have collapsed a lung, or just had the wind knocked out of him. He was fine, or he wouldn't be. I had to check the alley. I had to make sure we weren't gonna get flanked.

"Sar'nt," I said over the comm. Shouting to be heard through my mask. "Bad guys on the left."

Then Kurtz said something I'd never expected an actual Ranger to ever say to me.

"Take care of it, Talker."

Yeah. It didn't go right to my head. But this was a pretty far cry from where I'd started with them. Just tagging along for the ride. I was with the weapons teams because they were so often in support of Ranger forward operations. As a linguist, if I was needed, I could be kept safely among one of the most destructive elements of a Ranger fighting force and summoned forward when needed to do languages and stuff.

This wasn't doing languages. Unless RAH is a language. Which, in a way, it is. One I was gradually picking up. Bit by hostile bit.

Mag in and following my rifle, I checked the alley where the explosive had gone off, making my way through the floating smoke and dust. There were a lot of ruined bodies in there. But more importantly, more real live cat hajis were coming through there and if someone competent didn't do something right now, the gun team wasn't going to be effective at holding Highway One much longer.

So in lieu of someone competent... I started shooting. And for once I didn't go all amateur and move to full-auto mag dumps to get it done. The Rangers and Chief Rapp had gotten me a lot more competent with shooting. Single fire, I started shooting cats down as they rushed the alley.

Three in the first exchange of gunfire. Ironically, my shooting was awful.

I blame the mask. It's really hard to shoot inside a gas mask.

The first cat I shot in the gut and the thing doubled over, blood soaking through the sand-colored bedsheet ninja outfit it wore. It dropped its sword, which had a weird hook at the top of the blade. Kennedy would later tell me it's called a *khopesh*. I got excited about that foreign-sounding word in the way only true linguists do when they hear one for the first time. Not because it's a sword with a hook. But because getting exposed to the word *khopesh* meant someone was about to start studying a new language.

Egyptian.

If I survived, that someone would be me.

I missed the second guy, and he fired an arrow that would have gone clean through my skull if not for my FAST helmet. All I heard was it *crack* and shatter, and it felt like I got a good solid *thump*.

But I've had that before with these helmets.

They're great.

So then I shot him several times and some of those rounds hit. The main thing was he was dead, and also, I had no idea how much ammo I had left in my magazine.

So I just started squeezing on cat number three who, I kid you not, flung his hooked sword at me, started cartwheeling, and produced two wickedly curved daggers as he came the last ten steps before leaping to plunge them into me.

Like a cat ninja in a movie would do. Or just a regular cat with a human body because cats do crazy death-defying stuff.

Problem for him was, I had shot him a lot as he came at me, and really he was just going on pure momentum by the time he got to me. He was bleeding from everywhere and all I had to do was step aside as the cat, its eyes wide and unfocused swung at me, just tumbled forward and landed face down in the weeds where I'm assuming it bled out and died in the next minute or so.

At that point I had to make a choice.

Keep shooting with no rounds. Never a good idea. Or get a mag in.

I was going for mag-in, because more cats were coming down the alley, when I remembered grenades are awesome. Mag in, I stepped back into the courtyard, let my MK18 dangle, and started deploying grenades into the alleyway.

The comm was so wild with what the dragon was doing and the firefight at Highway One, but I just held the alley. As a member of the detachment, I had to think for myself. I knew what the mission was. Maintain the cordon and make sure nothing could get in to help the dragon by harassing the Ranger kill teams. And make sure the dragon couldn't get out.

That's what I was doing when the dragon rammed straight into the palace and hit the assaulters and breachers with everything it had.

CHAPTER SEVENTEEN

THE battle went kinetic at the palace as Tanner yanked Brumm by his drag handle out of the road where he'd been knocked down and exposed to volley arrow fire and targeted fire from the cat hajis.

Soprano was on full rock and roll, working the attackers pushing us, firing short bursts and then suddenly going full savage high-cycle as he devolved into speaking only Sicilian curse words and insults. He furiously rocked the incoming Saur troopers who were now moving forward behind heavy shields that deflected some fire. This enraged the tiny Italian gunner further and he made them pay by going completely Roman on them with the two-forty. Their shields stood up a little bit until the traversing fire slowed and Soprano spent more time disintegrating each phalanx, brass and linkage flying away frenetically in bursts as he swore.

One of their priests got close enough to hit Kurtz with a targeted volley of sidewinding streaking magic meteors and did just that. The strike smashed into the weapons team sergeant's plate carrier and instantly melted the carbine he was using to engage close targets with while screaming at the two-forty gunner to concentrate fire here or there, depending on who Kurtz wanted to die next.

One of the cat hajis came down off a building, landed in our midst, and caught the gunner's attention. Fatal intentions were clear. Soprano stopped firing for half a second, yanked his sidearm furiously, and handed it to Jabba, shouting, "*Puliscilo*, little monkey!"

Clean him, in Italian.

Little monkey, in English.

The tiny goblin grabbed the sidearm, winced as he racked the slide with his overlarge goblin claws, and pointed the Glock 19 at the cat haji rushing toward them with an upraised *khopesh*.

"*Andiamo!*" shouted Private Soprano as he returned to street-sweeping the bad guys with high-dosage, high-caliber, armor-piercing murder hornets.

During all this I was still holding the alley, hugging wall to avoid arrow fire, head on a constant swivel to check both the alley and the fight in the main street.

Full-gangster Jabba pulled the trigger a lot. The sidearm wanted to cant in his unnatural grip and yet somehow he hit the fast-moving feline guardian of the Saur's most sacred place enough to knock it down in the dirt of the street. And once it was down, the goblin was on it with a homemade shiv none of us knew he had, stabbing the thing repeatedly and squalling with murderous goblin glee. His tiny sharp teeth wide in a grotesque smile and snapping at his victim.

It was disturbing. But much appreciated.

Kurtz had just shucked out of his ruined carrier, the tiny bright red starbursts burning within it, and heaved it into an abandoned building in case the ammunition-laden mags within started cooking off rounds. He shouted at Soprano, "Where'd he get that thing?"

Meaning the shiv.

Soprano either didn't hear over the belching roar of the two-forty or didn't understand.

"I been teachin' him marksmanship, *Sergente*. He shoot-a ugly. But he good, no?"

Several explosions erupted from the palace behind us and the ground shook like a brief earthquake had just taken place. Then there was the sound of a building, or part of it, collapsing in an unexpected crescendo of ruin. A chain of explosions and all of this mixed with the sound of our gunfire as now more Saur came into view farther down the street pushing what looked to be a mobile ballista.

"Private Soprano... work that field piece over!" shouted Kurtz. He then turned to Tanner, who was getting a needle decompression ready on Brumm, who'd been hit so hard one of his lungs had collapsed.

"His ribs are all busted on this side, Sar'nt!" shouted Tanner above the chaos of battle here in the dusty street of ruins. "Swelling's pushing on his heart. Gotta do the needle D now or we lose him."

Secondary danger from a tension pneumothorax is it deviates the trachea from air venting into the lung cavity, pushing the airway against the muscle wall of the neck, in effect strangling the wounded man. This trapped air and blood also crowds the lung, making it impossible for it to inflate because there is no space for it to fill. The needle decompression vents some of the blood and air, allowing the lung to return to its own space, bringing the deviated trachea with it.

If it didn't, the situation would be absolutely fatal to Brumm in the next few.

We had arrows raining down on us. A Sicilian mobster working the gun with an indig goblin as his assistant gunner. Our SAW gunner was down with a collapsed lung. Our sergeant had just been hit by a real live magic spell and looked like he had third-degree burns across his forearms. The only other guy besides myself was busy attempting to start a needle decompression—which means jabbing a huge needle between the fourth and fifth rib to relieve building pressure from the lung on the heart—and oh yeah, the guy doing that was technically dead. And then there was me, the linguist, holding the left flank and not doing languages… except to note, in the part of his brain that can't help but observe and categorize such esoteric niceties no matter how danger-close death presses in on all sides by arrow or magic spell, that somehow a goblin now understood Italian.

Have I got all that down?

Yeah, I won't tell you at that moment I wasn't jonesing hard for coffee because even though everything was really, no matter how bad things looked, going according to Captain Knife Hand's plans and contingencies, coffee is my dark master. It's how I cope with stress.

But things *were* going according to plan. In broad strokes if not specifics. It might have felt like total chaos, but the Rangers were in total control of the battlefield and the situation. The dragon was seriously on the ropes despite the ominous sounds coming from the kill zone on our six. The Rangers were dealing out as good as they got. The enemy was reacting to the trap just as the Rangers had planned for it to do. And if all that kept happening, no matter how violent Lizard King got, its death was inevitable.

And beyond that… even if the Rangers ran out of 84mm rounds, mortars, and 7.62… then they were going to go after it with knives, tomahawks, and all the other weapons they'd scavenged from the Ruin. This was gonna end for one side or the other today, and the Rangers had come with the intention of grilling up some dragon steaks. No matter how desperate it got, they were going to get it done. All we had to do was follow the plan and run our game.

"Let me do it!" shouted Kurtz, and we all knew why. But he said it anyway. Brumm looked mad as hell lying in the dirt unable to breathe much.

"He's my little brother!" hissed Kurtz.

Tanner held up one hand, he'd shucked his assault glove to do the work, and no, no one was using plastic gloves. Ain't got time for that when arrows and lizard men are trying to kill you forward of your position and a dragon is being hunted behind you by bands of heavily armed Rangers.

"Your hands are shaking..." managed Tanner as he got the needle out of its wrapper. "You'll screw it up, Sar'nt."

Kurtz, whose control and focused rage in the form of his iron will hadn't noticed how badly his hands had been burned, stopped. He was all about the killing. Now he looked at his hands and saw that where they weren't burned badly, blackened with flesh peeling away, they were blistered horribly. And the shaking—it wasn't just a tremor but a full-on quake. The damage was that bad.

Kurtz didn't say anything as he skinned his Rampage from its sheath and got ready to defend the gun while Tanner saved his brother's life.

"Do it!"

That was when the call came in from Corporal Sims who was acting as the ground force commander's commo.

"Warlord Two to Gun Team Alpha. Warlord Actual needs linguist ASAP to his loc, Golden Arches. Corporal

Monroe will link up at the arch to the kilo zulu to get Talker there."

Golden Arches was the tag for the palace. Once the scouts had tagged the Saur temple as the In and Out, most every other location the Rangers needed for the hit had gotten some kind of fast-food identification.

"They hard. But they miss the junk food," Tanner had quipped to me during one glass house. "Me too. I could go for a chili dog real bad, Talk."

I looked at Kurtz whose hands were burnt to hell despite him gripping the sawed-off shotgun he used now as it caused the blisters to pop and leak. Part of his assault gloves had melted onto some of his fingers. How the man was just crouching there getting ready to repel the next wave of Saur and cat hajis as the belt got swapped out on the gun, and not screaming from the pain, I had no idea.

I guess he had better things to do than be in pain right now.

Tanner pushed the needle in and Brumm grunted hard as the next volley of arrows slammed into the ancient masonry all around us.

"We got this, go now," Kurtz hissed at me.

And I didn't want to leave them. Didn't want to leave my... brothers.

Man, I never thought I'd say that. But life is a long, strange journey, and you get a lot more than you bargain for if you just go for it.

I'm glad I had. I'm glad they let me hold the flank for them.

Now... it was time to do my job. Whichever one that was.

CHAPTER EIGHTEEN

I linked up with Corporal Monroe at the arch, which was really the old gate that led from Highway One into the Ivory Way. I saw the big minotaur hugging wall this side of the arch, watching the kill zone. He still had a gas mask on, but as I approached he pulled it off and let the M60E3 dangle on the sling. The massive light machine gun looked like a mere carbine on his eight-foot frame.

The gas here wasn't as thick but the scent of chlorine coming through my mask was still heavy. I was hot and the mask lenses were constantly steaming up. So I pulled it off. If Monroe was managing without it, then maybe I wouldn't die in the next fifteen seconds. I needed air.

"Here's the situation, Talker," Monroe said in his husky rumble, scanning the courtyard where the battle had taken place. It was littered with dead staks and ruined stone. "Dragon just pushed the palace hard. We got wounded but the assaulters repelled and held on. Kennedy says the dragon figured out it can't take the well, so it attacked the main body inside the palace, hoping to get whoever controlled the explosives and get them to go ahead and det. How it figured that out, no one has any idea. Probably means that scumbag SEAL is around and has comm with it."

There were groups of lizard men on the far side of the district, moving in with spears and what looked to be cross-bows.

"The dragon fell back and took another structure," huffed Corporal Monroe. "It's inside there now. Sergeant major thinks it's wounded badly, but the captain is going to wait it out and see if it's waiting on the hajis to break through our cordon. So we ain't got a lot of time to do what the captain wants us to do. The SEAL could be putting together a bigger force to push on us, Talker."

One of the snipers shot the stak leader over there and suddenly the lizard men were pulling back, dragging their leader away. Other snipers took shots and ruined more stak as they came to assist.

"So what's the plan?" I asked.

"Captain wants to assault the building the dragon is in before the OPFOR can break in. What he needs to know is... is the dragon outta breath weapons and what its mind-set is. He wants me to get you close enough to... well, to read its mind... if you can do that. Is that possible? With that thing you can do and all? The trick. Psych-onics or something. If it's outta gas, then the assaulters breach and clear. Then we fade."

Is that possible?

I have no idea.

"If the dragon's outta breath weapon attacks, which PFC Kennedy thinks it might be," continues Monroe, "and if it's used up a lot of its magic, which Vandahar believes it has, then we can go kinetic on it directly. But we need to know. So I'll take you as close as we can get, and then you can... you know... reach out and use the Force or what-ever. I know it sounds weird and all, but hey, I'm half bull now. And it's cool as ice. So we gotta close and find out what Lizard King's status is. Sergeant major says for you to try."

I'm no hero. But I didn't hesitate.

"Let's roll."

CHAPTER NINETEEN

ALL we gotta do is get me close to the target building to mind-meld with a dragon in the middle of what looks like a crossfire hurricane of arrow fire, ballistae exchanges with the weapons teams, magic meteor strikes, and all the outgoing lead the Rangers can do whenever the Saur push from the east end of the palace district.

The kill zone currently looks like this. Highways One, Two, and Three come from the north, northwest, and northeast respectively. That's where much of the ruined city sprawl sinking into the swamp lies. Where most of the irregular forces of the Saur, supported by a significant cat haji element, are pushing from. All three highways are held by Rangers weapons teams. Teams with the two-forty bravo medium machine gun are suppressing any enemy advances along those routes. For now, they're supplied thanks to the over-supply weapons and ammo caches the sergeant major made sure were located all over the battlefield and easily accessible to the teams in the field. Despite the condition I left Kurtz's weapons team in, all three teams are indicating *in it to win it* as both sides jockey for the final conclusion.

The dragon is pinned down and needs its hajis to come in and det the well so it can get back inside its lair. It most likely doesn't know or understand the six acetylene bottles down-well that will cook the entire underground. The

Rangers want the dragon to make its move, but they can't wait for the hajis to detonate the explosives around the well or get the dragon out of there, because there's a chance the detonation could activate the acetylene bottles down-well and devastate the district and teams fighting there. If that happens, the dragon survives and either goes back into the underground, or out into the swamp, breaking out of the cordon.

There are three drones in the air. All controlled by the pilots at various times. Drone one is close air support and is now making gun runs on the push from the north. The drone comes in low over the streets and unloads from its two M134 Gatling-style miniguns. In its wake it leaves a lotta dead stak in the dusty streets and ruins.

Problem is, it seems like the stak are coming out of the swamps in droves now. Kennedy had said that was a serious possibility. That we were not getting an accurate enemy count because the lizard men are amphibious and most likely have underground grottos where they sleep and hide in larger numbers.

They have some organization. But they're pushing hard everywhere and sooner than later that's gonna be a problem. Drone one is almost Winchester... meaning out of ammo and getting ready to either RTB, return to base, or get crashed into something significant like the catapults and ballistae that are now coming from the east down the Ivory Way like some kind of light mechanized force to relieve the dragon trapped in the target building the Rangers want to assault.

Which I'll get to in a sec.

The Carl G teams are E-and-E'ing, escape and evasion, inside the kill zone, using buildings and alleyways to evade the hajis and Saur teams now advancing to try to wipe out the Rangers. The snipers are working these, but the Saur have deployed magic-using priests or wizards, and weird stuff is happening out there. Waves of fatigue or even sleep. Dancing lights that disorient. And of course, magic meteors.

The Carl Gustaf rounds need to be saved for the next fight with the dragon and so the gunners are running, and their rear security is suppressing the stak trying to locate and destroy them. Ranger snipers are moving along the rooftops and tower walls, picking off targets of opportunity when they can.

One sniper got hit by a magic meteor and fell, busting both legs. Chief Rapp, leading the Lost Boys, moved in to recover the downed sniper under heavy arrow fire and supported by the Ranger snipers. It looked like the sniper was going into shock, so the chief, and I heard this from Daredevil himself who was on overwatch trying to keep the Saur and cat hajis rushing the sniper off and back, the chief pulled off his assault gloves and held his huge worn Mississippi-mud hands up to the sky, at which point they began to turn into small burning suns. Then he... this was the language used as related to me... the SF operator *laid hands* on Sergeant Kresdyn, the wounded sniper, and brought him out of shock. The Lost Boys stretcher-carried the sniper out of there just as the Saur rushed and the dwarves came out of nowhere, having moved into position with all the stealth of the scouts and Lost Boys, and hit the Saurian charge from the side, outnumbered five to one. The dwarves slaughtered a number of the taller Saur and then managed to fight a rearguard action back to the protection of the palace and the Rangers staging for an attack there against the target building where Lizard King was hunkering, waiting to be rescued, or to make his last move.

About that target building. While I was still at Highway One before I got summoned to go mind-meld, Lizard King slammed into the palace, gassed the front entrance, and rampaged through the main halls. The Rangers pulled back into the more abandoned areas of the palace and its crumbling antechambers, firing and using grenades and rucksacks full of claymores against the giant beast. The dragon collapsed a series of columns and brought down half of one wing of the old Dragon Elven palace, almost burying alive the defending Rangers inside.

Ssruth was pretty comfortable playing cat and mouse with the Rangers until Sergeant Joe deployed the flamethrower the Rangers had prepped and brought along for close encounters. The Forge had specs on its hard drive for a DARPA-developed flamethrower that was never field-tested, being that flamethrowers are against the Geneva conventions. But those died about ten thousand years ago and PFC Kennedy had put forth the hypothesis that because the green dragon was considered a "forest creature" encounter, there was a chance it had power over the local plant life and could attempt to use vines or even the swamp itself to attack the Rangers.

The sergeant major thought it would be a good idea to "forget the weed killer the Baroness is developing and just burn everything… if we have to."

So three flamethrowers were cranked out by the Forge and tested by the Rangers. They did what flamethrowers do.

Burn everything to ash and deny escape or routes of access.

Now, with the Rangers trapped and fighting for the palace and trying to keep the dragon from getting the detonators or causing the well to suddenly explode, explosives were a no-go inside the palace because they could bring the whole ancient and ornate ruin down on everyone. The entire structure was already groaning and collapsing in various sections as the Ranger assaulter teams fought room to room against the dragon, pulling hit-and-run raids as fast as they could before sections collapsed in on them. Trying to drive the dragon out with not much luck.

So far, no casualties.

Then Sergeant Joe went full pyromaniac and ran down three huge halls and through what looked to be a mausoleum to get up on the dragon from its three-o'clock position in the main hall. He ignited the flamethrower and sent flaming gel all over the dragon's flanks. It reacted instantly as its scales began to melt from the intense heat and flames, and its tail thrashed and busted open an ancient mural-covered wall as the dragon fled out through the side of the palace across an old royal graveyard with monuments sinking into the swampy ground, racing for what Vandahar told us was called the Hall of Immortals.

One of the Dragon Elves' most fabled monuments.

The Hall of the Immortals was like something from the lost ages of sometime prehistoric. As though Stonehenge and Easter Island had hired the builders of the pyramids to create their death hall. It was one of the larger structures besides the palace itself, here in the palace district of the ruins of Tarragon, and where the Dragon Elven royalty buried their greatest kings. It was the size of the Parthenon and surrounded by collapsed mausoleums among the standing ones along the outer porch. Within the walls of the giant necropolis was a vast dark space lined with a sea of Dragon Elven sarcophagi, and rising from the center of this vast dark space of death was a monument to the greatest king of Dragon Elves, the founder of Tarragon, Thrayis One Hand.

The structure was stronger than most of the other ancient buildings in Tarragon. It was far older and far more sturdy. The massive temple roof and thick walls were solid enough to withstand the Carl rounds and mortars. The only way to kill the dragon there was either storm the hall or recover the acetylene bottles and roll them in there and detonate. But right now, the Saur had ranged fire trying to hit the well and the explosives there. Going out there to recover the bottles was most likely fatal.

The dragon had two options. It could fight from the hall. Or rush the well. It was, by all reports, badly wounded. But still very dangerous.

The Ranger master breachers had lowered the six bottles of acetylene into the dragon's well during the lull in battle, moving out under covering fire from the assaulters and the weapons teams. Pulling back as the Saur began to hit the district from the east. And if the assaulters didn't kill the dragon, then the acetylene bottles were the last chance to kill it. So they'd be left there as the final shot the Rangers had to complete the mission. Those six bottles would crater much of the entire palatial district, and it was doubtful many of the buildings here would survive. The Hall of the Immortals... maybe. It looked more than capable of surviving due to its monumental structure. But the blast deep down in the well would be close to a micro nuke with no fallout or radiation. If the dragon managed to make it down into its lair, the acetylene would be ignited and devastate much of the underground tunnels and structures where the dragon lived, including a vast underground dome where it kept its hoard.

"The loss of those artifacts and that knowledge would be... devastating," Vandahar had whispered softly.

The Rangers didn't care about that.

"We're here to eliminate the target," Captain Knife Hand had said. "Those things, though they might be helpful to your cause, or of some value to your people, are secondary to eliminating a threat to our survival. If we have to go with our doomsday option, Vandahar, then we will."

The wizard had said nothing after that. Only watching the Rangers. I had a distinct feeling that somehow, he finally understood the difference between them, and normal men.

Later that night he came to me and said as much. I was brewing cold brews for the next day. So of course, he wanted some. It didn't bother me as much as it had once. I enjoyed listening to him. He was full of interesting tales if you were patient enough to listen carefully. He was good company.

"They look like normal men, young Talker. But they are not."

He was sipping my coffee. Making smoke rings with his pipe in the late night. I watched them drift up and play among the stars we could barely see through the miasma of the surrounding swamp.

It was quite pleasant.

"They are, Vandahar. They're just regular guys. In fact, you meet a lot of guys like them, guys in other branches, and the first thing out of their mouths is how special they are. But Rangers rarely tell you right off the bat that they're

Rangers. They're just regular guys who do extraordinary things."

The wizard thought about that for a long moment. Then, "I understand that, young Talker. But perhaps your world was much different than what we are now, and I wish I knew more about it and how it was before... this Ruin. How it became the way it did. But in this world... kings have lost empires for the fabled artifacts that lie in the great dome beneath the city where we will fight Ssruth the Cruel. Where the dragon sleeps. This is not to mention all the gold, and gems, of the fabled Dragon Elves who were rich beyond the dreams of the mighty, that he has taken for himself in the sack of Tarragon. All of it was for the dragon's taking when he sacked this city and made everything his. I believe your captain, and your fellow Rangers, understand this. But to them... they would rather kill Ssruth and lose the hoard than take a chance they might not get their prize when the battle finally begins. And in that... they are not ordinary men, Talker. They are extra-ordinary, in fact."

We drank our coffee for a long while, and when he was finished the wizard stood and stretched his back, groaning as he did so in the late night. By the firelight I saw how very old he looked. How tired he was.

"Perhaps extra-ordinary men are what the Ruin has lacked. Why evil has flourished in these dark days. Perhaps that is why the dreams of the Nether Sorcerer are almost realized in this last of all hours before the doom comes, and soon, the great war against the Cities of Men will be at hand. And if that is lost... well, then there will only be that world the dead see, young Talker. And I know you have had your glimpse of that forsaken and howling eternal wilderness."

Then the wizard was gone, and I sat there for a long time afterward. Remembering how the ring that made me invisible and the *Book of the Dead* had worked in combination to let me see a vision of that dead world where nothing lived anymore, or would ever again. A Ruin beyond the Ruin. A final Ruin. Where the dead endlessly crossed an icy and lifeless landscape forever. Where we were the dead, serving a death god that cared not.

I shuddered and had bad dreams that night.

CHAPTER TWENTY

WE were on the move for the Hall of the Immortals when we ran into the first group of heavily armed stak skirmishers making their way through the remains of the battlefield. Even though the fight was in some sort of weird stalemate at the moment, where both sides were trying to figure their next move, and maybe that was just the psionics giving me the big picture, both sides were still shooting each other when they could. Mortars had been re-tasked off of the dragon and were landing out there in the big concentrations of cat hajis and stak, staging to get ready to come in and rescue their dragon.

I had a feeling McCluskey was out there even now. Rallying bad guys of stak and cat ninja to get in there and bust the dragon outta the situation it had gotten itself into. Involved and behind it all. Probably thinking up some pretty clever way to stab us all in the back. Hard to believe ten thousand years and a little vampirism had done that to him. We'd all started out together back at Area 51 on a mission to save the world. But here we were. The Ruin does reveal. Autumn was right about that. The snipers hadn't spotted him yet and if they did, they were gonna take his head off and let him *vampiric regeneration* his way out of that.

Kennedy explained that was a thing they could do. Regenerate mortal injuries. Chief Rapp agreed that with DNA nanomodification this wasn't impossible science. "Geckos can regrow their tails. Why not cells working together to get the body back to life? I've seen DARPA research that was leading toward this."

"Stak forward," huffed Monroe as I followed him through the rubble and watched our six, scanning the debris we were working our way through to reach the back side of the Hall of the Immortals. A second later, linkage and brass was trailing away as the big Ranger minotaur opened up, cutting down a cluster of stak in a sudden burst of frenetic gunfire. The others scrambled for cover and started lobbing sling stones and arrows at us as some kind of return fire.

"They're getting smarter," rumbled Monroe as he squeezed off another burst on two more that were dumb enough to try and flank, exposing themselves to brutal automatic gunfire. "C'mon, let's go this way. We can't clear that area without getting into something. Those guys mighta been scouts. Gotta be another way around this pile."

We began to work our way to the south of the remains of the old building and half-standing structure they were in and around. Pottery in broken shards lay everywhere. Cracked urns and fractured bowls spilled out into the rubble. I followed the minotaur, half-crouched and moving along a narrow crack that became a trench where some of the building's foundation had shifted from some past quake and exposed a path through the tumble.

Eyes out and watching my sights, I spotted the first stak ahead getting ready to come down into the trench. They were coming out of the darkness of a collapsed section of the skeletal remains of this place and looking to surprise us.

"Hold," I whispered to Monroe. "Bad guys ahead."

"Good spot," rumbled Monroe and crouched there in a shadow like some hulking demon with a light machine gun and all the ill will in the world. His bull's eyes watching the morning shadows ahead almost lifelessly in their new animal alien way. There wasn't a FAST helmet that was gonna fit his head now.

He pointed at both his eyes and then knife-handed forward, indicating for me to keep eyes on targets. Then he was working fast with a large suppressor he pulled from his chest rig and screwing it on the threaded barrel of the M60E3. He put one of his huge hairy fingers to his lips and leveled the light machine gun down the crack-like trench as the line of stak started moving through the morning half-shadows up toward us.

Long burst. Linkage and brass jetting frantically out across the ejection port and all over the trench. Then two more short bursts to clean up some of the still moving.

It was loud. But suppressed. Here in the rubble the noise was mitigated some, and there were the mortar strikes and the exchanges of sniper fire and whistling volleys of arrows.

The *BOOM BOOM CLAP* had stopped for the moment.

The drone recon was telling us we had teams of stak all over the area, which was now being tagged as Taco Bell.

"Two groups to your west. One group to your south. Both searching," said the air force blond ponytailed co-pilot flying the drones this morning. And of course, "Better make a run for the border, Big Boy."

Corporal Monroe was now officially Big Boy Actual.

We waited for a second to make sure there were no more movers or anyone else as we watched up out of the trench for more stak. Waiting for them to suddenly come leaping in like wild lizards thrashing and slashing for a kill. Overwhelming our ability to return fire.

Nothing. Just distant gunfire and more whistling mortars falling in and making thundering explosions out over the distance of the city.

Through the rubble ahead I could see the rising slope of the slate-gray slabs of thick stone that formed the wall of the Hall of the Immortals.

Taco Bell. The border we needed to run for.

I reached out with my infant's use of psionics for a second and got nothing in return. If the command team was waiting on me to give them enough intel to decide whether they could chance a direct assault on the dragon… then this was bad. Because there was a part of me that was feeling things. But that might not be the truth. Might just be what I wanted.

Purity of raw data was what was needed right now because the next move for either side was going to be one hundred percent fatal.

You could feel that in the air. This was the endgame.

We were on the move again, working our way out of the scree and ruin toward the end of the trench, and low-crawling up through dead stak and bloody sand that had been made so by one of the mortar strikes in the initial moments of the battle. Crawling through the dust and blood, keeping low to avoid the enemy scouting elements the drone pilot was telling us were moving into the area now. That was when I got my first contact with the dragon.

Suddenly I saw things that made me break out in a cold sweat. I saw destruction and ruin and things I don't think any man was ever meant to see. It was horror personified.

"You okay?" huffed Monroe, looking back at me as we crawled closer to the cyclopean wall of the ancient structure.

"Fine," I muttered distantly as the flashing images came fast and rapid-fire now, shaky and hot. A thousand photographs were suddenly exploding across my mind. I had to wonder if this was an attack on my psionics, or was I blind and feeling an elephant for the first time. Swimming through dark waters in an unknown ocean at midnight and feeling the brush of the scales of a leviathan unimagined or comprehended. I was in trouble. Fear. But the Rangers needed to know and so I crawled forward unable to see, and able to not see at the same time. Seeing what I was seeing inside my brain, and at the same time seeing an almost grainy or smudged picture of what reality was like going on all around me. Knowing, mindlessly really, that I had to get close to the Hall of the Immortals if the Rangers were going to have a chance of knowing whether to assault or go with the doomsday acetylene bottles.

Right now, I was seeing a movie trailer that I knew... and I know this sounds crazy, but it was like falling into the Grand Canyon and I knew I was gonna die. But I knew communication would come...

... when I touched the outer wall.

It was like the structure itself was some sort of conduit and the dragon hadn't just come here for giggles and an easy hiding place. It was getting something here. There was a reason for *here*.

But first the movie trailer. The worst movie trailer ever. The one that scared you to death and made your heart stop and your mind unravel.

And still, like some dying man craving water, I crawled through the dust and blood to touch the stone of the hall. The Hall of the Immortals.

I saw the sack of Tarragon.

Saw it in the day just before the dragon came. It was a late fall day. The days getting shorter. High clouds and wind. Pennants and banners rippling in the wind. The Dragon Elves expecting nothing but endless success and eternal prosperity as though it was theirs by divine right. They were a prideful people. With much to be proud of. Tarragon was an epically beautiful place no major blockbuster movie could have ever captured. The stone-white marble rose in slender towers in every direction. Bronze and silver minarets shone in the daylight and dazzled, though the day was cold. The sculpted palaces spread geometrically, and life abounded in these places. The warriors were arrayed in silver ceremonial armor, wearing blood-red horsehair plumes in their Roman Centurion-like helmets. Their breastplates shining. Their cruel lances dancing up and down as they canted forward on magnificent war stallions. The elven women watched them ride through the streets as though they were rock stars or movie stars.

And despite the scars of battle they wore on their clean elven faces, these warriors, each and every one, looked like action heroes. They were no easy enemy, and it was clear they knew what they were doing.

There were children. Families. The harvest of a good summer being stored away in houses of plenty. Wealth in abundance as far as one could see. Think of the highest moment of a society, the best of its days, when everything was in abundance and there was little to fear from anything external. Or even internal.

Which is always a lie. There's always danger. There's always someone who wants what you have. I've read enough history while studying languages to know when you're prosperous, that's when you're probably in the most trouble. When you need to watch out.

There is always evil though it makes no sense.

This was prosperity in that moment before the coming of the dragon, and it was... endless in that moment I looked upon it.

I saw the *Mindon Elen* how it once was. The Tower of Stars. Knowing through the gift of psionics it was almost as old as the Hall of Immortals, except that wasn't right. The hall was older by orders of magnitude. One of the more ancient places in this world now called the Ruin. Rising in the Thousand Years of Darkness, as it was known in those desperate and horrific times, just after the Ruin began. After we left and tried to save the world.

And failed.

Naked and afraid, the near-paleolithic hunter-gatherers that were the Dragon Elves then, had begun to use great magics to drag the stones together to form this incomprehensible monument now called the Hall of the Immortals. Making a deal with something they called Bethoc Lightbringer. Something one of their kind had met in a darkness never meant to be explored.

In their High Tolkien they called it...

Calima tulu.

Calimatulu.

Light Bringer.

Before the Tower of Stars was built, before the Hall of the Immortals, there was just a lowly priest of the Hidden King. The original religion of these elves who would come to call themselves the *Angoquendi*. Dragon Elves. That dark and defrocked priest had gone forth, deep into the Crow's March which was little more than a howling wilderness of ghost-haunted mountains and werewolves baying in the forest.

He'd been driven there. An outcast and heretic who dreamed dreams no one should dream.

They called him *Thauron. Abhorred.* But that was the ancient form of his name. Abhorred was what they called him when they drove him out. When he went east, and east was always cursed according to them and others.

There was a strange and ancient giant there in what would be called the Crow's March one day but was just a howling dark wilderness then. He was called the Nameless One and it was said he had come from the Before. He was one of the Eld of old.

The strange and silent giant taught the priest the ways of Bethoc. Communication with one called the *Calima tulu. The Light Bringer.* When the priest returned once more to the tribes of elves he'd been driven out from, elves that had no real name for themselves in those early days, just elves who for a thousand years had lived in caves, migrating over land and sea to arrive in what was once known as France, he taught them lost knowledge acquired from the Nameless One and the Light Bringer. The wielding of great magics.

It was Thauron who dragged the stones of the Hall of the Immortals into place. It was he who gave them the Way of Destruction. The gifts of Bethoc. The arts of war and war magic. *Calima tulu.* The Light Bringer. Then great war clans of the Dragon Elves arose in the years that followed. The wars against the rising of the Black Prince in the East. Wars against the Stone Kings. Wars against the Cities of Men. Wars against the Saur.

The Dragon Elves were born, and the dragon cult rose once more. A schizophrenic nation that still worshipped a god they once knew. But listened to a whispering demon from the outer darkness that gave them power and conquest and magic. Tribute and slaves were their pay. They grew great in power and made other cities and mighty weapons of renown. They threw down their enemies and laid siege to foreign cities, leaving ruin and piles of skulls as they rode away. The black smoke of destruction covering the sky.

But then on that fateful day I was seeing now, even as a thousand flash photographs of their history exploded across my mind, in that last of fall before winter's cruel embrace began, the dragon swept out of the cold winter-coming sky, bringing ruin and chaos to the Dragon Elves. Gassing the soldiers and knights and starting fires in the Garden of Wonders that was Tarragon.

Within an hour the city was aflame. Dragon Elven archers formed on the walls to fight the dragon, but Ssruth the Cruel was here, and then there, his mighty wings lifting him high and up out of range, and then he would suddenly swoop down out of nowhere, ruining a line of bright and shining cavalry and smashing their mighty defenses with flame strikes and fireballs that were magic destruction due to his sorcery. Landing among the knights he would laugh his dragon's roar as their lances snapped against his mighty and impenetrable scales. His tail sweeping and dragging them. Smearing armored elves against the white marble stone while spear and foot troops choked to death on toxic gas.

And just as soon as the attack had begun, it was over and the dragon hauled himself off and out of battle, letting the fire do its work that night. Destroying towers, ravaging vast sections of the city as they fought it in vain.

At dawn the dragon came once again, diving out of the sky with a tremendous howl and giving battle in the markets of Tarragon. All trade routes of the Ruin led to shining Tarragon in those days. But the city was finished. The Crimson Ranks came out to make their stands, war priests making prayers and appeals to silent Bethoc, sacrificing their finest cattle and even children, but the battle in the great market was a slaughter, and when Ssruth flew back into the sky once more the corpses of the brave littered the ruin he had left in his ferocious wake.

I was just a few feet from the wall as I saw all this. Willing myself forward, though I knew it was something dangerous. A rattler hissing. A brown recluse in the dark under the rotten boards of a long-abandoned house. A place one should never go. A boiling kettle on the stove. Hearing Monroe distantly telling me to keep quiet as I struggled to move. I was mumbling all of this, I think. All I was seeing. The stak were close. Snipers were taking shots to keep their scouts from finding us.

The drone came in, dumping the last of its twin 7.62 miniguns as Monroe called target plots for the mortars who were nearing Winchester and being redirected to support.

I heard the minotaur rumble, "Get it done now, Talker! Clock's burning. Ain't much left..."

But I was there at that last night of the city of Tarragon. Watching from the dragon's eye as he circled over the city, high above, in the night mist and blue fog. Listening to the lamentations of their women. Seeing the spreading flames and the crumbling glory beneath.

At dawn, the last Dragon Elven king came out to make his stand and defend the city from the terror of Ssruth. Wielding the great blade known as *Coldfire*.

It was not a dwarven blade as McCluskey had lied to us. Of course. It was the sacred sword of the Dragon Elves. The sword of the dragon kings. And it had done battle along the banks of the River of Night far to the south. Against Sût himself. Sût the Undying.

Some say he is Eld.

Some say he comes from the Before.

An enemy of the Spider Queen.

All these things are meaningless to me. I am nothing and I know nothing. They just came at me, the details and the tears of destruction as I watched Tarragon burn at dawn long ago, the last king making his stand against the dragon.

He came out with *Coldfire*.

Ringaruinë.

Cold fire.

To fight Ssruth the Great. Ssruth the Terrible. Ssruth the Cruel.

To fight the dragon and die.

For even *Coldfire* could not stand against Ssruth.

CHAPTER TWENTY-ONE

"HUMAN..." rumbled the dragon in my mind as I touched the cold stone of the prehistoric monument called the Hall of the Immortals. The trap Thauron had laid for the Dragon Elves to forsake their god and serve the dragon who would one day destroy them all. The monument's dark history and the blood shed within it had been flash-fried in my mind. The lamentations of the elven women for the dead. The keening as the dragon took the city and slayed them all. The dark cult that had hidden within the hall all along throughout the Dragon Elves' rise to power...

It was like touching a live wire filled with deadly electricity. And graveyard stone at the same time.

I watched the destruction of Tarragon fade from my mind and the long years of hoarding that followed as the dragon took it all for himself. All their wars of conquest. All their loot and plunder. It was all his now. Payment for the dark knowledge he had given them.

"Human..."

Its voice was tremendous in the stillness between our two minds. As though spoken from some vast and cavernous space that filled up the dark gulf between us. I could feel the hot stink of Ssruth's breath, though I was not there with him inside the hall. I was still getting images. Starbursts. An endless howling waste. A vast steppe of fire and flame. A dragon greater by orders of magnitude than this one that spoke inside my mind now.

The name was not just Bethoc. The real name was unutterable and unknowable to the human mind. I knew at that moment that what Vandahar had once almost casually said during a briefing about dragons not being of this world, about them being *other*, that it was the truest statement I'd ever heard. More true than even the old wizard had known in the moment he'd said it.

They weren't just dragons. They were other.

I shuddered and felt small and tiny here in the darkness.

"You think you've won?" it said. Ssruth. Ssruth the Cruel. The dragon snorted and its snort was like a hot desert wind sweeping through the parched and dying lands of the scrub and saguaro of the southwest I'd once known. Like the wave of an atomic blast scouring the desert.

"Perhaps you have. Perhaps... you have," mused the melancholic titan.

My psionics were instantly pitiful. This thing had them. Knew them. Was the master of them. And considered them little more than a trick.

"The gift..." it spoke, as it searched my mind. Finding my abilities and tossing them aside like some junk man looking for prizes and finding nothing.

I had a momentary vision of how vast its intelligence truly was. It was like the biggest wave on the angriest ocean ever heading right toward the shoreline. A wave that towered over the skyscrapers of New York, dragging oil tankers and ocean liners with it like mere flotsam and debris as it crested and broke over Manhattan.

And I was a small child in the taxicab streets holding a red balloon that bobbed above my head.

Helpless.

Nothing really as the world ended. Just as Tarragon had ended.

I watched as the wave of the dragon's massive mind swept those ocean liners and supertankers crashing into what I thought was once epic and was now little more than nothing compared to the dragon. The skyline of the greatest city on Earth was about to be drowned.

I never cared for it much. New York City.

Don't fence me in, my dad once said. It was a song. An old one.

The old ones are the best, kiddo. That's where the truth is.

The wave was going to crush completely all of New York and everything. And me. And then I'd be nothing anymore. Nothing ever again. Like all the corpses of the dead the dragon had slain that were even now tossing and turning inside the glassy seafoam-green face of the giant wave of destruction towering over New York.

I heard Vandahar whisper something from far away. From the forest of fae we had first walked through. But... the wave that would be my destruction was too fascinating. Too loud in its rumble and roar. This was...

... the last of me.

"Foolish mortal," spoke Ssruth. "I have swam in the seas of other worlds. I have seen things. Dark and dire things you would scream endlessly with the knowledge of. Your mind is no match for one such as me, child. Ruler of Tarragon am I. Wanderer of the Endless Stars, I have been. I have seen things... child."

The wave swept up taxicabs and mothers running with their children in the streets. Just like my mother would have run to save me. Even if there was no hope. I could feel my tears on the sand and blood I was lying in. The blood-soaked sand where the Saurian infantry had been obliterated by Ranger mortar fire as I put my hand on the wall of the Hall of the Immortals.

My last thought was…

… I never should have done this. The Rangers will die because I'm not enough…

I was looking almost straight up as the wave swept the Twin Towers down and I watched them crash into the street and foam as a wall of destruction knocked everything into the waves. Tankers and ocean liners careening into buildings. Spilling dead elven corpses and many other creatures out into the chaos.

I am… never enough.

"The red balloon," whispered Vandahar on that hippy walk when this all began. And little boy me in a soldier's uniform stared at the balloon that didn't care of dragons and tsunamis and the end of the world or a sea of death inside a wave. That little balloon bobbed and waved and reminded me I was light as air. Because that is the way of children.

Then suddenly it was carrying me up and away. Over the dragon's intellect. Over the wave of destruction and away from it all. The sea-green wave of ocean foam and churn that was Ssruth the Cruel. Enslaver. Destroyer. Demon.

I could see everything now from high above where the sky was warm and blue.

How badly wounded he was. Ssruth. The Rangers had done a number on him like no one ever had.

Death's door. But still dangerous.

I looked closely into the wave that was below me now. Bouncing into the sky on a red balloon that didn't care about dragons and death. I could see he had no more breath in him. That he was almost finished now. But also, that he had one last card to play.

One last doomsday song.

He'd seen into my mind as I'd stared up at the trick of his intellect. When he tried to enslave me. The tsunami of him before the red balloon carried me away in our duel of psionics.

Hadn't Kennedy said that? In the game. Hadn't he said green dragons delight in the act of enslaving fae creatures? Like the elves.

He had tried to enslave me, and he'd seen inside my mind while doing so. Seen the imminent assault of the Rangers. Everything Corporal Monroe had told me and how the Rangers would go in after him. Tossing flashbangs and shooting to kill. Spreading out across the tomb in a killing line.

He'd seen the explosives lined at the well's edge to his lair. Denying him from ever reaching his lair. His hoard. His empire.

And then the acetylene bottles.

"Clever, children," he rumbled in the darkness between our minds. Ssruth the Cruel laughing like a demon's croak.

He was a being of incredible darkness. Jealousy and spite were all he'd ever known. All he'd ever know. He was cold. As cold as distant stars in the gulf of night.

"The way I see it…" Ssruth rumbled across that vast and cavernous space where our two minds fought. Where I floated above the New York that never was and watched his great green seafoam form toss and churn in anger and wrath as the city was drowned. The dragon was hoping for a last bit of spite and jealousy to pay out his assassins with.

"Those magic bottles with the wrath of gods you have waiting down in my lair… for me. I set those off now… and you all go with me. Every one of you, child. And if I don't make it to… detonate… you call it… then Triton surely will do my bidding. I broke that one long ago. And faithful a slave he's ever been."

Ssruth's laughter was the howl of a mad thing.

But his revenge had shown me something that changed everything in a flash. Not for everyone. But still everything, nonetheless.

Yes. The dragon broke souls and made slaves. There were many down in its lair. Still. Living in dusty prisons of slavery. Mindless and half-mad for many long years. Suffering for nothing more than the dragon's mere satisfaction and taste for it.

Now the dragon would pay all it could back in one final act of terminal revenge. It would rush the well now that there were no options left.

The ultimate suicide bomber.

An IED vest we'd made for it out of acetylene bottles.

Killing all of us.

And… killing the one who loved Last of Autumn. Not me. The guy before me. The one with the right to.

The prisoner of Ssruth the Cruel we'd never known about.

I looked at the carefree red balloon above me, realizing it was just like the one my mother had bought me on a day in Central Park. The day of the almost hot scalding.

She was trying to tell me something then.

Give me something. Save something.

But I was just a child then and what do children know of death and terror and the abyss a parent looks into every day and especially in the night when they can't sleep. I think she was saying a red balloon can take you away. Like a dream. A balloon is a dream. A better thing than reality often is.

I smiled and watched it carry me away from the dragon's mind. Thinking... moms, we never know how much they truly love us. We never...

***

I came back, lying there in the sand and lizard blood. Hot brass hitting me as Monroe laid down fire from atop the pile of scree and rubble. The stak closing in on us. Mortar strikes falling danger close.

I used everything I had in me to tap my comm.

"Warlord Actual," I gasped. "Go. Go now. You can't let it leave the target building... it'll kill us all. It's going for the bottles."

CHAPTER TWENTY-TWO

I was stumbling back toward the palace. Mortars raining down behind us and Corporal Monroe helping me get my feet back under me as we moved fast to get away from the stak overrunning that section of the ruins.

Yeah. All I was thinking about was coffee. I'll admit that here and now. I was outta gas after all that dragon mind-meld apocalypse. I had half a canteen of Portugon cold brew with magic Kungaloor sugar left. It wasn't enough. Could never be enough.

The Rangers were already tossing flashbangs into the Hall of the Immortals and I'm going to put down what one of the assaulters told me happened in there as the breaching teams went in to clear out the dragon before he could reach the entrance to the well and blow us all to kingdom come.

But right now, as I ran for the palace, my carbine was just dangling because I didn't even have the strength to keep my gloves on it as I gasped for air and tried to comm with the sergeant major over the net.

"Sergeant Major... we gotta get... down into the well... fast... try to get them... outta there... before it blows..."

My imprecise use of net protocol or proper terms was overlooked. Things were happening fast.

The sergeant major was aware the dragon was going to try and break out and det the well himself, taking everyone and everything in the district with it. But he wasn't aware of something else.

"SEAL…" I gasped. "He's… down there. McCluskey."

The sergeant major stopped me right there.

"Big Boy, get Private Talker to the well. We'll link up there to fast-rope in, secure hostages, and deny the bottles."

The unspoken part was that the sergeant major was going to personally whack the squid on site. You could feel that in the transmission. It was like the promise of a thunderstorm in August. Ominous and imminent. His voice was pure murder.

Corporal Monroe yanked me to the left and we were racing down a shattered alley filled with sand and carved runic stones to reach the end of the Ivory Way and the well down into the dragon's lair.

"Stop!" I huffed and bent over like I was falling out of a run in Basic. Something I'd never done. I'd shown up to Basic and RASP a runner. I'd never been run into the ground once. But I was close now. My battle rattle felt like it was a hundred pounds heavier and fifty degrees hotter.

"Can't fall out now, Talker!" bellowed the Ranger minotaur as he tried to drag me toward the next location. "Hit times are going down. We need every—"

I yanked my canteen out and guzzled for all I was worth.

"Coffee?!" bellowed the corporal. "I'd heard about you, but…"

I handed him the last swallow, gasping, "Needed it. Magic sugar."

He snorted and it was like a laugh and disgust in the same moment. Then he grabbed the canteen and drained it.

I heard him rumble and almost bellow like a bull charging. He suppressed it though.

"What, exactly, was that..." he said very calmly after a second.

"No time..." I panted. "Gotta move... now."

We made the well, and the gunfire from the Hall of the Immortals was absolutely psychopathic. Or at least what could be heard above the dragon's bellow within as both sides fought to the death. Thunder and lightning clashed within the tremendous cavern of ancient mono-lithic stacked stone that was the Hall of the Immortals. It was like a box full of monkeys with automatic grenade launchers.

We made the well and the sergeant major was dragging the end of one fast-rope out from the palace. Kennedy was with him as part of his Reaper force. So was Sergeant Kang along with two other Rangers.

A volley of arrows came from one of the buildings the Saur had taken across the way, slamming into the ground all around us and nailing one of the Rangers right through the thigh. Kennedy chanted something and threw up a shimmering glassy shield. The next downpour of arrows snapped and shattered against it. Then the shield collapsed with an audible *pop*.

"Sorry," said Kennedy emotionlessly. Which was his way. "Vandahar says I'll get better."

The guy who got hit swore as Corporal Monroe sup-pressed that building. Fast-moving cat hajis were trying to flank us, and the snipers began to go to work on them. Kennedy turned and pointed the dragon-headed staff, fir-ing a string of fireballs in that direction, detonating hot burning plasma all over the ruins the hajis were using for cover. From down the Ivory Way, one of the ballistae fired with an ominous singing bass-note twang and a huge arrow streaked over the top of our heads and slammed into the palace, exploding accent marble and masonry in every direction back there.

"We're goin' in," bellowed the sergeant major over the noise of battle, magic, and gunfire. "Everyone on security until we get the bottles up. They're located at the bottom of the well on the remains of an old stair carved along the well. Inside an OD green det bag. We get that secured, and we'll rope it back up and get it out of here. Sergeant Kang, you're on that. Corporal Monroe, maintain exfil security while we're down there."

Monroe slid the sixty to his back and grabbed the massive rope, giving it a tremendous yank to where it had been anchored at the palace.

It came free. Not because the swoll Ranger corporal's strength had caused it to do this, but because the ballista shot had taken out the centuries-old pillar the rope had been secured to during initial operations.

"That's not good," said the Ranger who'd been hit through the leg. The arrow had been pushed out while we were under fire, and now the other Ranger was using high-speed tape to seal and put pressure on the wound being that there was no arterial bleeding.

"You good, Ranger?" asked the sergeant major.

The pale-faced Ranger who'd lost some blood nodded and grunted, "Good to go, Sergeant Major," as he hobbled up onto his good leg. "In it to win it!"

That was when the sergeant major noticed the fast-rope had come free from its anchor. He swore and looked around for something that could hold us on that rapid trip down into the well. Something to get it anchored to quickly.

"I got this, Sergeant Major," bellowed Corporal Monroe. "You all ain't nothin' for batt squat king."

The sergeant major didn't hesitate, but I could see he was doing the math of weight-to-strength ratio in his eyes as Corporal Monroe wrapped the thick rope around his massive eight-foot hairy frame, walked back, and dug in to anchor us for the insertion.

Sergeant Kang didn't even hesitate. Dashing from cover to avoid arrow fire, he grabbed the heavy coil in a fireman's carry and heaved the end of the fast-rope over a chunk of debris and down into the dark well where the dragon lived. A well lined with explosives. And even worse by orders of explosive magnitude down below.

I'll say this right now.

The diameter of the well was as dangerous as it gets. There were enough explosives there to flat-out vaporize us instantly. But the Rangers knew one thing. If those acetylene bottles detonated now, it would kill a lot of Rangers moving through a wonky ancient city that would basically get a nine-point-oh earthquake in the butt and collapse a lot of structures right down on top of them. And maybe some of them knew there were hostages down in there. The Shadow Elves the dragon had enslaved.

Yeah, the Rangers could've run. But they didn't. You wanna know the difference between everyone else and heroes? Heroes run toward the danger.

They don't hide inside and get an achievement award for nothing.

They get out of the boat.

They run toward the gunfire.

They go down into the darkness.

"On me!" shouted the sergeant major, as more Saurian artillery sought to find our range and arrows whistled in from all directions along the line of battle. "One at a time. We get perimeter security established down there and then get the bottles up. Then we do the SEAL."

Then he was gone, knitting his feet around the rope and going down into the darkness, the rope's length whipping through his hand.

There was immediate gunfire.

Kang went next.

Then the other two Rangers. Kennedy.

Then…

"Good luck, Talker," growled Monroe from the anchor. "Get some for me!"

And then me.

I knew what to do.

Four seconds later I was in a wild gunfight with a Navy SEAL and a dozen orc archer assassins. Enough explosives to make a small moon crater right there in the Ruins of Tarragon turning us to nothing but fast-moving dust on the other side of it.

And I was out of coffee.

CHAPTER TWENTY-THREE

THE Rangers hit the dragon with everything they had before he could move on the well. Both sides ran head-on into each other inside the massive Hall of the Immortals. All the planning, all the scouting and observation, all the run-throughs had led to this final moment for one or the other. Everything the Rangers had trained to do for this pump over the last six weeks had ended at a wheelhouse moment for them.

This is what Rangers do better than anyone. Kill high-value bad guys inside the place where they've been found.

Yeah, the Rangers had made plans to get it with a tower, mortars, snipers, explosives, and even a Stinger ground-to-air missile.

But as the breachers threw their flashbangs, first teams entering and establishing a base of fire as the grenadiers, those with the M320, started landing grenades all over the dragon at the far end of the massive temple monument, Ssruth had no idea *this* was what Rangers did best.

They were the best at door-kicking. And the dragon was about to find out why.

The battlefield inside the monument was composed of old sarcophagi and crooked mausoleums. Above all this, within the temple dark, the fractured remains of the statue of the Great King, the stone likeness of *Coldfire* upraised in his hand, struck up into the dark reaches of the ceiling where giant spiders lived and waited. It was around this great statue to all Tarragon had once been—conquerors of empires, warriors without peer, the Dragon Elves who'd made the first empire—that the old wyrm curled back in defense as the Rangers stormed the hall.

Ready to make his final stand. Perhaps find an advantage and break out for the well. Perhaps his wings would work. Perhaps he'd kill them all. Perhaps he wasn't done yet...

Dead Dragon Elven knights and heroes, covered in rotting vines, pushed off the lids of their dusty cursed sarcophagi, raising rusty swords and fabled weapons, moaning endless curses in long-forgotten dialects. The Rangers gunned them down without hesitation, disintegrating their mummy wraps and rotten armor in sudden violent sprays of automatic gunfire.

This was violence of action. This is what Rangers do. Speed. Surprise. Maximum aggression.

What you saw, if you were watching, was the Rangers taking immediate advantage and control of the battle. Captain Knife Hand, his combat leaders, and every Ranger absolutely in control of the organized chaos and maximum violence.

Vandahar entered after the last team. Rangers breaking left and right to cover sectors. Shooting down dead knights summoned for the dragon's last battle.

"*Natsë!*" shouted the wizard triumphantly, and suddenly the dragon's bloody and ruined right claw was enveloped in sticky webbing. It bellowed and shook the roof. Useless to cast spells anymore.

Sergeant Thor entered, standing and firing rounds from *Mjölnir* right into the dragon's skull when he could get the shot. One of the Rangers told me he took out an eye. The lizard snaked its serpentine head away and behind the statue, ducking the incoming kinetic violence, and suddenly a huge thunderclap went off with a sonic boom inside the Hall of the Immortals.

Stone and dust rained down on the Rangers as the captain led an assaulter force forward with C4 packed into rucks and strapped with claymores.

The Rangers savaged the no longer flying dinosaur's armored belly with fire from the XM25s using detonated airbursts to blind the dragon further as its head slithered out from behind the monument. With the smart weapons, the statue was little cover.

The Rangers were gonna find you wherever you were, and then kill you. Old Ssruth must have finally realized the mistake a lot of dead bad guys had realized too late.

The Rangers had stayed up late thinking this through. Thinking about you. As if to say, "You're our favorite bad guy and we got you a little something…"

Seconds later, the explosives were lying right up against Ssruth's wounded frame. The captain had gone forward and placed the explosives himself under covering fire from the assaulters.

Then just as fast as they had appeared, the Rangers were backing out of the hall. Fading and ready to detonate.

Ssruth must have known what the plan was at that moment. For in that last instant he charged.

Thousands of years and who knew how much endless time he'd acquired from the *other* before he came… now it was just seconds to get some revenge in the end. Bad guys are bad guys for a reason. It was all he had left now. Spite and hate.

Because his bulk and weight were so much, there was little the Rangers could do to stop him as he rose up and heaved himself forward like a mad bull, raging for the last advance to death.

I saw a picture once. It was called *Blood on the Sand*. It was about gladiators, but it made me think of bullfighters. This was like that from what the Ranger told me about what happened in there.

The dragon roared and charged...

CHAPTER TWENTY-FOUR

I looked up as I fast-roped down into the dragon's-lair darkness beneath the well's edge. It was like speeding down into a massive gothic sports stadium from the roof to the field in an instant. Ancient and old with strange demonic statues, torches, and stairs leading off toward dark arches, was what I saw as I fell toward the gunfight at the bottom. I looked below my boots at the last second and it was all darkness with islands of firelight here and there.

In and out of these shadows moved those orcs like the ones who'd defended the fortress walls when we'd taken FOB Hawthorn. Shadow archers or something. Monk-like archers with rags and robes. Using poison arrows then. Who knew now? They'd been killers. They were here and the Rangers securing the insertion point were firing in all directions to bring them down and establish a foothold to get the acetylene bottles out.

What was Ssruth gonna do...

Probably bite down on them and blow us all to hell.

I fell fast and smashed into the ground, felt something in my foot twist the way it shouldn't, and then lost my hold on the rope and smacked my good old FAST helmet right into the mosaic floor down there.

Not lights out, but my bell was rung for sure and for the second time that day I was getting hit by hot expended brass.

I could hear McCluskey laughing from the shadows all around us with his vampire's cackle.

"Come out to play, Rangers?" he catcalled from the darkness not too far away.

The sergeant major turned and mag-dumped full-auto on the darkness as Sergeant Kang hauled me to my feet. At that moment I got hit right in the chest by one of the orcish arrows and it shattered on my plate carrier. Splinters of wood cut my face.

"With me, Private," said Kang. "We're going to retrieve the bottles now."

Calm. Like this was just Tuesday. Tuesday for Rangers. "'Cause sharks don't dread Mondays," Tanner would tell me Sergeant Joe would say. "You just wake up and do shark stuff. But Tuesday is a very special day for sharks... because it's like a second Monday and you get to be a shark all over again... so says the Book of Joe."

At the same moment, he was telling Monroe on the comm that we were all down and to get another rope down to us to haul the bag full of acetylene bottles up and out.

I followed Sergeant Kang, my ankle screaming and trying to catch my breath from the arrow strike that had basically forced the breath out of me.

My ribs didn't feel good.

I watched as a dark shadow grabbed one of the other Rangers and dragged him into the darkness, away from us fast. It moved like smoke and lightning.

McCluskey.

The kid didn't scream, he just yelled, "Frag out!" as the vampire bit into him. That freaked McCluskey out because he knew what that meant, thinking the kid was gonna do himself with a frag rather than get turned into something bad. The SEAL vanished like a streak of smoke, racing across the main floor and re-forming not far away from the sergeant major.

That was crafty of the Ranger. He hadn't popped his grenade. He'd just known that someone who knew grenades, like a former SEAL, didn't want five hundred fast-moving fragments moving straight through him, regardless if he could regenerate his form or not.

"Gotcha!" shouted the sergeant major roughly, and he put many, many rounds into McCluskey, who just ragdolled from the impacts of green-tip five-five-six, taking steps backward as each round tore through his Ren-Faire-Tragedian-Robin-Hood-Prince-of-Thieves outfit.

We saw him full in the light at that moment. Exposed by the torchlight and rapid flash of gunfire down here in the dark where he'd been hiding.

The eye where I'd shot him was missing. His skin was ghostly and greasy. He looked more like a ghoul than a vampire. Gone was the cool-guy SEAL from Michigan, Mike McCluskey.

His eyes had deep dark circles. Even the one I'd shot out.

He was absolutely stunned it had gone so horribly wrong in an instant.

Nearby, Kennedy sent a fusillade of magic meteors into two archers who were about to shoot the sergeant major. They screamed as hot fire burned them alive.

An arrow from the darkness went into the sergeant major's plate carrier and he didn't even flinch as he drew his sidearm, maintaining control of his primary as he did so.

He was firing at the SEAL near point-blank when the earthquake suddenly struck. Not a regular earthquake-like shaking for a few seconds. More like the ground just dropped six inches.

Stone and masonry came down from the ceiling.

Kang had the bottles and was running back toward the center of the room as the other two Rangers fought off the orc assassins. The earthquake sent the sergeant major down on one knee and I watched as McCluskey, shot to hell and all, suddenly moved like liquid lightning in one swift motion. Like he had on that long-ago day on the C-17 back when he first told us he was a vampire.

He was truly that fast. Putting the blade right up against Chief Rapp's throat in the blink of an eye on that day we first met him when we were new to the Ruin and completely surrounded.

This time he took the sergeant major's hand. Right off clean in one sweep of *Coldfire* that came out of the scabbard on his thigh and right through the air in one swift samurai-like cut.

Bullet-riddled and all.

Battles between pros happen that fast. Ain't like the movies. Real killers killing each other… it's over in a second before you even know what's happened. Thinking back… I think that's what Quentin Tarantino was trying to say in *Kill Bill* at the ending. It's over that fast when the pros meet one another.

And they both knew it would be that way all along. Even when they first started out on the trail of revenge.

Someone was going to die in a heartbeat. An eyelash of a second.

That's how it should have happened as McCluskey took the sergeant major's hand, holding my weapon we'd exchanged long ago.

That's how it should have happened...

I swung my carbine up without thinking. Automatic pilot. Just doing Chief Rapp's school of trick SF gunfighting as McCluskey raised *Coldfire* back like it was a baseball bat and prepared to decapitate the sergeant major for good, regardless of how many holes he had in him...

... and I drilled him right in the head.

One shot.

Right in the center of McCluskey's skull.

He fell over backward like I'd just put his lights out forever. But when I was standing over him a second later, the sergeant major was grunting in pain because *Coldfire* wasn't just a weapon... it was a magic weapon. A fabled blade that left the pain of its cut for a long, long time to come.

To let you know.

To drive you mad.

It was cold fire.

Ringaruinë.

I picked it up and felt... something. Something deep. Something for another time.

The sergeant major knelt next to McCluskey and let his bloody stump go as he snapped off the arrow that had landed in his plate carrier. The SEAL watched the whole time. Even though he'd been shot in the head, he was still alive in there. The one eye darting back and forth as his vampiric powers of regeneration tried to get him back online fast.

But there wasn't enough time for that. Time had run out.

The sergeant major reared back and drove what remained of the shattered arrow into the SEAL's chest, plunging it right down, and through, his black heart.

That's how you kill a vampire.

Apparently the sergeant major knew that.

McCluskey's eyes opened wide at the last second. Wild fear. Horrible knowing. The abyss opening up.

His mouth working and my mind, my psionics could hear him saying, "No! It wasn't supposed to end this way! You were supposed to die. You Rangers... You..."

His body was turning to ash before us. Turning into dry paper that began to catch slow fire.

He was shrieking in my mind. But in reality, his mouth was just opening and closing silently. Mouthing pleas that could not be heard.

I brought *Coldfire* down on his neck. Severing his head from his body.

Ringaruinë.

Done.

Finished.

Tango down.

Time's up.

"NET CALL NET CALL NET CALL. Lizard King is down. We got him."

EPILOGUE

I could tell you what happened after that. But it wasn't anything good. At least for me.

The Rangers took something close to twenty-five million gold coins out of there. Double that in silver and miscellaneous other strange and foreign coins. Weapons. Many of the Rangers now had magic weapons and armor.

Strange chests, ancient scrolls, bizarre maps, spellbooks, and other fantastic things of wonder and value.

Old Vandahar laughed with each new revelation of each new wondrous thing. Then he found the scrolls and grew quiet. Mumbling, "At last. Now, perhaps, young Talker, we have a chance. For if these are what I think they are… then the hour of change is upon us all."

I asked him what he thought they were.

"Why… the earliest fragments of the *Book of Skelos* I have ever encountered. This is how it all began. This is the story of the Ruin."

We needed what we found for where we were going next. There was a war on. A great war between east and west. Between life and death. Good and evil. We had struck a great blow against the enemies of the Cities of Men by killing the dragon. Now we had a chance to go up against the prime movers, according to the old wizard the Dragon Elves called *Wanderer*. Vandahar.

On the last night, before we left the ruins of Tarragon forever, what remained of it would now sink into the swamp sooner than later, Vandahar told us all about it. All about the forces of darkness, as he put it, gathering in the east. About the Black Prince of the haunted Crow's March, Sût the Undying of the Land of Black Sleep, and the Nether Sorcerer who is from the *Other*.

It was a lot to digest. Weird stuff I will tell of later. But as the old man told the captain, "Now begins the grand adventure you Rangers were sent for. Because I do believe… someone, perhaps even the Hidden King himself, saw fit to lend you extraordinary men to the extraordinary cause that doesn't have much of a chance without you. I'll be honest about that."

He looked around in the firelight, his ancient eyes resting on all of us.

And I watched her, Last of Autumn. Autumn. I watched her for a second.

She saw me and turned away.

That was over now.

"Allies you have," continued Vandahar. "Some know of it. Some not yet. But they need you just as much despite the ignorance. Stone King, will you make pact with these Rangers to stop the darkness rising against the last of the good?"

Wulfhard Ravenslayer stood, his grim dwarven features made more so by the flickering bonfire. He smiled.

"I thought we dwarves were the bravest among the good. But I was wrong. It is not the Rangers who would be honored to have the dwarves' weapons in their cause. 'Tis Stone Folk who are honored to stand in battle with them.

And that has never been said of any but our kind in the Halls of Stone."

Then he sat down and stared at the fire humbly though he was very noble in nature.

The wizard looked at the sovereign of the Shadow Elves.

He stood, their new king. He was weak. Many years he had been held captive in the dragon's dungeons. Now, haggard and ruined, he stood and looked around at those who had rescued him.

I'll admit this. He was a noble man. A quiet man. Once, long ago, he'd been the brash young captain of Night Watch. The sacred guard sworn to protect the Shadow Elven queen.

They had pledged to one another. Long ago. Before I ever showed up.

He was dead.

And now he was alive.

Last of Autumn, who had found and rescued the Rangers, helped him to his feet to address the Rangers and dwarves.

His name was Crazed Horse. But he didn't seem that man, or Shadow Elf, anymore. He seemed old. Wise. Haunted.

He cleared his throat.

"If I can..." he coughed. His voice was thick and not used to being used much. "... be as brave... as Lady Autumn... then... I owe Rangers... all the faith of... the Shadow Elves. We were... nothing. Scoundrels... lost... then... Rangers."

He bowed deeply to Captain Knife Hand.

To make it worse, I had to translate all this.

I kept it together.

Academy Award me.

But later I lost it. When no one was around. In the dark where you can't be seen. Late when no one can hear. Before we left in the morning. Under a full moon. Down near the edge of a beautiful silver-and-blue pond in the moonlight, I cried.

Then… I heard movement behind me.

Her horse.

It came and put its muzzle down on my neck. Just like my dad had done for that mare. Telling me I had to let go. To move on now.

The Rangers needed me.

I could read his thoughts easily.

She had given Sindamairo that last message for me. Telling him to be a friend to me now. To stand with me in the battles that would come. And that she was no longer Autumn, but Last of Autumn now. There would be no Cities of Men for us in the dream of the boat.

There would just be that dream. That was all. Nothing more.

In High Tolkien his name is *Sindamairo*.

Gray Horse.

THE END

OLD Vandahar inspected the first of the scrolls that had been recovered from the vast piles of dragon hoard within the great dome where Ssruth the Cruel had long made his home in the many years since the sack of Tarragon. He teased the ancient writings from the ivory tube, marveling at how well the parchment had survived the long years in shadow. Laying it out he began to translate the ancient runes, reading what had been inscribed in blood upon the roll of parchment. Marveling with each deciphered glyph at what was being now revealed... and what, for so long, had lain hidden.

"Hmmm, what do we have here. Curious indeed. Well then... Oh my. Oh my yes indeed. Might this... perhaps...? Could this be the earliest known copy of the *Book of Skelos*? The origin story of how the Ruin became what is now, from what it once was. What was forgotten. How it was made.

"I will translate it, and then ask that the young Ranger, Talker, make a copy for his record. A copy of what some said no longer existed anymore in these dark and final days. A record that might just destroy the Saur and set things aright again. We shall see.

"Now... this is strange and arcane to me. I'm sure—just as with the other fragments of the *Book of Skelos* I have seen with my own eyes—that the story is not entirely straight. That mysteries are hidden within. And that to those who possess all of the fragments, or at least enough, more may be known than a casual reader might see. But it tells a tale, and the knower will gain wisdom if one can follow the clues. Yes. Indeed.

"So, how does this begin for us? With the Spider Queen, Maker of the Forgotten Ruin... she of the most ancient of long-ago myths and legends. Oh yes, we shall see..."

The Scroll of Becoming

The Tale of the Spider Queen, The Ogre of Gaash, and the Beginning of the End of Everything that Was

Let us play a game for the end of the World...

The song woke her up and told her that love would keep them together, so she decided to tear the world apart to see if that was true. That was all she had left now. It was the only way to make everything right again.

"Love Will Keep Us Together" by The Captain and Tennille blared over the gym speakers during one of her physical therapy sessions at Serenity Hills, awakening her shattered mind to what she must do. And she remembered the beautiful boy. And the night of the secret he told her before everything that was a lie went away. Her spindly little legs were so atrophied by that time, from days on end of writing long strand equations of pure mathematics, that they, the rehab doctors, thought she'd never walk again. Not that it mattered much. She never left her workstation.

Ten monitors.

Two supercomputers.

One keyboard.

In all the years that had passed before the world as we all knew it ended, after they'd shut everything down and turned out the lights, she came back to the old place at the center after fleeing Serenity Hills. A little mad. A little crazy. Still very, very much in love.

Her body was breaking down.

At MIT they'd had to hire a nutritionist just to feed her.

At Dow Chemical's Nanobiology Research Lab in Zurich, with money arranged by the CIA and straight from the dark coffers of the Bilderberg Group, they'd had to hire a doctor and a psychotherapist just to keep her a-tap-tap-tapping at their keyboards. Tapping at those keys while the first teams began to watch, in almost complete bewilderment, what she was doing. Because what she was doing... well, she was the only one doing it.

Very dark stuff.

Tiny little machines like spiders making and remaking everything. Potentially. Remaking was the key. And the scary part. And how, in her mind when it would wake back up one day, everything would be made right again.

Later, at the bottom of the deep core no-name lab sixty-five stories beneath the back end of Area 51, under a big old piece of sunburnt granite rock way downrange and not on any map, they had finally put her in a wheelchair. She hadn't spoken to anyone, any human, in at least five years. Not a single word. Which wasn't entirely true. Some nights, when they didn't tranq her to the gills just to get her some sleep, during some bioweapon formula-binge, allowing her to stay up and go-go-go in the making of a new and groundbreaking way to annihilate mankind, sometimes she'd move her lips silently as she tap-tap-tapped at the keys. The team of analysts barely followed her trail, attempting to hopefully re-engineer just some of her equations, which were hundreds if not sometimes thousands of pages long. They theorized she was either mumbling to herself, or talking to the in-suite design AI.

Talking to the onsite systems management AI for the Doomsday Now Project she was currently being used on. Talking to SILAS. Y'know… like he was a person.

After three years of that she just broke right down. Or to be more correct… she was broken. The Defense Department had seen it before. The brightest burned like a white-hot light bulb, then at the last, snap… or pop. Even crackle. Then you'd just find them in the lab one day, fritzed out and staring at nothing because their big old brain was all gone now. They'd never move again. Institutionalization. That was always the next, and last, step.

Warehouse 'em and forget 'em.

Bright bulbs that burned so hot, in the end the analysts were racing just to catalog and record everything in order to merely keep up and get it down for the permanent record no one would ever see. At least for the official record. Their next big brain could figure out what she'd done. Really smart people realized that some things, and people, were just beyond them. Especially if those things were created by the truly brilliant. The one out of an immeasurable number, let's say the one out of a billion.

So maybe on Earth right now there are seven of these. Unless they happened to be born in a third-world country where no one will notice, or they get aborted in a first-world one because nobody cares.

Except now she was useless.

Six months later, she walked out of Serenity Hills and was never seen again. Just walked out of the maximum-security wing, though it wasn't called that, and disappeared. The last image of her merely a grainy black-and-white CCTV image showing the storm and a small figure, spindly and pale even in the night rain static, wobbling and disappearing off into a slate-gray forest and the waiting dark beyond. Her very first time all alone in the world.

If anyone cared, had known her when she was just a child, they might have felt something. But they didn't. She was just a broken asset.

They didn't think she could even walk on her own anymore.

In Bangkok she hacked the hell out of China by sneaking in through an MSS operation that was being run against India's elite RAW section. China's Ministry of State Security spy portal was being used to run a currency meltdown against India's Research Analysis Wing, both top-tier intelligence agencies. Fourth and ninth respectively in the world. This gave her an all-access pass to all the R&D China was ever-looting from across the entire world.

Gene tech was what she was really after on that one.

Nanobiology and engineering were basically hers already. In fact, they *were* her. The world knew that. Except they knew it a different way. By another name. Knew her as the Spider Queen. That had been her code name. But really it was more of a brand by which they sold her products to the rest of the world. She'd been the patient zero of the entire nano movement, and when they sold her tech, Dow Chemical CIA and other organizations that should not be named in open chatter, that tech was always source-verified as having come from the Spider Queen. And weaponized accordingly.

Her real name was gone.

A very long time ago.

Sometimes though, in quiet half seconds as her mind paused between theorem and formula in some fifty-six-page rap sheet of complex calc she'd be reciting back to herself by memory because it had been there in the night when she'd awoken, her unconscious mind not knowing how to do anything else even when it was supposed to be resting, and even dreaming, sometimes she remembered that other name. And without touching the keys her bony fingers were hovering over, she'd type it out on the air just above. Quick. Like a passing ghost. Or a muscle memory. Never seen again. Except by her.

That other name.

It was an easy hop, skip, and jump from China's super-secret MSS servers into the byzantine Russian GRU databases. Deep down digging. Chemical warfare stuff. The buried Nazi stuff the Russians had been hiding all these years. Stuff they probably didn't even know they had anymore. But those Germans, those Nazi super-scientists and their thousand-year rule they'd designed for, they had known all about infection vectors and spread containments. Chemicals and bioweapons were their thing, and she saw, saw it all in fact, how close they were to actually wiping out the rest of the world back in '44. And I don't mean in battle. Or with atomic weapons.

They were a few canisters away from choking out everyone in the world.

Kurt Vonnegut close.

Ice-nine close.

Science fiction scary close.

Then a tiny five-year wait, and it would've been all clear for the Reich to go forth and rule. They just needed the bunkers and the supplies to wait it out. The contaminant. Five years they didn't have because the 8th Air Force was bombing the hell out of Berlin. And some of their math was wonky.

But she'd fixed that. And a few other things. Nanobiology made things much easier and much more fun. The way they should've been.

After that, she'd headed back home.

Back to Viejo Verde.

East into the dawn where it all, for her, began.

Arriving at LAX in the middle of a hot day a few years back, she passed out in a boarding lounge from lack of food and sleep. In all the think tanks and secret labs, they'd always taken care of that for her. Time to eat. Time to sleep. Time to make. Later she woke in a security office. A kind man and woman in uniform were offering her orange juice. Looking at her like she was some lost old woman.

She was forty.

She said she was fine. Her voice, long unused when she worked in the bunkers and think tanks, was scratchy and rough. Like a rusty gate whispering on a wind-struck night.

They let her go and she went straight to the nearest bathroom, other pretty airport travelers all around, fixing their makeup… or taking care of a child. Young and beautiful and full of life.

Full of life.

Full of life…

Like.

She.

Could've…

She looked in the mirror and saw indeed that she was a hoary old woman. A harridan. Crazy thin, white hair. Tight skin. Gaunt cheeks. Watery washed-out blue eyes. Red-rimmed. Liver spots. Pale.

She looked at her bony and withered hands.

The fingertips were flattened from so many, so many, so many keystrokes. Uncountable keystrokes.

A tap-tap-tapping.

They'd taken everything from her for want of a better day after tomorrow. Everything.

She caught a cab. Took it south. Held out a wad of money. Didn't totally comprehend what she was doing.

At first things weren't familiar in the way they should be for someone who was going back to where they'd grown up, after all these years. But eventually as she went, she seemed to recognize things and places and even smells from long ago. Sudden bursts of wedding white, spring blossoming, honeysuckle still growing in the old landscaping. The heavy road-washed scent of sweet eucalyptus in the long stands guarding the shrinking orange groves that had once been so wide and large and everywhere. She did not smell the night sage as she did so long ago. Because it was not night yet. And then all the memories that were important came flooding back.

Her parents. Frozen and afraid. Just kids really. They'd loved her. The tiny child her. Precocious and far more intelligent than anyone they'd ever met. Genius was a word they, her parents, had understood, but it did not describe their tiny little girl-child accurately. You'd have to put a word like "super" and a hyphen in front of it to get it right. She'd discovered and uncovered that much in the records.

They'd divorced after she'd been voluntarily taken away. Her mother had killed herself. Her father might as well have. They had never been a part of the project in the way some of the other parents had been. Her parents had just won the "we had a wunderkind and the military-industrial complex scooped us up for their secret project" lottery back in the seventies.

Some lottery.

More memories came racing out from the places she passed along the suburban street of thirty years later.

The boy. The handsome beautiful boy was the only memory that meant anything to her. In fact, it meant everything. She saw him as he was and not as he surely must be now, though she'd seen all his files and had known at any given moment exactly where he was in the world. She'd had that kind of access all along. She'd kept her queries and searches hidden from the analysts who watched her. Along with many, many other things they'd never dreamed she was thinking up and working on all along.

She saw him as he was then. Tall and tan. Swept hair. Blue eyes. That shy smile. And the way he'd looked at her.

Her frail hand was pressing the cab's passenger window as they passed the old place where the game store had once been. As though she were waving at someone. As though she was reaching out to touch his face. As though it were all real again. The place was now a liquor store and an automated bank teller kiosk set within the long center of shops and stores. A plaza, they had called it in those days.

Where he'd told her his secret.

Where her life had begun, and ended, in the same early dark of a single summer evening.

"Is this the place, ma'am?" asked the cab driver a few blocks later.

Yes. Yes, this is the place.

She is staring at the washed-out remains of DataSys Development. A spreading one-story corporate sprawl with a wide sunbaked parking lot that's rippling and buckling and chained off to the public. And empty. And deserted. For a very long time.

The watchers.

In the sixties this was where they planned. In the seventies this was where they implemented. In the eighties… this was where they watched.

Project Tomorrowland.

She pays the cab driver, and he pulls away, leaving her outside the old forgotten place. Streams of cars shoot by along what was once a quiet manicured parkway in the center of Viejo Verde, planned community of possible futures.

Mainly just the one future.

The nuclear annihilation of the world as it was known then.

No-holds-barred, toe-to-toe nuclear combat between the Russkies and us. Y'know… the Cold War.

Everything seems vaguely familiar. And yet it is all really gone, she thinks. Everything that once was, is gone now.

But not forever.

She violates the rusty old gate and the thick doors that lead deep into the dusty place and all of its seventies military-industrial complex glory. Aerospace fonts along the walls and placards. Orange carpet. Futuristic chairs. Deeper in she finds the NASA sixties vintage moonshot control rooms. Complete with actual built-in ash trays. For the next five years she will tap-tap-tap from within here. This place. Only rarely does anyone come by. Just some outside maintenance crews really. To keep it from being overrun by the planned community landscaping gone wild. The whole place is supposed to be bulldozed and sold. But she keeps that from happening by running amok, quietly, inside the government's databases. They never find her when they come here. Even if they look around inside. Because she's deep down in the basement. With all the computers that used to watch her and everyone else. In the doomsday bunker that's deeper and bigger than anyone could ever imagine. They locked it up and left it. Just in case.

Beyond endless mausoleums of file boxes full of information and test scores on everyone she once knew...

Buried far below all the old relics of a lost civilization that was once her childhood...

Deep down in the bedrock. Within her very own Cave of the Unknown...

... the Spider Queen is back. Building an invisible web of a specially designed plague that will change the world in a day. Or at least start it changing on that day. Change it back into what it once was. Make it into something it should've been all along.

Take back what was taken.

She watches the news and studies the world to decide who exactly gets what. Because there might as well be a little justice as she goes about getting her revenge and finding what was lost.

She has an eye hemorrhage. One eye is filled with bloody popped veins. She's been working not just for days... but for years.

Tap, tap, tappity tap tap...

But first, everything has to go dark. That's how the plague must begin. That's how the world has to change.

Love needs a second chance, even if the world's got to burn.

Love will keep us together, she thinks. Because she really needs him.

They owe her.

The Scroll of Blindness

I'M blind.

Everyone on board the 787, flight 206, inbound from Indonesia, had the same thought seconds after they all went blind. It would've been an understatement to say they panicked next.

Mason heard a lady shriek from a nearby seat, her voice raggedly hyperventilating as she sucked at the dry pressurized cabin air. A baby was wailing bloody murder somewhere in the seats ahead as everyone collectively lost it above the dull hum of the massive engines now spooling up into an urgent whine. It was in that moment Mason finished a thought he'd started back in 2002. Back when the helicopter he was in, crashed.

What was it all for?

That had been the thought inside Mason's head as the pilot of the CIA helicopter auto-rotated the falling chopper right down into the Palacio Del Carnivale marketplace. As the operation to snatch Hugo Chavez went up in smoke, chaos all around, and a failed coup and a riot seemed to intermingle and become something singularly Venezuelan.

What was it all for?

Mason hadn't even been thinking about dying in that helicopter crash as at first the Palacio Del Carnivale spun into view, then the slums, then more slums, then some high-rises off in the distance. Then everything once again as the downward spin continued through the bright and golden South American afternoon. The co-pilot and pilot simultaneously freaking out and trying to control the crash, while alarms and bells competed for presence among that "last moments" madness.

He'd been thinking about a game. About the summer of 1985.

About the game shop.

About Viejo Verde.

About his parents.

And his friends.

He was thinking about everything that was supposed to have meant something. Once. That was what he was thinking about as what looked like the last seconds of his life spun about him in a wild twirl while that falling whirlybird fell.

It was all a big lie.

The slums swirled into view again as the co-pilot of the helicopter swore and said something about watching out for a construction crane.

"It was all a big lie, buddy." Or at least that's what Charlie Schwartzsky had revealed beneath the orange light of a parking lot in nowhere Minnesota as snow swirled down outside the bar he'd met Mason at.

Shrimpy Charlie. The kid with asthma and a chest brace. Charlie from Little League back in Southern California, 1979 and another world ago. The Charlie he hadn't seen for twenty-two years. He was gray now in that falling snow-orange light. A chain smoker whose dry rasp could be heard in the white snowy silence each time after he pulled at the coffin nails he kept lighting one after the other. Chain-smoking as all was revealed and everything began to change for Mason like some picture that was really a picture of something else. So much so, you couldn't see the other picture anymore.

Charlie had looked like a drowned rat. Like he hadn't grown since being the worst kid on their childhood baseball team. Like all the years between that meeting in the dead of winter 2001 and the last game they'd ever played together in summer twilight had only managed to shrink Charlie and turn him into an old man long before his time.

Back in the jetliner of the blind, the tired voice of the captain on the inbound to LAX jetliner came over the inflight intercom. It had been maybe five minutes since everyone had gone collectively blind.

"Ladies and gentlemen... it seems we have... a situation."

People who had gone silent at the initial appearance of the captain's voice now returned to penitent wailing, panic-driven screaming, and helpless sobbing as their minds filled in the blanks of what "a situation" might entail. Nothing good, surely. They tended toward the dramatic in their imaginings. That doom they'd all been promised had finally arrived like an unwanted winter guest.

Mason gripped the armrest, tightened every muscle in his body, and held his breath as he counted down from ten. Then he began to release. Just like he'd learned in the army. And then again in spook school. Relaxation under extreme stress technique.

"Oh please... oh please... oh please..." a woman repeated over and over off to his left. He still couldn't see. He remembered a pretty woman in that vicinity. A businesswoman. Chinese. Maybe that was her now, he thought to himself. Chanting the mantra of "oh please." Maybe.

"We have engaged the automatic landing system," said the captain. "And we're getting confirmation from the control system tone indicator that we are indeed locked onto the approach glide scope for landing at LAX. This is a 787, folks. She's state-of-the-art. She'll fly herself if she needs to. And it looks like…" the captain sighed and let a pause hang in the air above their heads like an unclean carrion bird. "It looks like she's gonna need to do it without us this time."

Silence overwhelmed the cabin. Stunned silence. There was some sobbing, but it was low, and distant, and pitiful. Like the moaning of galley slaves destined to pull even when the ship was a wreck, on fire, and surrendering to the waves. As though there was nothing but the fate you'd been assigned once the irons had been placed on your legs and arms.

"We should be on the ground in about, uh… about ten minutes, folks," said the captain.

The silence that followed indicated he had nothing more to say.

But what could one say when you've all gone blind at the same moment, at thirty-five thousand feet, in a screaming jetliner? What can be said about such things?

Everything'll be okay?

Don't worry?

Sorry about all this?

The engine noise changed pitch. People screamed suddenly at this. The plane began to bank. The screaming increased. It banked harder. Weeping burbled beneath the screams at each change in speed or pitch of the airborne giant as all the passengers were thrust back into their seats or slung off to one side of the cabin or the other, as unseen things began to fly about, or someone cried out in pain. Every sensory input was stimulus for a new unseen and much-imagined horror.

Someone began to babble incoherently. They're losing it, thought Mason. He'd seen that before. Seen hardcore killers suddenly lose it under fire. They'd begin babbling gibberish, high and hysterical. Out of their minds and long gone as the bullets filled the air like locusts.

There was an unannounced *thunk* beneath their feet somewhere in the belly of the aircraft. Everyone groaned, minds imagining the worst. The death roll. How would it really be? Fire? Impact? They'd never know. They couldn't see their end hurtling toward them at five hundred miles an hour. They were blind. But they knew it was coming all the same.

Mason's mind tried to unravel along with those of his fellow passengers. Tried to fray and finally snap in the high winds of panic. Someone a few rows back, a man, screamed, "I can't take this! Please make it stop!"

Mason clenched his teeth and locked his mind down even tighter. He went back to 1986. Back to the game. Back to his half-ogre fighter. Sixth level. Kal Tum. He tried to remember the feel of his *Player's Handbook* in his hands, its thick cardboard front. The hollow sound it made when you rapped on it with an impatient finger. May... no, June, he thought, and smelled magnolia from his mother's garden, or was it the businesswoman's fear-pulsing endocrine glands pumping out sweat and tears and the magnolia scent of her no-doubt expensive-from-Hong-Kong perfume?

The Cave of the Unknown.

A rumbling, grinding whine screeched beneath their feet.

"This is it!" the gibbering lunatic laughed. "This is it!"

Landing gears. It's only the landing gears, thought Mason.

Then he tried to go back to that long-ago summer and not this almost certainly final moment of his life.

He fought to go back to that last of all summers.

That last of his youth.

And the lie.

The summer of the descent into the Cave of the Unknown.

Everything... everything had been possible then. And he hadn't even known it.

"Ladies and gentlemen, everything is looking... sounding, I should say..." interrupted the captain over the kingdom of hysteria in the passenger cabin. Then hesitated. "Everything is... proceeding. Fasten your seat belts now. We're about to land."

What was it all for? Mason asked himself again in another falling aircraft and wondered why impending death by sudden deceleration impact always brought out the question from the treasure chest he kept deep inside. He knew the answer. He'd heard it in the first few minutes of blindness. Moments ago, within himself. He was just an ex-spook analyst, mandatorily retired, coming home to nothing and no one. He'd finally heard the answer he'd been carrying all along inside himself to a question he'd been carrying for just as long. He'd finally finished that thought he'd started in the falling helicopter. The thought that had started long before 1986. Maybe started sometime around 1968 when the military-industrial complex dreamed of a world on fire and a future after the ashes. They had dreamed very big back then about the end of everything.

Most people didn't know the half of it, and that was an understatement, thought Mason.

What was it all for?

Outside, speed brakes deployed along the wings as spoilers and flaps shifted into position, obeying the commands of the onboard computer to slow the falling giant.

"No, not now, please!" wailed a woman. "Not now, not now, not now, not now, please!"

Now, thought Mason. Now.

"Please," he heard her whisper again and again. "Please."

What was it all for?

Mason paused in the moment between flight and not flight. In the moment when the ground is so close you can actually feel it through the floor of the cabin. And also the moment when the thing you're flying in can't possibly fly any longer. It's too large, it's too big. It must fall. In the last moment of your life as you knew it.

It was for nothing, Mason answered.

And then the tires squealed, and the aircraft seemed not even to bounce once as it settled all three gears down onto the runway. And people were crying and weeping even though the plane was still going so fast and making horrible noises, noises it always made, but no one had ever bothered to hear because they'd always had their eyes to see their smartphones instead of what was going on around them. But they wept and rejoiced nonetheless as the careening aircraft braked hard, throwing them all forward in their seats.

"It was for nothing," Mason whispered.

"Thank you," the woman nearby murmured, her voice dreamy. "Thank you. Thank you."

The Scroll of Disaster

THE passengers remained frozen in their seats, in the dark, or blind, no one really knew. After the landing roll slowed to a crawl, they'd felt the plane begin to bounce and shake as the pilot told them he hoped he was taking the massive aircraft off into the grass median between the runways.

"Now... ah, we need to get off this plane, folks."

Mason felt his face move into an involuntary tired smirk. It was the same smirk he'd felt on his face any time the State Department had gotten involved in some company op.

The engines had fallen silent. Outside they heard another aircraft go thundering by on the runway.

There were no emergency sirens.

"Is *everyone* blind?" wondered Mason, emphasis on *everyone*, as he undid his seatbelt. He heard other people starting to do likewise. Metal clinks resounding here and there throughout the aircraft.

"Can anyone see?" yelled Mason across the unseen tight volume of space above the seats. His voice seemed not to carry among the sobs and whimpers and occasional murmur. No one replied. Someone asked if he, Mason, could see. Mason didn't reply.

Mason entered the aisle and began to walk, letting his footfalls thump heavily up the aisle to announce his passing. He knew people would stop what they were doing or get out of the way. As he passed, people asked if he was there to help them, or from the fire department, or SWAT.

"Uh… ladies and gentlemen… I'm hearing from the tower… one very brave lady in fact, that this… ah, blindness we're currently experiencing seems to be… widespread."

There was a pause.

"No, Dave," continued the captain as though talking to someone else close by. Mason, trying to estimate how far he'd gone up the aisles from business to first, realized the captain had inadvertently left the mic open. "She has no idea how many planes are inbound as of right now," the captain continued over the open mic. "She's just trying to get them to turn off the runway at intermittent lengths and angles, but it sounds like a disaster in the making."

Someone—presumably Dave—said something the mic didn't pick up.

"Hell yes!" replied the captain, closer to the mic.

Mason felt a gap in the seats to his left. He stopped. He waved his hand around in that direction and tagged someone in the face. That someone shrieked.

Mason demanded, "Are you sitting next to the emergency door, sir?"

After a moment, the man replied that he was. Mason knelt on all fours and began to feel his way toward the door. He found the safety handle and held on to it.

"I don't think we're supposed to open it." The man paused. "You know, without… someone telling us to."

Beyond the walls of the cabin another aircraft thundered by, its near passage causing the massive 787 to rock back and forth. Seconds later they heard engines suddenly screaming followed by a loud rending metal crash… and then a massive explosion. The 787 rocked back and forth again. People began to scream afresh.

"We have to get off this plane now!" Mason yelled.

A lady nearby screamed at Mason. He could tell she was close. He felt spit and breath on his face as she shrieked, "Help us!"

I'm trying, thought Mason, and he wasn't thinking about the summer of 1986 anymore. He wasn't thinking about meaninglessness. He was thinking about not being in a fuel-laden jet about to be hit by another jet and burning alive. He was thinking about that as he tried to understand, with fingers alone, how the emergency door might open.

"I have to get the door open and deploy the emergency slide. Otherwise..." said Mason, hoping one of the flight attendants was nearby and would either help him or crawl over and do it for him. He found a solid metal pin near the bottom and pulled. Halfway up the door, his hands racing back and forth frantically, he found a handle but decided it was too big. That would just open the door. He needed to deploy the slide first.

"Who is this?" It was a deep feminine voice at his back. Mason felt a slender hand resting on his shoulder.

"I'm trying to get the door open," said Mason. "Where's the mechanism that operates the slide?"

"I'm a flight attendant. Let me help." Mason felt the woman move along his body hand over hand as she made her way to the emergency door. Then he could hear her fingernails scrabbling across plastic above the growing pandemonium in the cabin. In the distance, beyond the reigning panic, everyone in the cabin could hear another aircraft coming down the runway.

A moment later, the door swung open, and Mason heard a loud bang as the slide popped away from the aircraft and began to inflate. A hot breeze sent grit across his face and acrid smoke up into his nostrils.

"Wait!" screamed the flight attendant, digging her nails into Mason's back. "It needs a moment to properly inflate."

Behind them, people were screaming and fighting, pushing to get away from the sound of the unknown aircraft of surely approaching doom.

Thrust reversers on the unseen aircraft began to howl. Its brakes began to screech.

Blind. A riot happening behind him. A runway full of landing and burning aircraft ahead. Mason tightened every muscle, counted to ten, and dropped forward onto the thick, heady, chalk-dust-filled rubber of the emergency evacuation slide. He careened down the chute, throwing himself sideways to try to control the descent.

He rolled out onto dry grass. He could smell stale rubber, burning jet fuel, and the scent of the grass, heavy and dusty, it too smelling vaguely of jet fuel. He crawled away from the slide, knowing all five hundred passengers behind him on the behemoth 787 were desperate to follow.

"Crawl," he ordered himself. "Away from the runway." Or at least, that's how he saw it all in his mind. He saw the massive aircraft he'd just flung himself from. Saw it run off on the left side of the runway after they'd landed, even though he had no idea which side of the runway the aircraft had actually gone off. He crawled atop dry prickly grass. He saw himself crawling away from the calamity of twisted burning airplanes and bodies along the sides of the big concrete runways. He heard passengers behind him screaming and crying as they began to fall down the slide completely blind and utterly terrified of the unknown awaiting ahead and below.

"Move, boy!" he heard an old drill sergeant named Ward growl from thirty years ago. During his first live-fire exercise. Bullets in the night streaking overhead. Drill sergeants yelling for the recruits to crawl forward into tracers above and the maelstrom of heavy machine-gun fire ahead. It was the only way out.

Mason crawled forward much like he'd done thirty years ago. He crawled and crawled, feeling his hands go numb from sharp gravel and the dry scrape of dead grass. He crawled until finally a hand touched another runway. Maybe. It was rough concrete at least. Maybe a taxiway along the sides?

At that point, Mason chose to stand. If he was going to cross a runway, or a taxiway, or a road where vehicles of any type might come screaming along, it would be better if he were standing. Someone might be able to see him before they ran over him. Hopefully.

But we're all blind.

Maybe some of us aren't?

Once he was standing, Mason shuffled both feet forward a few inches at a time. He was hyperventilating. He slowed his breath. Heard his heart thudding inside his chest. Willed himself to calm.

"I've been in worse spots," he told himself. But he couldn't remember when. Then, "This makes no sense." By which he meant everything. Not just the blindness.

He started forward across the wide stretch of concrete, shuffling his feet, waving his hands. "Inch at a time," he muttered and repeated with each step. "Inch at a time."

He couldn't count his steps because he was shuffling. A few moments later he heard another plane. High and away. Engines whining. Off to his left. Another one coming in for a landing. Mason shuffled faster as the plane's engine roar swelled to a deafening shriek.

"This is not the way I get it," he told himself through gritted teeth. "Not the way at all." He'd said something similar almost twenty-four hours ago in an airport bar on the other side of the world. He'd said it to AD Halloran. Said it about the package in the belly of the 787. Except he'd said, "That's not the way to get it. Not at all."

The approaching aircraft's tires erupted in a short distant squawk as they nailed the surface of the runway. There was a pause and then a set of rubbery squeaks. The airplane must've bounced, Mason guessed. He continued forward, willing himself to move as fast as he thought safe.

I can always run, he thought, envisioning the emptiness of the average runway. All I have to do is get off the landing strip.

No. Not this time. The out-of-control airliners are being piloted by blind pilots, they're running off into the grass just like yours did. The grass is just as dangerous as the runway.

Reverse thrusters kicked in and screamed into an eardrum-splitting squeal as some captain sightlessly leaned on the brakes of the unguided aircraft that had to be coming for the blind man known almost to no one left living, as Mason stood in the middle of a wreckage-strewn runway on the last day of civilization. Or at least, that's what it felt like.

"Not the way to get it..." he whispered again and moved forward. Hands and fingers stretching out.

A massive explosion pushed him to the runway facefirst. Behind him he could hear people screaming, reaching a new level of terror and fear that might have seemed impossible less than an hour ago. The passengers from his plane? But he didn't think the 787 had been hit.

The package was still safe in the cargo hold.

"Does it matter anymore?" he muttered.

Fear howled at the bars beyond his mind cage as he inched forward into the unknown and across the seemingly endless concrete surface. He heard another distant high-pitched urgent mechanical whine. An engine still running? More explosions beyond all this? He continued to inch forward, his hands out in front and waving at unseen obstacles.

I must look ridiculous, thought some distant part of his mind. The part that's always watching. Just as it'd been trained to from before he'd ever known he was being trained to do anything.

That fear beyond the bars felt like a rising maniacal laugh coming from deep within him. He knew, down in his heart, deep down inside, that if he let that laugh out, let that beast that howled like a wild animal loose from the cage he was standing within, he'd lose control. Totally and completely.

"Does it matter?" he asked himself again. Or heard some other familiar voice ask. And…

What was it all for?

Then there was the gentle give of dirt beneath his shoes. He felt the end of the concrete and the comparative softness of hard dirt. He shuffled on and felt spongy grass a few feet later beneath one hard-soled dress shoe. He took a deep, much-needed breath through his nose and smelled the heavy scent of dry grass beyond the burning jet fuel and coastal salt air.

He continued on through the grass, and after a time, its expanse seemed like a never-ending stretch as the world continued its cacophonic end all about him in darkness. Or blindness. He pushed all thoughts of Owen Matthew away, the other long-ago friend who'd begun to demand remembrance, and continued to grope, blindly, onward across the end of the world.

The Scroll of Death

THE last time Owen Matthew spoke to Mason had been in Singapore. At the Peninsula Bar. They'd had beers. Their last beers together. Cold beers in the sweltering afternoon, and then the night had come on as Owen waxed eloquent in the scented breeze by the pool no one was in, his voice high-pitched and annoying even to nearby eastern strangers of business and industry.

It was a voice Mason had known since he was eight.

"The big blue carpeted concourse stretches before the man, Mason," squeaked Owen. "Like a wide road. Empty, unspoken, and undeclared at three in the morning. He is tired and his suit is wrinkled. Expensive hand-cut fabric smells of taxis and cigarettes, hotel soaps and coconut."

Owen has only ever had two modes of conversation. Even when he was a boy in short pants waving a wooden sword and a trashcan shield, proclaiming himself to be Strider the enigmatic ranger. Either questions—ceaseless, endless at times, and seemingly without sequitur—or monologues that miss the mark just about as much as they strike center target, dead on. Regardless of whether the target screams in agony or not.

"At three of three in the morning. Who is the man, Mason?" Owen wonders loudly to the rest of the people at the end of the bar. He continues. "Who is anyone at the great places of in between? Lying neither here nor there. Destination both coming and going. Who is anyone and how can they be explained when one is still going and not yet arrived? Justified? They cannot be. They can be merely guessed at. Supposed of. Painted, photographed, and even captured. But never explained. In the great places of in between, there is simply not enough time. Flights arrive, baggage is simultaneously expelled and inhaled. Cold metal carts smell of jet fuel and rattle with the cheery jingle of tiny bottles amid the merry jongle of soda cans as they are trundled aboard past the banter of ground crew and the chit of stewardesses mixing with the too-hurried chat of gate agents. Warm aircraft cabin air stands boldly against chill winds seeking entry off the engine-swept tarmac of the ramp in late night."

Owen pauses to drink and wipe his lips. His eyes are alight as he sees just how he will chase this particular rant to its finale. Or so that's what Mason thinks in these "Owen's eyes alight" moments. Like a Da Vinci. Like a Socrates. Or maybe just some lunatic beyond the last streets of Anytown, USA. Out near the edge. On the other side of the train tracks.

"But some planes stop here, and somewhere high above, other planes pass by. Are they going to land? Has some quiet voice, night-tired and cigarette-burnt, called out, mechanically, the closing of this particular haven of planes for the night? High above, captains and co-pilots listen, staring into the dark ahead, faces washed by the warm red glow of a million ticking readings and overachieving indicators, each humming with efficient and quiet complacency. The tired night-burnt voice, up and down the wires of information, signals the end of day and the solace of night. Captains high above, ice-blue eyes and iron-gray precision hair, examine great metallic watches, verifying the official time. The co-pilots, expectant, nod, and the planes continue on into night away from this forgotten no-place. Passing by, too late or never early enough, to stop. It is gone, and the airport where Mason finds himself retreats beneath the existence of winged knowing."

At this point Owen drained his beer and raised two fingers at the Asian bartender. The man gave Owen a distrustful look, but Owen, short, annoying, eyes wide, pleads for another. The bartender is fast and efficient, a smile now as the bar is wiped down once more as though a fresh start and clean slate have been extended. The salty bar mix is not just freshened but replaced altogether, and finally a cold beer lands on a heavy, white, logo-embossed cocktail napkin.

Owen drinks deeply and continues.

"The man, Mason, wanders past a long-closed snack bar. The scent of forgotten hot dogs sings of glories past as the heady butter of bygone popped corns loiters like some high school big-man-on-campus quarterback recalling glories gone a year, or even five ago. Fading from the current memories of just yesterday. Mason, the man, passes on and wanders first the blue concourse and then the green. The red concourse is dark tonight, the airline that once ruled those sands having faded from the era of transport trade."

Owen leans close to Mason.

"Its darkness is too dark, even for Mason. The night beyond the windows is too much like the eyes of the dead Mason has known. And so he returns to the blue concourse, which is now under assault by vacuum. And this sound, this sound of mechanical cleaning accompanied by the occasional glissando of some someone whistling away the night's loneliness, comforts Mason, oddly."

Another sip from the glass of beer and Owen wipes his lips before continuing.

"And so, who is Mason? Who are you, constant watcher, curled up between three seats in the boarding lounge, attempting tantric sleep, drifting, never really sleeping and all the while realizing you too are also far from home? If only you knew where home was. And the realization, the great realization that the normal people who stay in small towns all their lives never know is: You are never farther from home than when you are attempting sleep, elusive sleep, at three in the morning as you curl this way and shift the other in hopes of striking some bargain, being granted some miracle of undeserved sleep. You rise, you stretch, and you lie and convince, wander and stroll, splash water, read some, chew gum, and brush. This Aztec night will never end. It is that night which has finally fallen on all the world, forever. You are trapped here in this airport, and in its dry clutches you know some kind of eternity that might just be the appetizer plate for the full menu of hell. You will never again eat pancakes, drink cold milk, and slip, tucked by a patient and understanding loved one, beneath crisp clean sheets again, drifting quickly into sleep, mistakenly thinking you are still awake when in reality and in deed, you have long been asleep. That will never come. Night has fallen forever for the wicked, and you've been carried along with the tide of a wrecked world."

Owen looks around the bar as though searching for someone before continuing with this next bit. A few high-class hotel hookers pass and cast eyes at Owen and Mason. Two middle-aged American businessmen. One short, one slightly above average. Neither reeking of success or money.

Owen doesn't pay them the slightest and they move on, always in search of the bigger, better deal.

"Are you one of those?" Owen shrieks, and the bartender issues a sternly enigmatic rebuke of not-bemusement to the little man at the end of the bar with the bandsaw voice. Owen ignores him, but continues sotto voce. "Are you one of those? From behind weighted eyelids do you see the man Mason passing up this concourse and then down that one? And do you make a game of guessing him? Guessing who he is and what series of failed selections have left a man with almost-model everyman good looks wandering these concourses at this time of not-night and never morning? Did Mason's charm and wit, read easily on the tired yet friendly face, lead to early success in sales? Yes, sales! That's what anyone who did not know the man Mason would think if they saw him in this place, at this time of night. Only... it would be sales of a product gone belly up. A fading, once brand-new promise. Only a few gather now to purvey this past-prime product where once great herds of salesmen and saleswomen roamed the plains of a Golden Age and a heyday of that particular product, when it was all the rage. Making their mark, making a killing, making a mint at selling aluminum siding, computers, mortgages, junk bonds, dreams, et cetera, et cetera... and can I get a double shot once more of et cetera? Does Mason remember those halcyon days when the cash was everywhere as he partied with strippers in Caribbean climes, returning home across these then day-lit concourses of hope and opportunity and that bright word everybody thinks about all the time: the Future? Is Mason returning to Italian marble kitchens in glass block mansions? Is his position leveraged, and is his capital marketed? No. That's not the Mason they see. They see the Mason *after* that Mason. Bygone and belly up, he wanders the concourse on this forever night and remembers those Big Game yesterdays, while the reformed stripper wife of the tramp stamp and two point five kids slumber in another city not this one and dream their dreams of baseball and school project dioramas and soccer camp and play dates all financed by Mason's court-ordered and garnish-threatened wages."

Owen takes another sip of beer. His voice, still off-pitch, squeaky and annoying, has tuned down to the morose in the most minor of keys he can work. Only Mason would know this because he has known Owen longer than most.

"And the man Mason wanders," squeak-whispers Owen. "A modern man of poetic material sculpted in tones of Robert Louis Stevenson and even, if things had been different... Dumas." Owen throws his tiny hands wide, encompassing everyone in the bar. "Adjudicated by you, sleepy traveler. Painted by you, and finally, categorized, organized, and placed on the shelf of your collected observations, by you all. Mason is fate in repose, and you witness his forlorn concourse wanderings. You pity him, and if you knew how to pray, you would pray for him. Because your life has no reformed stripper wife, no tramp stamp, no failed ambitions, no lost Halcyon Days. No Big Games bygone."

Owen pauses grandly.

"This is Mason."

Another pause. But only for a moment.

"And it is not," Owen adds in a whisper, so only the two of them can hear this last part. "And it is not at all. Is it, buddy?"

They both know it never was. That was just the cover that allowed Mason to pass the world invisibly and do the dirty work of government that always needed doing.

Later, out by the cerulean pool, shimmering in the night beneath towering palms, lying in chaise lounges and nursing more beers beneath a swollen moon, Owen starts again. It's his last monologue. His last truth for this lifetime. His last words to Mason. Though neither knows it.

"Three days ago, POTUS awoke," squeaked Owen. "He woke up and lay awake in the dark, frightened to death. POTUS is awake! Should someone be summoned? Awakened? Told of the POTUS's sleeping crisis? Would anyone consider this a crisis? I mean, given the current state of affairs, and there is always a state of affairs current, maybe the POTUS should be awake. Lie awake, wander the halls of the White House, awake. America would probably sleep better if he were awake, or at least they thought he was awake, solving, handling, resolving the latest crisis."

Owen kicked off his tiny loafers and neatly rolled up the legs of his pressed slacks. He groaned tiredly and stepped into the pool a few feet away. Then he continued. There was no one else about.

"America would sleep better if they knew the president of the United States of America could not," he said to the pool and the night and Singapore.

"Everyone hates me, thinks the president. And you know what? He's right. Everyone hates the president of the United States of America. Americans hate him. The Chinese hate him. The Germans, Muslims... even the Canadians hate him. The president has reached such new heights, or lows if you choose to be that kind of person, of hate, that there are now thirty-nine credible active death threats against him. Not the thrill-kill-for-celebrity I'll-ambush-my way-into-infamy-with-a-small-caliber-handgun-and-win-the-love-of-father-mother-insert-movie-star-here love. No…" says Owen in almost a low moan.

Silence, other than the gentle waves lapping at the sides of the pool from Owen's circling of his tiny feet.

"No, these death threats are the kind Jack Bauer should be handling! These death threats are backed by highly motivated groups with a long history of getting their way regardless of law, morality, or expenditure. In fact, these aren't even threats. When someone is really serious about killing you, they don't call up the Secret Service and say I'm going to get you, or write long pages of erratic freeform craziness with passages from overrated coming-of-age novels as they cherry-pick their alliterations, juxtaposed against anger manifested in the person of their grandfather's voice. No. These groups are serious. These threats should be read as promises. These groups are made up of 'hard men' who do the 'hard things.' The only chance you have of ever getting them, if you've got a Jack Bauer, is in the early stages of planning. Way up the food chain… back when Contact A is shopping for armaments in Moroccan Weapons Bazaar B and gets a little too Jägermeister'd and spills the beans about Nefarious Group Zed with cryptic ambitions about code name 'That Guy.' Then, and maybe only then, Jack Bauer, the tip of the intelligence iceberg, ends up months later lethally eviscerating the active hand of Group Zed. All the mid-level and low-level players who might have actually purchased, handled, and even paid for the weapons that were going to be used against code name 'That Guy' are dead, globally speaking, and Jack Bauer has once again saved an unaware America. Once again."

A strange bird cackles in the Singapore night. The silence that follows is otherworldly and pleasant. Mason is used to these long Owen monologues and has enjoyed them since…

… since when, he wonders. Since…?

"But the low-level and the mid-level of the highly motivated aren't the top-level or the Main Guy. Those people go on. Maybe just the act of putting the low-level together with the mid-level was their only aim. Maybe being discovered was their aim. Because intent sends a clear message regardless. Intent speaks volumes at those levels. And while the mid and the low get shot up, stabbed, interrogated, tortured, and beaten, well, the high and the mighty never really do, do they?"

Owen sighs deeply. As much as his tiny frame can. The sound reminds Mason of their childhood together. Of Owen's brief yet daily bouts of ennui juxtaposed beside his frenetic highs of zeal, industry, and optimism.

"There are thirty-nine of these, on this presidentially sleepless night, Mason. Thirty-nine!" squeaks Owen.

Then whispers, "But there aren't any more Jack Bauers. Are there?"

In the silence that follows, Mason knows Owen has finished for the night. Owen stares at the dark sky and seems to hum one phrase over and over to himself. It is then Mason asks Owen the question. The question he has been sent to ask. The question that requires an answer.

"The world's darkest day is ahead!" shrieks Owen, refusing to answer.

And in the morning, Owen is dead.

The Scroll of Doom

WHEN Mason comes to the chain-link fence, feels its dry, rough wire beneath his questing fingers, he stops. He's heard three massive, metal-rending explosions behind him in just the past few minutes. He can feel heat and flames and hear people screaming in the distance as though he has just fled some terrible rock concert turned riot for the solace and silence of the parking lot.

Mason turns and leans his back against the fence. It gives, surrendering to his middle-aged solidness as it bows outward and away. He tries to think of his next move. Should he slither along its length? Or go over it? Or sit tight? None of these options seems right as he weighs the cons of falling into a ditch somewhere at the end of each choice. Or getting creamed by another runaway jetliner. Or walking into a field full of flames he can't find his way out of.

There are no sirens.

No police or fire.

No one is coming to help.

"The world's darkest day is ahead!" Owen had proclaimed in his high-pitched squawk in the hours before his death.

Indeed, thinks Mason as he waves his unseen hands in front of his face once more.

He tries to calculate the current time but the flight from Indonesia has him all turned around. He remembers waking up to morning light over the Pacific and the stewardess telling him they were just an hour from LAX. He'd had orange juice after that. He can taste its sour sugariness in the back of his mouth even now.

They were supposed to land at just after nine a.m. So, it's sometime mid-morning. Mason tries to feel the sun on his face, but the heat of the flames coming from somewhere nearby competes and won't let him get an exact position fix.

How could everyone go blind all at once? Not just his plane, but every plane. That's what he's thinking. He keeps landing on the "terrorism" answer. Not the dire promises of Owen the hotel bar prophet.

There was nothing on anyone's radar about a mass attack using blindness. NSA. CIA. FBI. Homeland. Department 19. Nothing.

"Our darkest day is ahead!" warns the once-living Owen, and Mason pushes that thought and its near-final vision of his childhood friend away from himself. Pushes Owen away. Pushes the package down inside the belly of the 787 away.

I'll have to worry about that later, Mason thinks.

When he surmises the grass nearby is burning, its crackle echoing across the unseen void between the flames and where he stands, Mason decides it's time, and probably for the best, to climb the fence and get farther away.

He knows there will be barbed wire at its zenith. Razor wire to protect people from other people getting onto the runway. He reaches up to the top of the fence and feels along its edge. Nothing. He reaches higher and finds the first prickly pear razor in the strand.

He takes off his coat and feels the heat of the nearby flames against his sweat-laden dress shirt as he turns and places his coat over the three strands of barbed wire above and unseen. Then, just like he's done before in places both domestic and abroad under cover of near-total darkness, he climbs up and feels a pant leg catch and tear on a defiant razor as he goes over the other side, hoping there's not an open pit beyond and below.

He falls onto hard dirt and rock.

The flames are getting closer.

He starts to crawl and soon finds himself scuttling down a sandy slope through thorny grass that smells dry and, again, slightly of jet fuel. His hands move over sharp rocks, sudden washes of sand, and long stretches of hard dirt as he crawls forward. In time he knows he's no longer going downhill, and after that his leading hand feels the rough paving of a road.

The sounds of fire and screaming and smashing jetliners have faded. There is only an intense quiet here, and occasionally, distantly, the soft hiss of an intermittent white noise.

He stands and starts out into the road, waving his hands.

If everyone's gone blind, he reasons, then no one's driving.

But you don't know that, Mason, he hears Owen bleat. Owen was always bleating about something that was obvious only to Owen. Always lecturing. Always hectoring. And always right.

"No, I don't know that," grumbles Mason, and hears the dryness in the whisky bass his voice has become in middle age.

Ahead he feels only cool air, and behind him the dry grass and flames that will consume him. The road is at least some kind of protection. He decides to cross the road. He guesses it's at least two lanes in each direction. Not a highway. Just a normal, old-school, LA county road.

He thinks of the layout of LAX.

In his mind he knows it's near the water. How many times had he watched the runway and the world falling away from him as the plane climbed, and then suddenly the brief strip of sandy beach appeared and then the ocean and the white waves lazily rolling in toward shore like flights of homesick birds?

I must be heading toward the water then, Mason reasons. The air is cooler and… yes, he tastes salt in his dry mouth.

He leaves the road and starts off through squishy, almost rubbery plants. Beyond the ice plants, he finds the other side of the road and in time is crawling up a steep sandy slope. At its top he gets a full blast of salty ocean air. He can hear the waves, and their white noise consumes everything.

This ocean is the white noise he has been hearing since the fence along the runway. The surf of the Pacific Ocean rolling onto the wide flat lonely stretch of this Southern California beach. Unused because of its proximity to the airport.

He smells smoke in sudden shifts of the wind, but the breeze is generally coming from the ocean, blowing onshore. So at least, he hopes, that should move all the fires in the other direction. Away from him.

The winter sun in California at noonday feels pleasant. Feels safe. Mason lies down in the sand atop the dune and begins to breathe deeply.

"You were probably almost killed more times than you'll ever know today." That's the thought he keeps repeating to himself. He thinks of the sudden blindness in the aircraft. The landing. Then getting away from the aircraft before it was hit, or destroyed, or whatever happened to it. Crawling…

He's sleeping and he doesn't even know it. He can't tell the difference between the darkness and sleep. He wonders if it's permanent. If he's blind forever.

"Our darkest day is ahead of us!" proclaims Owen.

The Scroll of Sand and Fog

THE past is a Tuesday afternoon.

1984.

Spring.

They are all playing rubber-band wars on the small greensward called "the Gazebo," because there is a gazebo rising in its midst, that lies in the center of the neighborhood. The younger boys are hazing an older, dirty-blond-haired boy named Gary. It's Gary versus everyone. Gary, a surfer, can dip, duck, and turn and twist to avoid all their shots while still firing rubber bands almost point-blank into their faces. But they chase him anyway.

And occasionally they corner him and assault him with volleys of rubber bands scoring direct hits across his lean chest and lanky arms.

Then he is away, scavenging fallen rubber bands in the verdant green of the lawn just as they do, and firing at them again. The boundaries are the grass. Everyone must stay within the grass to keep firing. The sidewalk walkways, gray concrete, are out of bounds. How this was decided, or when, is unknown. That it is such, is known.

Owen and Mason are fourteen.

Twilight is coming on. They are hot and sweaty and itchy from the fresh-cut grass they have rolled in. But still the rubber-band war rages on. It reminds Mason of the part in *The Fellowship of the Ring* where the orcs chase Boromir and the two hobbits. Then the orcs put tons of arrows into

Boromir who blasts his trumpet. Not surrendering. Even in the face of certain death.

Mason liked that part.

He also liked the orcs. The Uruk-hai. They seemed like real warriors even though they were supposed to be the bad guys.

Later, in a purple twilight, mothers begin to call out across the neighborhood as long blue shadows settle along the grass around the gazebo. Around the battlefield, warriors turn back into boys as they depart one by one. In time Gary leaves, and Mason and Owen, friends, sit on the cool grass beneath the twilight.

Mason goes to public school.

Owen goes to a private religious school.

But they have been friends since they both started living in this neighborhood. Mediterranean Heights. A planned community in a city of planned communities. Stucco and wood-frame houses that arise in angular 1970s architecture shapes, sheathed in colors of beige or sand. All trimmed in dark brown. A squat dark brown circular light post along the walkway near the gazebo, postmodern minimalism, flickers to life in the evening's first breath, making a small electric hum in the quiet.

"Where'd you go on Saturday?" asks Mason, who'd had two Triple-A little league baseball games that day. They'd planned, last Friday, on playing rubber-band wars again on Saturday evening before dinner.

"Oh," says Owen, who is smaller than Mason. Smaller and pudgier. Not an athlete like Mason. "I found a game shop. It's over in that new center across the train tracks. It just opened. I finally got to play the game."

"How was it?" asks Mason. Owen has had a boxed set of Dungeons and Dragons for more than two years. A blue box. On the front is a warrior with a bow and green shield. A red dragon glowers from atop a pile of gold and treasure. There's a wizard too. They've never played. Mason likes rubber-band wars and building forts and dirt clod fights and of course, sports. But he knows Owen has been on a personal quest to find someone, anyone, to play Dungeons and Dragons with since he ordered the game from a small bookstore a few years back. No one they know actually knows how to play this complex game. It is not Monopoly by any stretch of the imagination.

"It was great!" squeaks Owen. "I got killed by a minotaur!"

"A what?"

"A minotaur. It's a bull that walks like a man. He had an axe. I was on the third level of the dungeon, we were using these little figures, and they gave me a first-level fighter to play. I went off by myself and got killed."

"You shouldn't have gone off by yourself," Mason admonishes while pulling at handfuls of the razor-blade-edged grass.

"No risk, no reward," lectures Owen with a seriousness beyond his years. He is always suddenly sober when he delivers these bits of memorized wisdom. As though reciting a creed, a mantra, or a rule in the same manner and age as the source.

Owen always has some such bumper sticker of enlightenment ready for every occasion. His parents are the same way. Whole conversations are merely exchanges of found wisdom. Often the only thing they need is the impetus of a recounted failure or a related tragedy to start the wisdom roulette wheel a-spinning.

"How did the minotaur kill you?" asks Mason.

"He rolled a twenty. But he was way too powerful for me anyway. I looked it up. Minotaurs are like third-level monsters. I was only first-level. I had no chance. But I thought I could take him."

In the unseen dark a bat flaps its leathery wings, crossing the early night.

"If he was better than you, what made you think you could take him?"

"Listen..." huffs Owen as though explaining something obviously known. "I've never played the game. I thought it was like *Lord of the Rings*. I admit now... I had some preconceived notions about how the game could be played. But now that I know a few things, I'll do better next time. Now I know how the rules work."

"You told me it's just like *Lord of the Rings*."

"It is, and it isn't."

They wait. At any minute one of their mothers will call them home to dinner.

"Next time I'll know what to do," whispers Owen as he plucks up a handful of the dark green grass, considers it, and lets it fall from his hand.

"Next time?"

"This Saturday. They're playing again this Saturday. You could come too."

"Maybe."

That night, as Mason turns out his light after finishing *The Fellowship of the Ring*, thinking of Gandalf and the Balrog and the Mines of Moria and the Uruk-hai, he lies in bed, in the dark, and watches the night sky. He can see

Owen's room in Owen's house from here. Next door to Owen's is Scott Ott's house. His room is also on the second story. The blue glow of late-night TV flickers at the Otts'. *Star Trek* most likely. Both houses of both friends are in a row of almost perfectly identical tract homes just behind his own row of almost perfectly identical tract homes. He sees that Owen's reading light is still on.

"This time, I'll be prepared."

Mason awakes in the sand and fog. The air has turned cold and damp. He feels mist on his cheeks. He is still blind. He smells burning rubber and other chemicals on sudden violent shifts of the wind. He can still hear the waves.

He has no idea what time it is.

He has no idea what to do next.

The Scroll of Revelation

THE temperature drops and Mason finds a few sticks and some dry grass because he has begun to shiver. Night, he thinks. He digs out a small basin in the sand, arranges the sticks, and builds a fire using his Boy Scout training.

Everyone was a Boy Scout back in Viejo Verde. It was like a cult.

Scouts. Indian Guides. Baseball, swimming, electronics club, hunter's safety... the activities had been endless.

Now I know why, he thinks, and listens to the low dry crackle of his tiny blaze.

He sends his fingers out across the nearby sand and gathers more sticks, returning to the warmth of the smoky little fire. He is still blind, and he hears distant, larger flames and no sirens beyond the white noise of the constantly intermittent surf falling onto the shore like slow thunder. The swell has increased, and the waves are larger and Mason guesses this also must mean nightfall.

He stares only into the darkness and thinks about Owen. He's been thinking about his best friend a lot. Thinking about the past. About the games they played. About growing up in Viejo Verde. He recalls every memory of his oldest friend.

It was all for nothing.

He thinks about the time they made a dummy and put it on the train tracks with Scott Ott.

He thinks about those first weekends playing Dungeons and Dragons down at the game store.

He thinks about the summer of the Cave of the Unknown.

He wonders whatever became of them all. He'd followed news as best he could across the years. Scott Ott had gone to MIT. Last Mason heard, he'd become some kind of guru astronomer. That made sense. Made more sense, what with everything he knew now.

Since Charlie Schwartzsky spilled all the beans on their childhood.

The night seemed endless as Mason fed found driftwood into the fire. The cold dampness of the Pacific hung on his business jacket. He was thirsty. He licked his lips, and they were cracked from the constant buffet of the wind from offshore and the dehydration of an entire day without water. The sound of the distant flames was gone. There was only the occasional roar of massive waves falling onto the shoreline in the night. They'd grown in intensity and yet seemed slower in their short lifespan as they were born and then died a moment later against the wet sand.

Somewhere, distantly, he heard a foghorn.

"Must be socked in," he muttered and tried to visualize fog. Or mist…

He remembered the girl.

The girl who'd joined them that next summer at the game store.

What was her name?

Ao-… Ao-something.

No. That was her character's name. The elf mage princess. A princess.

Ao-something.

He tasted the name and remembered it. He laughed, once. Sharply. A laugh tinged with something else. He'd had no thought of that name since... well... since a long time ago.

His short laugh, in reflection, was more a dry bark of self-loathing, he thought.

Whenever Mason thought of the concept of "innocence," throughout the years of life being quite the opposite of that word, without ever thinking about it much, his mind had always pictured her even though he hadn't thought about the quiet, shy girl, since... long ago.

Now with his sightless eyes, he could see her once more. She was precious and made of porcelain. Delicate with the tiniest of soprano whispers. She had golden hair and large oval glasses.

"When did I stop thinking about her?" he said aloud to the surf and the night. And the world. Blind. Thirsty. And with no idea what to do next, he wondered aloud, "When did I stop thinking about her?"

In that moment Mason knew life was a far crazier thing than sudden life-changing blindness. Life was crazy enough to make you forget the person you'd first loved and thought you'd never love again. It was the blindness that forced him, allowed him, to go back to her once more. After all these years.

After West Point.

After both Iraqs.

After Somalia.

After Afghanistan and every other place the CIA had sent him to do intel analysis... and the occasional odd task.

He'd forgotten something important along the way, and he'd never known it.

He realized time was a thief. A cruel thief who steals only what you value most, and heartlessly, not knowing the stolen treasure's value. Caring little for what was once most cared for.

"You'll forget her," Owen had warned him on that hot August night when they roamed quiet streets together, talking. When they were just fifteen and the world was ending. "Because it hurts too much to remember. Trust me!" he'd squeaked in the silence. "I know about love."

The surf advanced and receded again and again as the night plodded through its courses.

"You were right, Owen," croaked Mason hours later after staring through the glass display case of his mind at so many lost memories. Seeing so many things once more on this long night of sightlessness. "You were right. As usual, Owen."

In time, he can feel the morning sun.

Barely.

At just after nine, Mason can see. The light stabs into his eyes. He holds his hands up as a shield and finds he is looking back at the long runway of LAX in the distance. Wrecked airliners litter the field. Some have even smashed into the terminal. Columns of black oily smoke rise up from the sea of apocalypse wreckage and are carried away by winter winds aloft. Beyond that, the city of Los Angeles itself is in flames. A massive anvil of black smoke climbs up over the sprawling city. He can see as far away as Beverly Hills and the low hills beyond. He sees the firestorms there also. To the north he watches flames racing up the sides of the Santa Monica Mountains toward Malibu.

Where there is not black smoke and fire there is drifting haze and ash.

He tries to find the 787, flight 208, inbound from Singapore, somewhere along the sides of the runway. But all the airplanes have smashed themselves into each other and are burned or burning. Only large tail sections or massive, lonely engines remain within the stretch of scattered disaster. Everything else is gone, burnt to ash and melted tin, along with the body of Owen Matthew.

The package in the belly of the 787.

The package he was ordered to bring home.

The Scroll of Darkness

COSMO Van Roos started to feel sick two hours after he opened the letter. Cosmo would never be able to link one to the other. No one really would've been able to conclude that any of the seemingly harmless letters or other innocuous infection points were connected with the raging virus that would shortly devastate their bodies and change their lives. At first, they knew only that a horrible flu was assaulting them, violently. They had no idea about what was really happening.

This was three days before the blindness.

The letter had called him, Mr. Van Roos, a "monster." Nothing new there, Cosmo had thought. The whiners were always calling him a monster for the things he did. Deriding him for the ways and means he employed to win time and time again against the losers who could do nothing but complain because they were incapable of competing. Especially against him. Against someone who played to win, no matter what.

The letter had said, "Dear Mr. Van Roos— You are a monster." It had gone on to call him a "chaotic evil bloodsucker." He'd scanned the letter mostly. He got dozens a week. Mainly due to the fact he'd blocked development six months ago on a competing malaria drug patent because he had that particular market cornered in Southeast Asia and the new rival drug would have dried up demand by effectively reducing some of the more lethal consequences of Plasmodium falciparum malaria. So he'd bought the competing bright little biotech R&D startup with its big dreams of crashing his cash cow and promptly fired the researchers. When they tried to take their groundbreaking research with them, he had his lawyers seize everything for evidence in some heavy-duty litigation he was planning on drawing out for the foreseeable future. Probably he'd clear another two hundred million by the time everything got resolved. Or they'd give up because they ran out of cash to fight him in court. Either way was a win. For Cosmo Van Roos.

Whatever. Whiners. He was in the mood for some Wu-Tang Clan.

He threw the letter down on his glass-topped twenty-seat dining room table. The letter ended, "… you will live like the monster you are." Signed, "Justly, Eowen."

Four hours later, he was completely delirious. He'd barely enough presence of mind to cancel a Zoom call with two new researchers he was about to advance enough money to finish their clinical trials on a low-cost HIV retroviral they were developing for sickle-cell anemia candidates. It would be a huge relief to the ravaged populations of sub-Saharan Africa. After. Important word. *After* he'd marked it up one thousand percent and made the UN force all the NGOs to buy it for their relief work.

He had just enough presence of mind not to mess up that easy moneymaker by pulling a no-show for the online meeting. This flu is the monster, he laughed to himself, and felt his insides ache with a sudden soreness that seemed unwarranted. The two researchers were desperate for cash. Desperate enough to come to him because they thought they were smarter than him.

Laugh. Out. Loud.

Which he did, as much as he could without crying out in pain, as he downed half a bottle of NyQuil and then climbed the stairs to the master suite of his Malibu beach house. Casa de Scarface, he liked to joke.

"Cancel the girls…" he mumbled, his eidetic mind going through a snapshot of his daily calendar one last time before the biomechanical-induced fever carried him away for the next three days. The college girls, call girls, he kept on retainer would knock and knock, but in the end would go away when he failed to answer the door. Secretly they were glad because he was so creepy. They'd often remarked to each other they "didn't need the money that badly."

Meanwhile Cosmo fell into a strange and euphoric dream much like many would soon be having. Some would think of it as the most horrible nightmare they'd ever experienced. Others, a very few, found it to be a kind of paradise they'd longed for all along, and had given up hope of ever finding now that they were locked up for their various crimes against humanity. Of the five serial killers currently prowling the I-5 corridor, all five felt the same way about the dream as Cosmo Van Roos did.

It was beautiful.

The Scroll of Now

MASON hears the sirens before he sees the moving emergency vehicles. Some. A few vehicles moving in a long convoy. In the distance the fires seem to be growing. From his place along the sandy ridge of the dunes that watch over the beach, Mason can see lone figures and even clusters of people moving south. Away from the growing firestorm in the north and east of Los Angeles.

He tries his phone. He gets a signal. He gets his news feed.

The news is from yesterday morning. Nothing new.

An hour later the phone won't be working.

Mason kicks sand across the ashy embers of his fire and heads back down to the road. He walks along it until he comes to an intersection. He's dying for a drink of water.

Farther down the street he sees a small commercial strip mall. When he arrives, full-scale looting is in progress. People are running from a big-box home electronics store with giant-screen TVs. Sometimes even two. A few lie smashed in the parking lot. Mason spies a liquor store at the corner and crosses the dirty oil-stained and pothole-strewn parking lot. A man pushes a grocery cart loaded with beer and snacks away from the store and coasts, riding the cart across the parking lot before he hits a pothole and dumps his goods.

Inside the liquor store a fat guy behind the counter is holding up a large bottle of Jack Daniel's, the plastic drunk-proof kind, to his lips. It's down to a quarter of sloshy fuel-colored alcohol. He grins stupidly at Mason and goes after the rest with gusto. Mason hears the man smack his fat lips together after a breathy "aahhhh."

The water case is virtually untouched.

Mason takes a bottle and drinks. He finishes the whole bottle and takes another of the larger ones to carry with him as he walks. He grabs some beef jerky and Corn Nuts and stuffs them in his dress slacks and coat pockets. For a moment he thinks he should pay, but whoever should be paid isn't there and the fat guy behind the counter doesn't seem interested in anything other than the porn mag he's laid out on the counter as he starts to break the seal on the next drunk-sized bottle of Jack.

Outside, Mason checks his phone.

A car races by the strip mall pushing well over a hundred. It's a Lamborghini heading south along the beach.

PRESIDENT DECLARES STATE OF EMERGENCY

Mason stares at the headline. There's no story. Just the headline. A moment later, after he tries to refresh the page on his smartphone, he's looking at a blank screen.

Survival Mode.

It just appears in his head. Like an order. A command. And he knows exactly what it means. He knows there's no weekend fix to whatever's going down. There's no business as usual by Monday morning. Plans are canceled. The government, which has barely been of any real help to anyone lately, is offline. Indefinitely.

Survival Mode.

"Our darkest day is ahead of us!"

An hour later he's found a local mall. He loads up a hiking pack with freeze-dried snacks and what few other supplies he can cobble together. There isn't much else left in the store. They don't sell guns anymore in California and most everything else has been taken. Even the hunting knives. He does find an arctic-rated sleeping bag and he attaches that to his ruck along with a few D-clips he finds near the register.

As he's doing this, he smells smoke inside the mall. The fire alarms go off and then stop. Electricity fails inside the large bright space of the mall and it makes little difference due to the skylights above, other than the creepy feeling of knowing the power isn't there anymore. He looks out along the wide two-story concourse of the shadowy barely day-lit mall as looters come out from the stores, smelling the smoke, casting about for its source. When it's not readily evident, they return to the stores and their ravaging. Their piles of hastily assembled clothing, purses, and even video games.

Mason leaves the massive shopping complex and when he's reached the parking lot's far end, he sees black smoke erupting out from the second-story café of Nordstrom. The smoke rises too quickly in great huffs of black indignation. In no time, the entire mall will be on fire and Mason knows many of the looters will be trapped and burned alive.

Survival Mode.

Three blocks later, Mason finds the dead woman.

A gunshot to her head. She's near a bus stop. Along the bench of the bus stop a pile of loot waits, draped across the back of the bench. The woman lies in the grass behind the bench, in front of a dark Denny's. Blood is still running away from her body and down through the grass where it's begun to pool and congeal along the dirty sidewalk.

Mason knows from the state of the blood this has happened recently.

Just like Owen, he thinks, and then pushes that, and himself, away from the place he sees and the thought he doesn't want to think.

He's heading toward the freeway, walking east. None of the cars he's come across are working. Some even have the keys still in the ignition. But when he tries to start them, nothing happens. No crank, no stutter, no *click-click-click*.

Nothing.

The sirens he heard back on the dunes overlooking the wreckage of LAX are completely absent. He hasn't heard any since he entered the mall. Behind him, a few blocks back, the mall is now completely in flames. Smoke rises from other places blocked by the houses and businesses that line the street. And to the north, near Santa Monica, the evil vulture that was the black anvil of smoke has grown into a demonic mass of roiling oily dark hatred.

It's noon and the sun beats down from directly overhead. He raids another looted liquor store, stocks up on water and jerky, and takes a pint of tequila that has somehow survived the pillaging.

By three o'clock he makes the wide cut of the 405 freeway. The traffic jam that it always is at nine o'clock in the morning, when the blindness happened yesterday, is still there over twenty-four hours later. The endless cars are abandoned. People are walking along the freeway casting backward glances over their shoulders at the growing firestorm in the north. From atop the freeway, Mason can see dozens of pillars of smoke rising from downtown and many other places throughout the LA basin. Drifting ash falls like lazy snow. He takes the camping scarf he looted from the sporting goods store and makes a shemagh out of it by wrapping it around his neck and face.

Most of the people on the freeway are not looters. They're scared and they're moving toward safety. Wherever that is. Mason knows he's going to need a weapon soon. He knows things are about to get lawless. He falls in behind a large group and begins to move south along the freeway.

The Scroll of Evil

ON day three of the flu, Cosmo crawled from bed. Literally. He knew, dimly, that he needed food. Where was his smartphone? He was still wearing the Italian slacks and silk button-down he'd put on three days ago before the Zoom meeting with the geeks he was going to buy out and hike the price on their "miracle drug." It had been the middle of the day then. And he'd had various lucid moments since, where he'd popped back up to the surface of consciousness after almost drowning in a hot sea of sweat-fever. Popped up and saw that it was night, and the moon was out and sinking into the Pacific. He'd crawled across the moonlit carpet to his designer bathroom for a drink of cool water, but he'd been so weak and the blown glass sinks from Milan that had cost him a mint were so high up and out of reach from his current Italian marble floor altitude. So high up they might as well be a myth. The myth of cold water to drive away a worst-ever thirsty fever.

So yes, eventually he'd drunk from the closer-to-hand toilet. But it was so cool and refreshing to his flaming skull. So cold and...

Hours, or maybe another day altogether later, he'd awoken back in his wide and unmade bed. He was convinced he was dying. His mind felt as though it had been eaten alive by tiny insects. Or locusts. As though monsters had eaten all the higher functions he'd once so cherished and left his body with little more than a few caveman functions. He, Cosmo Van Roos, deep down inside and watching, was a puppeteer now. He felt as though he was pulling worn and fraying rusty wires deep within himself just to raise an eyelid, which, at that searing moment when the sun scorched the palatial master suite and bounced off the mirrored ceiling as it sank like a fiery sore, was all he could do.

You're being re-coded. Overwritten.

Your hard drive has crashed, gangster.

But that was just the flotsam of the material he'd been studying for the retroviral investment floating to the fever pool his mind was drowning in. That's what the new drug would do to the human immunodeficiency virus. The drug he would shortly own.

The money, money, money, money, money, money, money…

It was just what the miracle retroviral he was about to buy out was supposed to do to the deadly virus. It was supposed to invade it and then rewrite it, effectively making it useless. Nanobiotechnology. It would still be there. But it couldn't do any more harm because it had been rewritten.

These crazy thoughts about being rewritten were just work floating to the top of his brain in the throes of a fever. He was still him. He wasn't going to disappear. He was… not… a… monster.

"Sure," he mumbled and swooned, passing out for another three full hours before waking up with, "…'cause I was reading all their lit-literature. Not being re… rewritten. S-silly. S-silly."

It felt like streams of ice water were rushing through his shaking frame as the chills became violent. In a little while they'd be downright homicidal as they contorted and twisted his pain-wracked body. And he still hadn't gone to the Night Kingdom, not yet. But he was sick and getting sicker. Much sicker. And the gateway to the Night Kingdom was way down below. Right where he was falling.

The Scroll of Coincidence

IT'S later, toward a dusk turned hellish red, in front of which ash drifts like light sleet, that Mason and the other survivors he's been following crawl down off the freeway where it intersects with the 710 out of Long Beach and walk through a downed mesh fence into a wide and open area where ancient oil derricks have cleared a space within the unending urban sprawl.

They start a fire composed of brush and found oily wooden pallets as a few alpha types try to organize the rest and themselves. Business types with leadership skills and many, many management seminars out at the Airport Hyatt under their belts, Mason suspects. Many of the others talk of the blindness. Its sudden appearance and its sudden departure. Darkness falls and the sky glows red in the north like a furnace, or Hell, or a furnace in that damned place if such a place existed. Flames can be seen even at this distance, leaping hundreds of feet into the air. The glow reaches its zenith over downtown LA.

The skyscrapers must be on fire.

A man named Bill tells everyone they need to get some sleep and he asks for volunteers to keep a watch. Mason takes a shift toward midnight. He doesn't sleep before his shift and when it's his turn to feed the campfire and watch over the huddled mass of survivors, he does. An hour later he taps a guy he only knows as Ken on the shoulder, makes sure he's up and doing his job, then finds a spot on the ground and lies back without unrolling his sleeping bag.

He's seen the other survivors looking at his pack. Most of the things they've looted are useless and now lie neglected along the sides of the freeway. Better to be ready to move. Just in case.

He uncaps the pint of tequila and takes a small pull as he watches dark ash drift across the night-early-morning-late turned red and gray.

At dawn there is fog and Mason has been lying awake thinking back about Hell's Highway in Iraq. Thinking about Owen standing there amidst all the wrecked Iraqi combat vehicles and burning T-72s. Mason had been sent there to do an assessment update on what was left of the retreating Iraqi forces. Flame-mummified corpses hang from the hatches of a long line of shot-up BMPs. Pieces of random, jagged, heat-blasted metal lie along the highway. Vehicles that had tried to get off the road, out of the way of the tanks, as the avenging A-10s made pass after pass, shooting up the entire column.

Second Lieutenant Mason is trying to take pictures of some of the unit identifications on the scorched and melt-ed vehicles when he hears the squawk of his oldest friend behind him. The squawk he has known most of his life. Since those rubber-band wars. Those other wars.

"It was a success!" Owen exclaims.

Mason turns to find Owen in khaki fatigues and an olive shirt. He's wearing dark aviator shades and a pith helmet.

"Just like that time we killed the hydra!"

Mason smiles, which is difficult with his Kevlar strapped across his chin. But the intel platoon sergeant he's come out here with has regaled them all with horrifying stories of VC snipers lying among the dead back in 'Nam.

Waiting for the intel guys to show up so they can take a shot. So no one's taking any chances even though this battle is three days old.

Mason and Owen hug.

Two best friends from another "when" some still called Southern California, here, at another end of the world. Or so it looked back in 1991 with oil fields burning and jets streaking overhead.

Rocking everyone like a hurricane.

A long way from Viejo Verde.

"What're you doing here?" Mason asks.

"The company!" shrieks Owen. "Same as you!"

Everyone knows "the company" means the CIA. Second Lieutenant Mason is attached to the 4th Armored Division's intelligence section.

"I'm not with the company. I'm in the army, Owen."

Owen stops, thinks about this, and then raises his chin and nods once. "Oh yeah. Not yet. Soon though. Or at least that's what I heard 'em say."

Each turns to survey the damage to an entire Iraqi column done to death among the burning sands. The desert wind whistles through the 30mm Swiss-cheesed holes in the wreckage.

Mason has not seen Owen since that night when they walked the hot August streets and Owen told young Mason, fifteen years old then, that he would forget the girl he loved. Forget Ao-something the elven princess. A week later the game store would be closed, and Owen would be shipped off to the New Mexico Military Academy. Jeff Deacon would be in juvenile hall, facing murder charges. Then it's just Scott Ott and Mason. They would be best friends through what remained of high school.

Through what remained of the lie that was Viejo Verde. The facade that was reality.

"What do you mean, it was a success, just like the… hydra?" Mason shakes his head slightly, feeling like a teenage dork. He's an officer now. A fighting man. Their Saturday afternoon games were just that. Games for kids. Boys who'd read too much Tolkien. This was real war.

"Don't you remember?" Owen whines. "Don't you remember the sunken Tower of the Lizard King? It was just like that. Except this time, I didn't get crushed."

Mason shakes his head in disbelief. Somehow Owen is likening all this to a game, a role-playing game that had absorbed most of a couple of years. And at the same time, he's taking credit for all this death and destruction along some foreign highway on the other side of the world. Mason only vaguely remembers the event Owen is referring to.

But he remembers it clearly now, at dawn, lying in the dirt among the other refugees. In the fog and the drifting smoke, he remembers the details, and nuances, of the hydra and the Tower of the Lizard King.

The Scroll of Adventure

BUT before the story of the hydra can be told, there are all the seemingly endless days leading up to it.

"Seemingly endless… isn't that how we remember thinking about those days?" Owen had waxed to Mason in the hours before his death. "Those long days when we were young… they were without end in our minds. As though there was an unlimited supply of them and thus would be the shape of all our days. Or was it the 'seeming' part, Mason? Did we always know, then, it was all just an illusion? A facade?"

Did we?

Owen knew. Knew long before Mason and Charlie Schwartzsky. Knew long before anyone else.

Before the death of the hydra on that best of all Saturday afternoons, in days that followed the twilight in which Owen told of how he'd finally found someone to play Dungeons and Dragons with. Well, that had been a day three years in the making.

Owen had read *The Lord of the Rings* long before anyone else, before any of their other friends. One summer, while at his grandmother's house, he was told all about a game called Dungeons and Dragons by a distant cousin whom he'd only met a handful of times. From that moment on, it was Owen's personal quest to play at least one game of Dungeons and Dragons with someone. He found a small and quiet bookstore that was willing to order him a copy of the game. It came in a box. Three booklets and a module called "The Keep on the Borderlands." It was a fairly complex game to understand, and the truth is, what with the way Owen's mind worked, he didn't completely grasp it. Owen's mind was never good at logic. At step-by-step conclusions. He was better at the intuitive leap. The big guesses. Conceptualizing things other people hadn't even thought of. What business gurus would eventually call "thinking outside the box" in the twilight of American business before the Dark Age of its final days.

But back then, during the early 1980s, Owen tried to understand the mystifying game all by himself. Alone, day after day, studying the pages and handouts and arcane-shaped dice. Imagine moving from Chutes and Ladders, or Clue, to a role-playing game which is akin to acting out a movie but with math writing the script. As time progressed, even the eternally optimistic Owen knew he needed someone to show him exactly how to play it. He'd read every rule. Studied all the charts. Stared for hour after hour at all the intricate pictures and even daydreamed adventures of what he might do if he were in the place of each of the heroes represented in each of the pictures, or the scenarios contained within the colorful booklets. Attacking a green dragon in a swampy tomb. Confronting the surprised, unopposed, and evidently perturbed red dragon atop a pile of hoard as depicted on the box the game came within. Dealing with the mad hermit who lived in the tree or fighting the strange bear-shaped monster with the beak maw. He'd imagined each and every scenario and how he might tactically take advantage of any given situation, regardless of the dice.

Regardless of the chances.

Finally, that weekend, Owen, who was one for wandering long and wide back in the days when boys might rise on a Saturday morning and be out before their parents awoke and not return until near or even after dark without causing fear or raising alarm, found the quiet little game store in a recently built commercial center beyond the train tracks that cleft Viejo Verde in two, whether the Community Planners of the Future liked it or not. The railroad had weight back then. It was something to be reckoned with. Back then.

He'd gone into the tiny store, Owen explained to Mason, and seen some other boys gathered around a, "Campaign table!" he shrieked. A big plastic map was laid out and everyone clustered about a drawn diagram of a dungeon. There were miniatures and paper and multicolored polyhedral dice. "I need to buy a twenty-sider!" exclaimed Owen to Mason. "A lucky one even though there's no such thing as luck because you make your own," he added in his suddenly sober philosopher's tone.

"Is this Dungeons and Dragons?" he'd interrogated these boys in his high squeaky squawk.

It was.

Could he play? he'd squawked at them again like a deranged crow, or so Mason imagined. Crows always reminded Mason of Owen. Even now. Even more so now.

They, the nerds gathered about the campaign table, didn't seem all that interested in Owen playing with them.

"They weren't very sociable!" Owen announced to Mason the afternoon he held out the box containing the Dungeons and Dragons game. "But before I knew it... I was playing!" And then he was killed by a minotaur. For the rest of the afternoon, he watched the other boys continue to play without him. He was captivated and didn't mind being marginalized by death in the least. Even though he suspected they'd let him die just to get rid of him for the afternoon.

"Once you're dead, you're dead!" Owen lectured Mason. "But I'll be back!"

"Now," he explained to Mason that Wednesday afternoon, "I know what I did wrong. I felt I could influence events by how I did things! I had no idea the dice were so influential. They control the game!"

Mason had no idea what Owen was talking about as he examined the warrior and the wizard on the front of the cardboard box.

"It's a numbers game," Owen erupted as though he'd just discovered that the backroom card game he'd encountered at some speakeasy was rigged.

"But you're not good at math," Mason observed.

"I'm terrible!" Owen agreed. "But you're not. So this Saturday, will you come with me and we can try to play? If they'll let us."

Mason studied the warrior on the box. He was shooting an arrow at the peeved red dragon who would no doubt whip the wizard and warrior to pieces. In *The Lord of the Rings* he liked the warriors and the swordfights. He liked reading about Aragorn and Gimli and Legolas and even the Riders of Rohan and of course the Uruk-hai. All of them were "doers." That was a word his dad used a lot. "Doers." Men of action. The wizards seemed too bound up to ever do anything.

"I finished *The Fellowship of the Ring* last night. Is it like that?" Mason asked, referencing the game in the box in the boy's hands.

"Better!" Owen said. "But wait until you get to the Battle for Helm's Deep! That's pretty good."

That Friday night, the night before he would wake in the morning for an early baseball game and be back by noon and in his street clothes and off with Owen down through the lower sections of Mediterranean Heights, Mason was reading about the Battle for Helm's Deep. In the morning, Owen and Mason would cross the big green park near their elementary school, then down into the brush and over a small creek, out into the area known as "the Train Tracks" and then up into the new business center where the game store was. On Mason's desk nearby, Owen's box of Dungeons and Dragons waited.

"Study this!" Owen had ordered Mason in the gloaming with all the seriousness of a Lafayette to his drill sergeants. As though lives and the very cause of liberty, and the state of the world, depended on it.

As though.

Late into the night, long past midnight, Mason looked out his window after all the lights were out in all the other houses.

Except for Owen's.

From Owen's room in the house on the hill above his own he saw a lone light in the window.

The Scroll of the Ruyn

THE Night Kingdom.

When the invading virus really gets down to business, Cosmo is out of his mind, writhing, sweating, and groaning. But there is no one within his party-pad palace to hear the most aspiring of princelings of business and venture capital shriek in agony. To watch him is to think he is in that great amount of pain and suffering as so many wish him to be. That he is cognizant of his torment. But he is not.

Cosmo's silent palace never minds the blindness and the blossoming firestorms that ring Los Angeles. Its quiet is more mausoleum than palace. Except for the mindless groans and bouts of shrieking torment as though someone were stretched on the rack and their bones were being shifted. There is a dry crack, crack, crack that echoes within Cosmo's mind.

But his conscious mind has long been descended into the nether of his virus-clogged subconscious. His mind has swirled away from the pain and sunk into this feverish bliss way down deep in the howling night swamp that is his soul. On his way to some other place the virus never planned or knew of.

The Night Kingdom is always an unexpected detour on a dark night.

Here, the virus is not here, could not reach here. Here, wherever here is, is the Night Kingdom. Accessed solely by Cosmo Van Roos. The Night Kingdom is at once a swamp, and a city, and a quiet carnival if there can be such a thing. Van Roos is bathed in cold electricity as he wanders from macabre to macabre, thrilling at, and drinking in, each new delicious horror. He's drifted over pungent mushrooms that explode in eruptions of hallucinogenic poison, drowning the drug-addled gray wraiths all around him once more, much to their giddy delight. Who are these wraiths, he wonders as he drifts by toward that town on the hill above. Who were they? And the answer that returns to him out of the croaking cacophony of the hot eternal night is that they were him, sort of. In a way. He glides on toward the town on the hill knowing that its name is both ancient and home to him all at once.

Ruyn Towne on the old tor.

Ruyn Towne.

On the old Barrow Tor.

He slips along the silent twisting lanes of the village, passing thatched cottages somehow psychotically askew and insensibly off-kilter. Behind tiny framed windows, red guttering candles reveal horrific shadows doing terrible things.

The suffering and torment from within is like music to a drifting shade and he remembers, later, when he is not right in his mind but mostly back in his body, he remembers that those blue shadows along the crooked lanes were where he first understood the freedom.

The freedom.

The freedom to do anything. To be… anything. To do anything.

No longer restrained by law and morality… y'know, freedom like the kind only true sociopaths know. In that nightmare town beside the unseen babbling brook, as visible as a shade and as real as a threat, he would remember that knowing of a kind of freedom. Savoring it like it was a thing that could be tasted on the tongue and felt between the claws.

Expecting it like a lover waiting for the surprise to be revealed and for the lusty satisfaction surely promised.

He journeyed on, passing the tavern. He knew it was a tavern from the roar and cackle coming into the without where he waited. He knew there were monster-beings and demonic trolls delighting in the misfortunes, and savoring in the sufferings, of others there. The suffering of the weak was the bill of fare in that wonderful tavern. He was sure of it and he promised himself many a fine old time on its boards.

He promised himself this as he drifted on toward the "other side" atop the Barrow Tor. This was truly home. More home than any other home he could not now re-member in this deepest of fevers.

He knows this.

By the small bridge that crossed over the Drowning Creek, above the creeping moss-covered stones and the large rust-stained boulder, he stopped. Ahead was a howl-ing plain in the distance, swept by the winds of ruin. An undiscovered country just seen. A firestorm to play in.

It was the freedom.

It was night forever.

And the fever suddenly broke and the work was done, and he felt all the pain in every part of his ravaged body. The dry ache in the husk that had once been Cosmo Van Roos was gone. There was only a new pain screaming out from every nerve ending, as though his body had surely been stretched beyond the breaking point on one of those racks he must have passed in the village, that sweet village he could no longer remember the name of.

Surely…

He screamed in torment.

He. Screamed.

In utter torment.

And he was back.

The Scroll of Knowing

MASON and the other survivors walk through the drifting smoke and falling ash. There seem to be fewer of the other survivors from the night before. Some had wanted to start moving early.

"Let's wait and see if help shows up," a woman had pleaded with everyone.

But the fire in the north was getting worse, which didn't seem possible every time you looked at it. How could the most horrifying thing you'd ever seen get worse? Until the next time you looked at it and it'd gotten bigger, its bellows heaving like the chest of some raging dark giant towering over everything, rising thousands if not tens of thousands of feet into the glowing red and storm-gray sky.

Even if help showed up, lady, thought Mason as he tried to guess how high the anvil of black smoke that seemed to be moving toward them was, it wouldn't be enough.

They went back to the freeway, climbing up the plant-covered embankment they'd trampled down the night before, and continued south, weaving in and out of the ash-covered cars. Alongside the freeway, the urban sprawl was dead and motionless. There was no one out along the frozen streets. There were no lights, no electricity, and no fires, for now.

Civilization's ending was so fast, it still didn't seem real, even now. But then you looked closer and saw buildings without power, and corpses in the streets. Corpses no homicide squad would ever investigate, no morgue would ever come to pick up. No funeral home would ever prepare, no grave would ever welcome. No headstone would remember, and no tears would be shed over on the green grass all around a cemetery that the body would never rest in.

"The world has changed," whispered Mason under his breath and felt like he'd just made a gross understatement.

In time, lost in thought, Mason found himself alone along the freeway. He turned, wondering when the last of his fellow survivors had dropped off to the side of the freeway, probably in search of food, water, or a backpack like the one Mason had.

He had no idea.

He turned toward the south again. A long line of never-again-moving cars lay under a blanket of thick ash. He was in Seal Beach now, and he continued to walk and think about Owen and the game store and all the other past remembrances that awaited him on the road ahead.

The Scroll of the Night King

WHAT Cosmo Van Roos saw in the mirror, the day after the fever broke, when he was finally able to stumble into the palatial bathroom once more, was not a monster.

What he saw by the pale illumination cast through a high skylight was himself, his true self... and he was beautiful.

The tiny biomechanical machines that had invaded his system four days ago had mostly finished. They'd done their work both internal and external.

Where Cosmo saw pale perfect sculpted skin, the virus machines had savaged his melatonin to the point of zero viability, and as a nice touch they'd rewritten his DNA and added the code for the gene that caused porphyria.

Where Cosmo marveled at his almost perfect skin, the machines had again gone to work on the DNA, re-coding cellular regeneration's marching orders for a finite existence, this far and no farther, to infinite, renewing and renewing forever.

And when he smiled, almost giddy though he still felt weak as a kitten from the violence of the fever, as though he were some kind of weird lottery winner or airplane disaster survivor, he caught his first hint of the so much unseen that lay beneath the almost perfect and tightened alabaster skin.

What he saw when he smiled were the fangs.

They flashed slowly as his fever-weakened facial muscles automatically chose delight. But once they were out, an ivory white shining in the antiseptic light of the expensive designer bathroom, well, they were out. But beyond the visible, the machines had done so much more. His bone density was altered, the machines manufacturing virtually indestructible bio-ceramic out of an abundance of iron-rich blood, reducing the weight of the bones while at the same time strengthening them by a factor of almost fifty. The hypothalamus and adrenal glands were now manufacturing their very own versions of a DARPA-developed secret steroid recipe that tripled strength in the soldiers it had once been tested on. The nanobots had been able to improve on that significantly; now there would be much, much more strength available on demand. As long as there was iron, there would be strength and life seemingly eternal, which would seem, to the greedy Cosmo Van Roos, like a wish from a bottle for a greedy child.

But that was never what the genie had intended. Never ever. Cosmo Van Roos would learn and live to regret by design. Yes. Yes he would.

But not now.

And isn't that the best kind of prison? The one that seems a palace at first and a never-ending hell a little bit later. Forever, in fact. Isn't that the perfect kind of punishment?

Whoever Eowen was, she must've thought such.

No, right now what Cosmo Van Roos saw in the mirror was not a monster. He did not see a thing that would never again witness the light of day, though he was not aware yet of the porphyria raging across his cellular structure or realize that even direct, electrically provided light would, in time, prove far too painful as it left its first-degree burns after less than a minute. Not that there was much of that electricity left now that the blindness had come and gone and all those heat-twisted jetliners lay cooling among the ashes. Yes. Yes, the world had changed.

Cosmo Van Roos did not see a monster that would need access to protein-based iron in abundant amounts to survive, though there was something starting to ache deep down there in the hierarchy of needs as the limbic system began to make its survival demands on the cortex. He saw none of that and all that he'd been transformed into.

All Cosmo Van Roos saw was himself, his true self, and the fangs.

As though the fangs were him in full.

As though they were what he'd always wanted—no, *needed*—to do what he had to do to win. To become what he'd intended to be all along, right from the very start. To feed on the weak not just for life, because what was life… without power?

For power.

He saw himself, and he was beautiful.

And very, very… hungry.

The Scroll of the Hydra

THAT Saturday, that first Saturday, they finally arrived at the little game store that lay at the end of the small business center. It wasn't a strip mall. It was a center. It had a design. Dark wooden structures all laid out reminiscent of some type of quaint English village. There was a Chinese restaurant. A video store. A dentist. The bookstore Owen was a frequent lingerer in. An Italian restaurant no one ever seemed to go to. A quiet bank. The liquor store at the far end. And finally, just before that, the game store.

The game store was called The Game Shoppe.

Inside, polished glass display cases were filled with small hand-painted miniatures standing guard. Shelves upon shelves where all types of boxed games awaited purchase. The fronts of these boxes, and sometimes just thick booklets, showed battles ranging through every time period, or starships destroying each other, or a Cthulhoid monster's slithering tentacles clutching at post-nuclear war survivors. Near the back of the narrow store lay dartboards and accessories. Flights and tips and hand-tooled leather carrying pouches. And finally, in the very back, waited the wide campaign table.

An older man ran the game store. Owen smiled and waved cheerily at him as they entered, Owen charging and Mason slinking along behind.

"Hi, Boyd!" Owen exclaimed as he waved.

Boyd cast baleful, bloodhound eyes down at the tiny Owen and managed a tired wave of his thick mobster's hand toward the boys. When he replied with a "Hello," his voice was husky and dry from years of habitual cigarette smoke.

A group of teenage boys were gathered around the campaign table, all slightly older than Mason and Owen. Mason immediately identified them as nerds. The science club kids. Kids you'd never see going out for baseball.

"Hi, guys!" exclaimed Owen.

All of them turned at the startling appearance of Owen's unmistakable squawk, muttered something, and returned to their binders and charts. Some were unlatching cases full of tiny miniatures. Taking up a particular one and inspecting it as though they were jewelers appraising rare stones.

Owen and Mason stood there. Waiting.

"What now?" Mason whispered.

Owen shrugged and gave Mason a wide-eyed look. Apparently this was as far as Owen had planned. Or more likely, this part had not been planned at all. The game, yes. Getting into the game... no.

They waited.

"Do you guys have characters?" asked one of the nerds. A slight, thin boy with wispy blond hair. He was as pale as a lamb. His eyes were hard and piercing. Later they would learn his name was Kyle. Kyle Andersen.

"No!" squeaked Owen. And then, "We don't even know how to play!"

Several of the nerds, there were eight in all, visibly winced but continued staring intently at their tiny miniatures and papers, or thumbing through various bound books and then making annotations on paper with pencils.

Kyle sighed and dove into a large thick binder.

"I'm only giving you one, the other guy will have to copy. This is a character sheet," he said, holding out a piece of paper with arcane markings on it.

"I don't think René is going to let them play. This is a sixth through eighth module. They'll get killed," said one boy.

Kyle shot a hard look at the kid who'd questioned him and then motioned toward Boyd who seemed to be staring off into nothing out the highly polished glass window at the front of the store.

"It's a game store, Rob," said Kyle. "Emphasis on store. If they learn how to play, they might actually buy a player's handbook and the store will be able to stay in business, which means we'll have a place to play games instead of at my house."

Rob computed, then nodded, returning to his binder.

Kyle swiveled his intense and highly unnerving gaze back to Owen and Mason.

"Have a seat." He motioned toward some folding chairs and a place near him at one end of the campaign table. Once they'd unfolded and placed the metal chairs, Kyle pushed dice across the table at them.

"You can *borrow* these dice for today... Today only. You wanna play next week you gotta buy dice, at least."

Owen and Mason nodded. Mason had the distinct feeling he was joining something. Or trying out, even. He also had the feeling that given the slightest reason, they, he and Owen, would be denied entry and chased from the store. It would be wise, thought Mason, to remain silent.

"Can we buy one set of dice and share?" asked Owen.

The look Kyle gave Owen was withering. But he glanced up and over Mason's shoulder at where Boyd was sitting, perched like some retired ancient gargoyle still watching the sides of the cathedral for form's sake. A shrug or nod must have given Kyle an answer to Owen's imperceptive, if not impolite, question.

"Sure," answered Kyle curtly.

"That's good!" whispered Owen too loudly and elbowed Mason. Owen's parents were notoriously tight with money.

"Now, one of you is going to need to make a copy of the character sheet. Here's a piece of paper."

"Do you have any pens?" Owen squeaked.

"Pencils," ordered Kyle pedantically. "We only use pencils."

"Why?" Owen asked.

"Because things change. You might gain a level and then your stats would change."

"Or get life drained by a wight or a vampire," interjected Rob. "Then you'd go back down a level."

Someone groaned and muttered. Apparently they'd been life-drained recently.

"I wanna be a magic user!" Owen announced. "A wizard!"

Mason knew he wanted to play a fighter. Like the guy on the cover of a module called "Into the Unknown." A fighter with a winged helmet and a beard, carrying a spear. He liked that picture. Even though the green dragon in the picture looked wickedly tough, Mason was sure the fighter was going to mess that dragon up.

"Well, you'll have to roll some dice and then we'll see what kind of character you can make," said Kyle.

"You mean I don't get to choose?" Owen erupted.

"No."

"Why not?"

"Because you have to have the *stats* to play certain characters. You can't have a three intelligence and be a magic user. You'd be a lousy magic user! C'mon, guy!" He said this last bit as though this were common knowledge that surely everyone with a brain knew. The other nerds concurred, chortled, or simply snorted as they continued to labor-mutter within their binders.

"I'd like to be a warrior," mumbled Mason.

Kyle looked at him for a long moment. The look was almost kindly. Of all the people in the room Mason was the one you knew was an athlete. A jock. A cool kid. People liked Mason. They always had. Even if they didn't want to.

Now, trudging along the ash-covered 405, entering Huntington Beach alone on a smoke-dark afternoon that was turning strangely cold, Mason told himself, "People liked me when I was young. And I never knew it."

"Well, let's roll some dice," Kyle had said that long-ago day that was lost and now seemed found as Mason trudged along the silent highway. "And we'll see."

They rolled dice. They got to roll five six-sided dice and take the three best dice for each stat. One of the nerds, a chubby boy named Andy, told them that wasn't how you actually rolled up characters according to the rules. The rules said you could only roll three dice. But you had a tendency to end up with terrible characters that might have only one good stat. Such as a character with 17 strength and 5 dexterity. This made for an incredibly clumsy warrior.

One nerd, Wade, proclaimed to everyone he only ever used three dice to roll up his characters. Someone muttered, "Liar," and Wade merely pushed thick glasses back onto his bulbous nose and retreated into a bound book he was casually perusing.

The rolling commenced and each of them ended up with a middling array of stats with dexterity being the best stat for both Mason and Owen.

"You can play thieves," said Kyle bluntly.

"Aright," said Owen, again elbowing Mason. "We're thieves."

"I wanted to be a warrior like..." Mason paused mid-mumble. "Like Aragorn. Or the orcs... in Tolkien."

"You could play half-orc," suggested Wade. "But you'd take a hit to your charisma."

"Well," said Kyle, studying their character sheets with his powerful deconstructing-everything stare. "You barely qualify to be a warrior. I'd suggest thief... but... if you want to play a fighter... I guess you can."

"Warrior is second level by the way," added Andy. "You have to start out at first. Which is a veteran."

"Can he dual class?" asked Owen, his voice making everyone jump a little.

There was a pause.

"He can, but it's slow going," Kyle advised.

"Do that, buddy," Owen whispered so loudly that everyone could hear.

"I'll do that," whispered Mason back.

"It doesn't matter anyway, we're going up against the Tower of the Lizard King," said Andy from farther down the wide table. "You guys won't make it past the first encounter. I bet René won't let them play anyway. So it's a moot point."

"They can play!" bellowed Boyd suddenly from within a deep, almost catatonic reverie.

No one said anything else on that subject of permission granted/not granted to play and Kyle dutifully, if not slightly exasperated by Owen, helped Mason and Owen finish up their characters.

A few minutes later René entered the store. He was small and cherub-faced. He had a mohawk and wore a leather motorcycle jacket studded and then decorated in ghostly white lettering with the shocking names of various UK punk bands. In time they would find out that René was Swiss, raised in America, carried a 4.5 grade point average, spoke six languages, and could do most math problems in his head before people could enter the equations in their calculators.

René was the dungeon master.

Accompanying René was a giant. The two of them entered the store, René wildly recounting some story that seemed about another game of Dungeons and Dragons while the giant merely listened passively, his deep-set hooded eyes staring into the room and only mildly taking in its occupants as though they were beneath being noticed. The giant was dressed in a too-small sweatshirt, shorts, and large tennis shoes. He carried a briefcase. René finished his story with, "Then Callandar rolls a one and crits himself for triple damage. I warned him not to use it because the gnolls were storing massive barrels of oil everywhere. The entire level explodes and the party dies. TPK. Total Party Kill. I even rolled out all the damage. They were dead thirteen times over."

The giant nods. Then, in a quiet rumble: "Well, they wanted to go there. You know what they say, sometimes you get exactly what you wanted, even if you thought it was something else."

René moves to the head of the campaign table as nerds look up and smile at him or mutter some greeting.

"Well, victims, ready to die today?" asks the dungeon master René. Then with a smirk or a sneer, "Who're you two?"

As though Owen and Mason are stowaways on some ocean liner reserved only for the richest of the rich. Maybe the contempt is intentional, or maybe it's just part of his European background. Whatever it is, it's there. Especially for Owen, whom it seems René wants to physically eject from his presence.

"I'm Owen Matthew," announces Owen as though reporting for duty. "And this is my best friend, Mason."

Now, on the freeway after the end of the future with night coming on and feeling the cold and damp as the coastal fog surges inland, Mason remembers those words.

"This is my best friend... Mason."

For the first time since Singapore, Mason wants to cry. For the first time in a long time Mason feels something again.

Some best friend you turned out to be, he thinks to himself on this dark and friendless night, watching a lightless cityscape of shadowy outlines.

He decides to get down off the freeway and look for a place to stay the night. At least he'll be warm in his sleeping bag.

"They're first-level thieves, René. We could hire them to be our porters. They can carry our gear and treasure," offers Kyle.

"All right. It's your funeral," replies René after a brief sigh.

But it isn't their funeral. They survive. Mason and Owen, as Skully the Footpad and Rawg the half-orc fighter thief, survive where others do not. In fact, after a few encounters, it's Owen's natural ability that saves the day on two occasions. Owen's ability to think tactically and lead without actually possessing any kind of actual leadership authority. He is neither charismatic nor good-looking nor someone whose voice convinces others to follow him. He is the opposite of all those things.

But he knows how to make a good plan.

Andy has already been killed. His Ranger fails a save versus poison after they encounter a party of lizard men in the swamps of Uthanmarch. There is no way to bring him back from the dead, and Andy sits, sullen and watching as the party loots his corpse for a few magic items before entering the dungeon beneath the Tower of the Lizard King. It's an immense dungeon crawl that lies beneath the sinking remains of an old castle tower within the swamp.

The next few encounters go off roughly, and fast, as René gleefully distributes large amounts of damage in violent encounters with more lizard men and traps. Crocodiles, a gas spore, and some ghouls join in adding to the party's suffering, to the delight of the sadistic René. Mason and Owen as the two thieves, Skully the Footpad and Rawg the half-orc, hang back under the protection of Alrich the druid, aka Kyle the Game Shoppe diplomat-in-residence.

It's when they meet the hydra lurking under the waters of the sunken hall they must pass to re-enter the ruins of the castle and climb up into its tower to destroy the lizard king, that Owen takes charge.

"We're all going to get killed!" he shrieks across the table during an informal snack break in which everyone has gone to the liquor store for chips, sodas, and candy bars.

Mason is eating a Whatchamacallit.

"Said the first-level thief," snipes Wade. "I am a mage of great power. I can destroy the monster with a salvo of magic missiles and freeze."

"No, you can't!" says Owen. "Haven't you realized from every encounter so far, it's not what it seems? This guy," he nods toward René. "Is trying to kill you!"

René smiles and seems to enjoy Owen's heraldry of his homicidal intentions.

"No offense, I'm really having a lot of fun!" squeaks Owen to René.

"None taken," says René. "I *am* trying to kill them." He says this matter-of-factly while eating strange dried fruits and nuts from within a plastic bag he's brought from home.

"We know the hydra is in the water," continues Owen. "We deciphered the ruins on the monolith."

"And…?" says Wade.

"And," replies Owen in a squeaky imitation of Wade's haughty bridle as he jerks his tiny thumb at René. "This is how he operates. He tells you what the battle is and then switches it up." He pauses and stares at everyone around the table. He's standing but the table comes up to his chest. "He's a switcher!" he shrieks, and waves his hands in the air for effect. What effect isn't clearly discernible.

No one says anything until Kyle, who has been staring at Owen with his deconstructing glare asks, "So what do we do then, guy?"

Owen lowers his head. Mason is sure that in this moment, Owen is going to pray aloud. He does this often and everyone is generally weirded out by it.

But he doesn't, or he prays silently to himself.

"Let's see," says Owen, studying the map. "We're here on the east wall. This room is sunken... meaning that somehow, there is a hole in the room that goes down into the lower dungeons. On the other side of this room are stairs leading up into the castle proper. Is that right, René?"

René looks down and reads aloud the description he's written once more.

"You see a once-grand hall mired in swampy water. Tattered tapestries hang from the high shadows down into murky dark water. In the distance, fifty meters, you see a staircase rising into the gloom above."

No one says anything.

"But there has to be a hole in the floor," whines Owen. "Otherwise the hydra is going to appear in two inches of water, and that's just not possible according to things I've read about hydras in the Monster Manual."

"We have to kill the hydra to get its treasure," complains Rob.

"But if you kill the hydra, will you be ready to fight the lizard king?" Owen asks. Then answers his own question. "No, you won't be able to. That could be the trap, but I don't think it is. No, he has another trap here and he wants you to fight the hydra so the lizard king and his guards can kill you."

René says nothing.

"Again, what do you suggest we do?" asks Kyle firmly.

"If we disturb the water… that will probably alert the hydra to our presence. Then we'd have to fight it," mutters Owen as he studies the map.

"I'm already down to half hit points," says a kid named Warren. He's playing the dwarven warrior. "He's right. We fight the lizard king after this, we are dead meat. I say we leave."

"We just leave?" asks Kyle, his voice rife with disbelief. "Just leave now and go home with no real loot?"

"Yeah," Warren replies. "I just made eighth level. I don't want to lose this fighter."

"Wait a minute!" shrieks Owen. "Why don't we just boil the thing?"

"What?"

"Yes. We could boil him. He's in water. I don't think he has any kind of special flame resistance. We can use all our oil and flame-based attacks, I mean we have two magic users and the druid, and I think the cleric can do something. Plus, we get the water all oily, and I think in the supply room two encounters back, the lizard men had a barrel of oil. Then we draw the hydra to the surface and ignite the water. He'll take fire damage, steam damage if there's such a thing, and then we attack with our weapons."

No one says anything until Kyle turns his lamb-white head toward punk rock René and asks, "Is that… even… possible?"

René puts his hands in his pockets as he lowers his head and stares at something behind the DM screen. He pulls one hand out of his pocket and picks up an unseen die and rolls it. Whatever number appears is unknown to everyone but the dungeon master.

The giant who has been watching all along, quietly, sitting next to Boyd who occasionally leaves to smoke a cigarette outside the store, clears his throat.

Quickly—so quickly that Mason, who saw it and who has very good reflexes, as every shortstop must, barely catches it—René shoots a quick look at the giant.

Whatever passed between them is unknown to Mason as his back is to the giant. René once more lowers his eyes to the sheets and notes behind the screen. Then he looks up and his arctic-blue eyes are ice-cold.

"Is that what you guys want to do?" he asks the party.

No one says anything.

Then someone, a kid who hasn't spoken much, pipes up. He's running the cleric. "Seems like a plan to me."

Others agree. Wade holds out but goes along in the end.

"Once we get to melee," announces Kyle as Alrich, "we'll all need to attack, even you two."

"What's melee?" whispers Mason.

"Combat. Swords and axes. Maces if you're a cleric."

Mason looks down at his character sheet.

"I have a short sword. Is that good enough?"

A few of the other players snicker.

"It'll have to be," says Kyle and sighs.

A few minutes later, as Owen basically takes charge of the preparations and the magic users announce their flame-based attacks, the stage is set.

"How do we draw out the hydra?"

Everyone looks at Owen.

"I'll do it," he answers reluctantly.

"Well, it looks like you'll be killed again," Wade says. "This time by a giant five-headed lizard instead of a bull.

What character will you make next week?" He smiles smugly at Owen.

"Before I go," Owen announces, "I just wanna say, this is a dream come true for me. I have wanted to play Dungeons and Dragons for three years. It was everything I thought it would be, and more. Thank you, guys."

"Sounds like a farewell speech," Wade quips.

"It is! I'm probably going to get killed now!" squeaks Owen. "But you guys are my friends... and no greater love hath a man than that he give up his life for his friends."

Silence.

Then, "Aren't you a thief?" asks René with that same uncontained euro-contempt. "You obviously don't understand role-playing. So I'm nailing you for two hundred and fifty experience points for not playing your alignment. What is your alignment?"

"Chaotic neutral," Owen answers sheepishly.

"Well then, minus two-fifty for not role-playing."

"I *am* role-playing! I'm like Robin Hood."

René hits back quickly because his mind is sharper than most people on their best days. "Then I'll nail all of *them* for two-fifty times their level for being led by the equivalent of a pickpocket when some of them are almost ready to lead armies or start guilds in a couple of levels. How about that, kid?"

"At least they won't be dead!" Owen shrieks.

"We'll see," mutters René.

Then it goes down. Classic Owen, remembers Mason, as he picks his way down into the dark and dead city by the side of the silent freeway. Owen takes the lead. Mason has seen it all throughout his life. In dirt clod fights and kick-ball games Owen is there, at the forefront, leading though no one expected him to. Mason will see it in his best friend all the way up until Owen is dead. In fact, it will be the reason Owen dies. Leading when no one asked him to.

Owen declares to René, "I run into the room, but I don't stop. What color is the water?"

"Roll a twenty-sided die," orders René. "What's your intelligence?"

"Twelve."

Owen rolls a three.

"Is that good?"

René doesn't answer. Then, "The water is a murky brown as you enter the room, but in the center, it seems green and almost translucent."

René is rolling dice behind the screen. Everyone at the table, including Wade, is leaning forward. A quiet seems to pervade the game store beyond the normal muffled noise level thanks to all the boxes of games and game magazines and paper-bound modules and warm red carpeting.

"I go wide right. I'm steering clear of that translucent green area!"

"Make a save versus dexterity," demands René. "What's your dex?"

Owen looks down at his character sheet.

"Fifteen!" He takes the purple twenty-sided die in his tiny hands and shakes it between both hands closed. Then, triumphantly, a broad smile across his face, he tosses it onto the table, barely missing some of the miniatures.

Fourteen.

The DM moves the miniature representing Skully the Footpad to the edge of the area he has just drawn in to represent the translucent green area in the floor of the sunken hall.

"Close," someone mumbles.

"The water begins to bubble and froth," announces René. There is an evil malice covering a patina of joy on his face as he says this. He reaches into his backpack, a backpack adorned with more UK punk bands of the obscene variety, and retrieves something. He places it behind the screen.

"I'm running for the stairs!" yells Owen. "Be ready, guys!"

There is a pause. René turns to Owen. A slight smirk creases one side of his face. It reminds Mason of the Grinch in the Christmas cartoon that plays once a year.

"So, you are running for the stairs. I want to make sure of that, right?"

Mason is suddenly aware that all is not as it seems. Owen must be too because he hesitates.

"Five seconds. You're running. Decide. Do you stay in the water or take the stairs? Five…"

"Well, if I stay…"

"Four…"

"… in the water, I'll be boiled for sure!"

"Three…"

"Stairs!" shouts Owen. "I'm going for the stairs!"

"Good," says René.

"It's a trap," mutters dead Andy from down the table.

"Coming up from the pool," intones René with a new solemnity. "Beneath the water is the dreaded ancient guardian of the sunken tower of Uthanmarch."

René places a beautifully painted large miniature of a hydra into the center of the pool within the sunken grand hall. Every detail is exquisitely rendered. The individual scales have barely been outlined beneath the green armor of the nightmare's skin. The long multi-headed necks are flecked in splashes of gold. Burning menace glares out from each of the serpentine heads as the eyes seem to capture the light. He has even painted the pupils. The work is beyond master craftsmanship. This is evident as the breath of everyone at the table is collectively held. All bend forward to examine what must undoubtedly be the result of many patient hours spent with a fine brush and a magnifying lens. With skills well beyond their own. The hydra dwarfs all the other miniatures and makes them seem pale and poor by comparison. An overwhelming sense of failure pervades the room as everyone is sure for just a moment, that Owen's plan is a catastrophic failure and that ruin, and only ruin, lies ahead for them all.

"Meanwhile," says René as though tasting something particularly delicious. He turns to Owen. "You hear a rumbling coming from the shadows at the top of the stairs."

"Forget about me, guys!" yells Owen. "Boil that thing now!"

What happens next is typical of games being played by high-IQ children, and even adults. A war of rules is suddenly waged vociferously, and it is worthy of the most all-night epic filibusters in any house of government ever. At first René wants to negate the effects of all the fire-based attacks and the ability for oil to ignite on water. Wade, of all people, launches into an argument on the nature of fireballs and their similarity to US military napalm. Napalm burns at 2,200 degrees Fahrenheit, a statistic provided by Rob, a Vietnam War enthusiast. So, continues Wade, if water boils at 212 degrees Fahrenheit then this water has become scalding. Beyond boiling, in fact. René counters with well-stated arguments on the nature of dissipation regarding convection and annotates experiments with a microwave oven as performed in his AP Science class. But in the end he must concede that, yes, the water has reached a point well beyond boiling. Tables and charts are consulted. Suggested damage is forwarded by players scrambling through rulebooks, and an hour later, the discussion about how long the fire will last due to the burning oil but mitigated by vaporization concludes.

"Could the steam harm the monster?" ventures Andy as though the destruction of the hydra is some sort of payback for the death of his prized Ranger.

"No, it's a monster that uses gas-based attacks. So steam has no effect." René's been beaten by previous arguments and this one is given to him due to the almost petulant absolutism he has responded to Andy's query with.

The hydra fails the save versus fire and takes an immense amount of damage. Kyle quickly calculates it can't possibly have more than one round of attacks' worth of hit points left. Meaning, if everyone attacks it now and only half of them hit and do half damage, it will die. Which, everyone agrees, is pretty good odds.

"Is it stunned?" Wade asks.

René flips a die behind the screen and utters a flat, "No."

"Then we attack," says Kyle as Alrich.

"The hydra will have one round of attacks before you can close."

Everyone knows if the damage is distributed evenly, they can survive. But if the hydra goes after any one person, then that person is most likely dead meat.

"The hydra attacks Skully the thief," whispers René.

Silence overwhelms the room. This is payback and there is no doubt to anyone it is anything but. René begins to pick up many, many dice.

"Wait a minute," interrupts Kyle as he studies some rulebook, his eyes making hard furious movements across the page. Then, "The monster will need to turn around to attack... Owen."

René makes some quick unreadable face and then seems on the verge of an objection he hasn't fully worked through.

"He's right!" shouts Andy from down the length of the snack-cluttered table. "You placed the monster facing the party. See?" He points a thick Cheetos-stained finger at the beautifully painted mythical multi-headed beast that seems to loom over all the other drab and lifeless figurines representing the fantastic party of mages, warriors, clerics, and two fledgling thieves. "He requires one movement phase to turn around and thus attack the thief. If he does, then we get bonuses to our attacks for attacking a large creature from behind. Which should be quite sizable. Pardon the pun."

"You're dead," says René.

"Yes, but I'm Obi-Waning the party. And—"

"Silence!" shouts René like some Nazi prison camp commandant. Then, "Fine." As cold as an icy Swiss alpine stream, René continues. "Fine," he says again, if just for himself. Then he reaches out and turns the beast around. It is now facing Owen's figurine. Owen's Skully the Footpad who is at the bottom of the lines representing the stairs leading up into the tower of the lizard king. Owen who is all alone.

The giant behind them, sitting at the counter next to Boyd the silent keeper of the Game Shoppe, stirs. Shifting one of his massive legs and burping as he seems to watch the goings-on intently, and then not watch, in the same moment.

"All five heads attack with their breath weapon." René says this as he begins to gather up even more dice.

"But I still get an action," tries Owen timidly. His voice is the mewl of a defenseless kitten.

The grimace that passes across René's face is both dark and humorless. "Sure." Pause. "One action before I... before the monster attacks. Go ahead, kid."

Owen stares hard at his character sheet.

A few of the other players mutter words that basically imply there isn't much Owen can do.

The silence proceeds and everyone knows René is just on the verge of prompting Owen when Owen finally speaks up.

"I detect traps!" announces Owen triumphantly.

Everyone, including the murderous DM, raises their eyes. Everyone except Mason. The young Mason just watches everything in silent awe. He has seen this Owen standing in front of groups of people, arguing his point to the end. Throwing dirt clods back at overwhelming numbers of other kids. Standing up to bullies. He is always amazed by two things about his best friend Owen. One, Owen's inability to read the room and continue on, regardless of the perceived outcome. And two, his ability to stand his ground. No matter what.

He secretly admires that about Owen.

His best friend.

"Okay, roll some dice."

Owen does.

"Did I detect the trap?" he asks. "That is… if there is one."

René presses his lips together and sighs through his tiny nose.

"Fat lot of good it'll do you," he says, not looking at Owen. "All right." He sighs again and begins to read. "Coming down the stairs out of the darkness is a massive boulder. I'll even tell you that it weighs three tons. Remember *Raiders*? Well, it's way bigger than that."

Silence once again embraces the table and the game shop.

René's triumph, delayed, is finally at hand. He opens his mouth and raises both hands much like someone wielding a dagger might before plunging it into the heart of their bound victim.

"I think we need to roll for initiative." It's Wade. He smiles smugly at René.

"Fine!" huffs the punk rock DM with his fist full of dice.

The party rolls a four.

"If we can attack and kill the hydra before it attacks the…" Wade nods at Owen. "Then he might live."

René nods at Kyle and says, "Roll for me." His eyes are daggers. Kyle picks up a six-sided die and rolls a five.

René smiles. His satisfaction evident. He raises the handful of twenty-siders once more. When they fall, they will determine the effectiveness of all the monster's attacks. Skully the Footpad is clearly doomed. Everyone knows this now.

"Don't I get to roll for initiative?" asks Owen.

"No!" shouts René. "You're part of the party. The party rolled a four. I rolled a five. I go first. Die!" And just before he drops all the dice representing all the damage all five heads of the hydra will do to poor little Owen's first-level thief who only has six hit points, Owen says, "But the party's way over there." He waves one of his tiny hands at the campaign map, making it seem a vast and expansive space. An endless desert. "I'm here!" he proclaims. "We are not together," he lectures. "Initiative implies that a party acts as a team. I'm not near enough to influence their initiative, therefore I should get my own initiative."

René lowers all the dice behind the screen. He leans across table right into Owen's face and says, "Go ahead. Roll."

"What if I roll a five?"

"Then you and the monster do the same thing, at the same time."

"So I need a six." Owen takes up the die and only Mason notices that for the briefest of moments, Owen's delicate eyelids briefly flutter as he shakes the lone die back and forth in both his tiny hands.

And then he rolls…

… a six.

The room explodes. René even utters a Boyd-forbidden swear word.

The nerds laugh and jeer impolitely, seemingly oblivious to the DM's much-demonstrated desire for vengeance. If not today, if not now, then perhaps another time, his eyes seem to promise them all. But this has always been the weakness of nerds. Their inability to read such social cues and dire promises.

Six little dots stand out on the up-facing side of the die. Like a home run in the ninth. Or a touchdown in the fourth. At the last moment. When time was no longer a luxury, and a hero did something seemingly impossible that changed everything and let everyone know that some-times… sometimes it's called a game for a reason.

Because anything can happen.

"All right," says René, wiping his face in frustration. He picks up someone's half-drunk Cactus Cooler and takes a deep swig like it's gunfighter whiskey. "You go first."

Owen studies the map.

"Well," he begins, in his drawn-out, high-pitched squawk. "The dragon…"

"Hydra," somebody corrects.

"The hydra," continues Owen. "The hydra is going to kill me for sure. And if the hydra *doesn't* kill me, the big rock rolling down the stairs will kill me."

Silence.

There really is no win. The sobriety of the moment after seems to push the victory of the initiative from the table.

"I tell the party to stand back!"

"You *what?*" shrieks the DM.

Owen shrinks back. Involuntarily. Then, "I trigger the trap and yell for the party to stand back."

"*Why?!*" shouts René, his rosy apple cheeks and peach-es-and-cream skin suddenly flushed with anger.

"Well," says Owen, pointing toward the table and the map, the sunken chamber and the stairway leading upward into the darkness. "Once that three-ton rock hits me, a lowly first-level character, it's probably going to cream that dra—hydra next, right?"

Silence. Again. Everyone studies the map.

"Yeah, and now the hydra can't attack the party 'cause he's facing the wrong way," says Andy. He shoves a handful of Cheetos into his mouth and crunches them up confidently.

For a full minute René just stares at the map.

He'd labored for a full month on the hydra. He'd sketched it out before he'd even started painting. He'd brought it all the way back from Gen Con in Wisconsin last summer, where he'd purchased it from the premier miniature maker. An old beardy guy who specialized in one-of-a-kind miniatures. He had planned on wiping out the whole party with this thing. Because what they didn't know was that once most of the party had stepped into the room, the sunken floor would collapse, sending them into a watery grave. Some would drown. Others would have to engage in underwater combat with massive penalties and the hydra would win. Without a doubt.

In fact, there is no lizard king. The hydra *is* the lizard king. The local lizard men have based a cult around this thing, and they've been throwing gold and sacrifices into the pool. René had spent an entire evening randomly rolling up all the treasure lying at the bottom of the pool. It was an incredible amount. There were a ton of magic items down there. He didn't care, that's what he thought as he sat listening to Dr. Demento at his desk, writing everything out. They were never going to survive the hydra and the collapsing floor. They'd never get the treasure, and he'd even let them know how much stuff they could have had if only they'd survived the hydra. Which they never would.

It was gonna be great.

Numbly, he picked up the rock, a rock from his mother's garden, and placed it in the map at the top of the stairs.

Then he pushed it slowly across the map until it was in front of Owen's figurine. He raised it above the tiny thief with the ridiculously small dagger and then gently crushed it down on top of the lead miniature.

No one said anything, except Andy.

"Hey, that's mine."

René seemed not to hear and continued to press down on the now-flattened thief. Then he picked up the large rock and held it over the hydra. He paused. The rock held just above the mystically beautiful dinosaur snake-headed beast.

Everyone knew he would smash it down onto the most exquisite miniature any of them had ever played with. Had ever even seen. There was nothing in *Dragon Magazine* like this.

Deftly, quietly, and quickly, Kyle reached one slender lamb-white hand out and removed the hydra out from under the rock. René looked at him and some unspoken thing passed between them until René finally nodded and accepted that Kyle would hold on to it until the suicidal DM was in his right mind again.

René mumbled, "The rock hits the hydra and kills… her."

The Fragment of Revealing...

IT is cold outside the tiny motel room Mason has sealed himself in. Mason has pushed the entertainment console in front of the door. He's beginning to feel very heavy and tired. Sore even. He chalks it up to riding a desk for the last five years and all the exercise since LAX. Outside, before he shuts the curtains, the sky is gray with falling ash. It's almost full dark. Briefly he wonders if someone somewhere has used a nuclear weapon. He closes the stiff gold curtains smelling of dust and gets into his sleeping bag that he's rolled out on the queen-sized bed. In the darkness he sips his tequila and remembers the afternoon and the twilight walk home, when Owen defeated the hydra.

He's beginning to feel very sick.

ALSO BY JASON ANSPACH & NICK COLE

Galaxy's Edge: Legionnaire
Galaxy's Edge: Savage Wars
Galaxy's Edge: Requiem For Medusa
Galaxy's Edge: Order of the Centurion

ALSO BY JASON ANSPACH

Wayward Galaxy
King's League
'til Death

ALSO BY NICK COLE

American Wasteland:
The Complete Wasteland Trilogy
SodaPop Soldier
Strange Company